THE HIDDEN MAGE

Published by
Gallery 41 Books
3 Church End, London E17 9RJ
books@gallery41.co.uk

Copyright © 2021 Liz Berry
All rights reserved

Liz Berry has asserted her right under
the Copyright, Designs and Patents Act 1988
to be identified as the author of this work.

ISBN 978-1-84396-629-6

Also available as a Kindle ebook
ISBN 978-1-84396-630-2

A catalogue record for
this book is available from the British Library
and the American Library of Congress

No part of this book may be
copied or reproduced in any way or form
without the prior written consent
of the publisher

Cover design by Ken Dawson, Creative Covers
ccovers.co.uk

Pre-press production
eBook Versions
27 Old Gloucester Street
London WC1N 3AX
www.ebookversions.com

Other books by Liz Berry

JANEY AND THE BAND
SING THE BLUES, JANEY
BRIGHT LIGHTS SHINING
FOOL'S GOLD
EASY CONNECTIONS
EASY FREEDOM
MEL
THE CHINA GARDEN
FINDER
THE HIDDEN MAGE

CIRCLES OF BECOMING (Poetry and autobiography)
THE DARK GARDEN (Haiku poetry)

THE HIDDEN MAGE

Liz Berry

GALLERY 41 BOOKS

Rhianna is living with her grandmother in a small village at the edge of the Perilous Forest, hidden deep in the Summer country, remote from all the turmoil of post-Roman Britain, where the Bear, King Arthur, is battling rebellious war lords, and invaders from the north, west and east, to bring order and safety to his people.

Rhianna thinks of herself as an ordinary village girl, enjoying life with her animal friends in her paradise Forest, although sometimes she thinks she remembers another life in a great stone hall, and travelling on a ship with billowing sails, or is she just dreaming, as her grandmother insists? She seems to be surrounded by mysteries that her enigmatic grandmother, healer and wise woman of the village, will not explain. And what of her absent mother who never visits?

As she grows older, exploring and learning, Rhianna realises that her skills are not ordinary at all and can be very dangerous. Does she really want to be a healer too, or is there something else she must discover?

This is a story of a young woman, with a secret heritage, growing up in a shattered world of good and evil, and the choices she must make.

Liz Berry lives in London. She is a painter who exhibits her work regularly. She has been Head of Art in an East London High School, a careers guidance counsellor, worked in politics, and run her own small art gallery.

Part One

Aella 1

This morning I received a message. An extraordinary message – so extraordinary, I could not doubt that it was a message direct from the Goddess herself. But I am afraid I have delayed too long, ignoring and discounting many of the omens which have come to me in recent months. But this latest warning cannot be ignored, however much I would like to bury it deep in the surge of daily activities.

Very early this morning, just as the dawn light crept across the Eastern sky, I left Gwyneth's cottage, where I had been all night, delivering the surprise package her husband had left with her – not one child, but two, twin boys, howling and yelling into life. Good lungs. They should do very well. Gwyneth had begged me for a birth prophecy, so I tranced and read the Record for her (great warriors both of them), before stepping out into the icy ground mist that had blown in from the estuary. As I climbed the path, I paused to drag my old cloak closer around me and then it happened.

The mist swirled, thickened, and as I looked up to the overhanging cliff, a great white stag stepped from the edge of the trees, and paused, staring down at me. He was huge, shining white, bearing a great rack of silver antlers. He stood poised, regal, staring straight at me, demanding my attention, so that I could not doubt that it was me he was staring at, not just the track or the village.

I was unable to move, returning his stare, clutching my cloak. He tossed his head, and one forefoot lifted and descended noiselessly, and belatedly, I remembered my manners. I bowed deeply. 'Greetings, Great Lord.'

He continued to watch me, insistent, as though trying to convey an important message and then, uncannily, I realised I could see the trunks of the trees through his body, and he was gone, the mist drifting, concealing.

I was very shaken. I hurried up the track to our round house, which was the last in the village at the very edge of the Great Forest. I couldn't get the white stag out of my mind. I had seen him once before, many years ago, at the time of the most awesome and momentous day of my life. The Goddess had finally sent an unmistakeable message. I knew what it meant. Change. Great changes, and danger as it had before and I must prepare for them.

I remembered then the increasing number of uncanny happenings of recent months. Why on earth hadn't I taken note? Three lots of twins born in the last three months, in a village that had seen only one set of twins in the ten years I had been there.

It had started with the comet and the meteorite shower spreading against the sky to the North. Then. shortly afterwards, there was the unexpected eclipse of the moon in October. I had looked up and found a black shadow eating away the edge of the full, shining moon, and the hairs on my neck lifted as I remembered. It was all natural, I thought, although I knew full well, that no eclipse was due. And there was the Northern Lights, which seldom shone this far south, gigantic and brilliant, wrapping the whole of the sky. And what of the strange behaviour of the animals and birds, that had puzzled Rhianna? I had put all these away from my mind.

But now I knew. Changes. Warnings. Danger. A direct message to me. I feared now that I had left things too late. Perhaps several years too late. I should have spoken before. Explained everything to Rhianna. Suppose the omens indicated my own death, leaving Rhianna unprepared, ignorant of her history and destiny, unable to protect herself?

It will be very hard to speak of many things she must know. I thought of her eyes, filling with hurt and disbelief at my betrayal.

I am a coward. I cannot do it.

She is the child of my heart, dearer to me than even her mother. I saw her into the world, raised her, educated her and protected her, and I cannot bear to lose her through these old histories and misunderstandings.

But what if I write it down? She could read it and think about it. It would be there permanently for her to return to when she was older, and could understand high matters and adult feelings. She is still so young, barely thirteen years, although mature beyond her years and thoughtful. I must protect her as long as possible, but the information will be there for her when needed. I will begin tonight.

Rhianna 1

I am deep asleep, dreaming that I wake up and find that I am riding a great white Stag. I grip his silver antlers and I can feel his strong neck muscles moving against my knees, as he bounds through the mist – no, not mist, clouds, and we burst through, high in the upper air, to see stretched out below, to the horizon a golden land, threaded with shining waters, glowing with glory as the rising sun leaps upwards.

I am overwhelmed with awe and joy, and then we are plunging down into mist and I recognise the low cliff above our round house on the edge of the Forest. He comes to a halt, and shakes me from his back. I slide down his shoulders, and stand next to him. He is staring down intently, and I see my grandmother, Aella, leaving Gwyneth's house, smiling, and I am pleased that Gwyneth has birthed her baby safely.

Aella puts down her healer's bag and pulls her cloak higher against the chill of the early morning. She glances up, and stops, pressing her hand against her heart. The two stare at each other, immobile, for several long minutes. Then Aella bows deeply and says 'Greetings, Great Lord.' The White Stag does not move, still staring at her, then he lifts his right foreleg, and I realise he is losing his substance, disappearing into the mist. I drift back into sleep and dream of the golden land shining into infinity.

I must remember to tell Aella. Perhaps it is a message for her.

Aella 2

Rhianna, my love, there are things I should have told you, important things, that you will need to know. There have been warnings, omens – remember the owl and the two headed calf? – but I ignored them all. It is too soon, I thought, she is too young, wait another year... and another year...

But the Goddess has sent me a direct message, I can delay no longer, and I know now that I should have spoken before. Rhianna, there are great events afoot, changes, dangers. Perhaps my own death.

I think you will be angry and feel betrayed, but I hope, believe, you will forgive me when you know everything, and remember that I have had only your protection and love in my heart.

Rhianna, I have never lied to you, but I have evaded your questions, been silent. Let your assumptions go unchallenged. Fortunately, you have never thought to question me about my own history. All your questions are to do with your mother – and I have been able to make adequate explanation.

You know that I am a Priestess of Avalon, a trained healer

and herbalist. You know that I am your Guardian. From infancy you have thought me your grandmother. No one told you this, you just worked it out for yourself, and I did not correct you. Indeed, I feel that we do have that closest of ties. But I must tell you now that I am not your mother's mother or your father's mother. I am not of your noble line at all, and the name you know me by, is not quite correct. So how did I come to be your Guardian?

It is a long and difficult story, hard to tell you, hard for you to understand. Where to start, that is the problem, How to explain my involvement in such great matters? I was there. I can bear witness. But I did not choose the path.

When I was very young, there was a wandering bard, a story teller, who came to my father's Hall every year at Samhain. We all know that stories begin, 'Once upon a time' but he began his stories 'Little did he know that...' I am minded to start my own tale with those same words.

Little did I know that one day I would be living in a common round house in a small village, hidden away beyond the boundless Great Forest of the Summer country, on a tributary of the great Sabrina River, cut off from all learning and civilised society, cut off from the companionship of my fellow Priestesses, healing the sick, delivering new lives and most of all, protecting you, Rhianna, my love, seeing to your well-being and attempting to educate you in all the ways appropriate for a girl of your station. You should have been in Avalon, with other noble girls, but your mother would not hear of this and knowing what I do, I could not blame her.

It has been so far from what I expected my life to be, but I cannot say that I regret our life here. I am content, fulfilled, and full of gratitude to the Goddess. It has been safe and normal, better by far than more illustrious places would have been.

Sometimes I wonder what my father would say if he knew. And then I laugh with satisfaction and triumph. I have beaten him.

I was born Gwenaella, the third child of a minor King of Brigantia. I will not name him. He is not worth honouring in that way. He was a rapacious, violent, greedy man. Greedy for riches, greedy for power, and above all greedy for land, He warred constantly against his neighbours, seizing their lands and enslaving their peoples. And he was hated by all his family, including his second wife, my mother Aelwyn, a princess of the Cymry. I was the youngest and last child. My two brothers were full grown, and dead in my father's wars before I arrived belatedly, so I was very close to my mother. She was gifted, a wise woman and healer, who taught me well.

The Goddess called me early. She came to me in dreams as a child, and once, reflected in a pool in the wood when I was awake, and I saw and spoke with her clearly, with no possibility of doubt. I had no great gifts of prophecy or magic, but I loved the flowers and herbs of the field and forest, and healing, and it was always my dream and intention to go south to the House of the Priestesses at Avalon, a centre of learning and healing, to serve the Goddess there all the days of my life. I could not wait to get away from my father's brutal, miserable, court where the women were treated like slaves, and frequently beaten, while his warriors and sell swords filled our great hall riotously, and the women were forced to huddle away in their quarters full of fear. I waited impatiently.

My mother, poor tragic woman, died from a blow to her

head, when I was twelve, and then my father suddenly found another use for me. He told me I was to be married to a local chieftain, whose lands abutted our eastern boundary, which would give him an excuse to claim all of that land. I was horrified and despairing. He knew full well I was dedicated to the Goddess, and the chieftain was old and diseased and was known to have killed his two previous wives in drunken rages. I begged and begged my father, reminding him I had been given to the Goddess, but he and his warriors laughed and jeered when I said she would be very angry.

I prayed to the Goddess to save me, made sacrifice, and cut off my hair, but that only earned me a bloody whipping which nearly killed me and left lasting scars. But it brought me one good thing, a delay to the wedding until my hair grew and the cuts on my body were stitched and healed. Then I could delay no more, and once again the marriage went forward. Three days before, when we were all distracted, and the guards were sloppy and drunk from morning to night, the King of a neighbouring country, an old enemy, came against us in force with many more sell swords than we had, and better trained warriors. He came in revenge for my father's destruction of his family – mother, father, eight brothers and two sisters, as well as numerous clansmen, and he was not inclined to mercy.

The horde swept over our country, our Great Hall, our villages, all burned, the warriors slaughtered, the women raped, killed, or enslaved.

Of course, my father escaped. It was all his fault but he escaped. He rode off, taking with him two sacks of gold plate and a chest of golden coins, with a group of his clansmen, leaving his Hall full of women and children to stand against his enraged enemy. And me? Raped of course. Three of them, and when I bit the jaw of the last and called him a filthy pig, he slashed me across the face with his knife and left me for dead.

Eventually the raiders left, taking anything of value they could find. When it was safe my father returned, and set about building up his war band again.

My ruined face shamed him and he would not see me about his court. I went to live with an aunt, my mother's older sister, a wise woman, who tried to heal my ruined face. She lived beyond the village in deep forest, and thus escaped the raid, praise be. For a long time, I wished I had died in the raid. I bore a babe, but I was only newly come to my womanhood and the child was weak and not properly formed, and she lived only a week. I was barren from my injuries, and my body took a long time to heal, my mind even longer. I sank into depression under the heaviness of the fury and hatred which consumed me, a kind of madness. Well, I recovered. No, that's not the correct word. You do not 'recover', you survive. I survived.

Then my father sent for me: 'Come, or I will string up your old nurse.' We could not believe it – once again he was trying to sell me. But by this time, I had learned some useful skills from my aunt. We went to his Hall, and I stood up in front of him and his warriors and I spoke of all his crimes and I cursed him for each one. It was a long list and I remembered them all with a longer list of terrible curses, that went on and on, and there was silence. No one spoke, and I could see the fear in their eyes. He stared at me, until suddenly he lost his temper, and taking his sword, swung it at me. I swayed backwards, but the long sword continued its trajectory, and swept off the head of my poor old aunt, who was standing next to me. Her blood fountained over me and something, I do not know what, happened to me then.

'Die in agony, you bloody tyrant!' I shouted in a voice that wasn't my own, pointing at him, and flames leaped from my fingers, licking over his robe and up his neck to his face.

He was screaming, writhing on the floor trying to put the flames out, shouting for help, but his surrounding clansmen stood staring and made no move, transfixed with terror.

I laughed and laughed, hysterically. Nothing like that had ever happened to me before. The Goddess herself had truly come to my aid. And then I walked out of that place, never to return.

I am not sure what happened after that. I was out of my mind again, but one day I found I was on the road, walking south, covered in blood and crying for my good old aunt. I have never recovered from the guilt of her death, or my hatred of warriors.

I hardly know how I survived to reach Avalon safely. The roads were dangerous, full of thieves and robbers, masterless men, bandits and the war bands of the great Lords. I hid, like a wild animal, stole food when I could, and never stopped walking south. The Goddess must have guided and guarded me. Good people along the way helped me sometimes, giving me lifts in their farm waggons, or fed me, or tended to my hurts. All I know is that it took months. I was broken, ragged and half mad, but I am forever grateful to those, who gave me what help and love they could.

One day I found myself staggering along a rocky path, running along the bank of a wide lake. It was late, dusk, and mist was spreading over the water. A half-fallen tree blocked the way forward. I was totally exhausted and had not eaten for three days. I sank down by the tree and just lay there. I was finished. I had tried so hard to come to the Goddess, but now I knew that it was not to be. I could go no further. I knew I would never rise again.

I must have fainted or slept, and I dreamed that there was a woman in the mist kneeling next to me. She took my hand, and folded it around a thick rope hanging from the tree. 'Pull,' she said. But I had no strength. She held my hand between both of hers, and, lifting it, kissed my broken knuckles. She said, smiling. 'One last try.' And suddenly a wonderful warmth and strength flowed up my arm and I was able to tug the rough rope before blackness swept over me again. Without knowing it, I had summoned the Avalon ferryman. Praise the Goddess! They found me and without hesitation, they saved me, this filthy, utterly destitute, broken, mad thing. They fed me, bathed me, healed my cuts and bruises, and held me tightly when I howled with despair and madness.

It was many weeks before I came to myself, and even longer before I began to live fully again.

Aella 3

I had finally achieved my greatest dream. And Avalon exceeded it in every way. I lived in an atmosphere of love and joy, and in complete acceptance.

Avalon is on rising ground, near Glastonbury Hill, a very large isle in the middle of a lake, long sacred to the Great Goddess in the Levels of the Summer Country. A huge palace-villa, it was built by a wealthy Roman General, Lucius Severus Vespasianus, using the finest craftsmen, intended for his retirement in the last years of the Roman occupation. He intended to settle in this country and he married a British princess, Morfran, who was also a Priestess of the Goddess. The palace contained every luxury, beautifully painted walls, mosaic floors, heated beneath, hot and cold baths, and a vast library of many scrolls and books, collected by Lucius, for he was a scholar and writer as well as a soldier. Lucius died unexpectedly, and Morfran inherited the large palace and the surrounding farms and villages and turned it into a settlement for learning and the worship of the Goddess. She was a very learned woman herself, proficient in Atlantean magic, far seeing and famous for her prophecies. She said that a time would be coming when our religion and language would be under threat, and that our knowledge and culture must be guarded for the future. She established a community of women, following the moon rituals and magic of the Goddess, where we could study all the arts – philosophy, poetry, languages, mathematics, painting, weaving, embroidery, music and literature, and of course, medicine, and healing for the community and all the surrounding villages.

It is self-governing with a High Priestess and nine senior priestesses, and many sworn priestesses, and acolytes. The High Priestess, Vivienne, Lady of the Lake, was and is, famous throughout the land and beyond, for her prophecies, her learning and her wisdom. She has great influence with all manner of people – the Kings and Queens, High Druids and the Priests of the White Christ. She corresponds with Rome and the Franks. I helped her secretary-scribe for a while and you would not believe how far her word spreads. But above all her loving presence like a jewelled net, covers Avalon and the surrounding country and it is magical and safe like no other place in the world.

She had given me back my life, and as far as I was concerned, she could do no wrong. I would have done anything in the world for her.

When I had recovered my health and mind, to my joy I was assigned to the healing hall and herbarium, where I spent the next seven years, studying, and learning my trade with my dear Sophia. She was very old, a great healer from an old Atlantean line, full of magic and wisdom. She became like a mother to me. Everything was given to me: Protection, love, self-respect, which had been utterly destroyed, every help to learn and practice my craft; time to explore the books in the great Library, one of the secret wonders of Avalon. She even healed my ruined face. The knife slash had cut deep, diagonally from my forehead to my chin, narrowly missing my left eye. The knife was dirty and the wound would not heal but continued to fester and break open again and again. People could not look at me directly, But Sophia worked on the wound with herbs and the ancient magic and gradually only a light scar was left. You can still see it, a little, this pale hairline here, beside my mouth, which you have often asked about. Now you know!

I was thirteen when I came to Avalon and twenty when I finished my apprenticeship and entered joyously into my full vows as a Priestess of Avalon, and began the deeper studies in the High Atlantean magic, which is Avalon's legacy and great purpose, and which I have begun to pass on to you.

Aella 4

As the time passed, I became very close to the Lady of Avalon. I was something of a pet and she often asked me to do small jobs for her. She knew I loved her dearly and was delighted to help. I found books in the library, took messages, copied ancient scrolls, and assisted her secretary with the voluminous correspondence that came from all over the world. Several times I went on short journeys for her to local chieftains with private messages which she did not want to be generally known, and then when she knew I was reliable and discreet, on longer journeys to the courts of Kings, perhaps to fetch their daughters to their studies, for Avalon was a school as well as a Temple and community, and many Kings sent their sons and daughters to be properly educated in languages, the healing arts, music and mathematics and philosophy, to take their places as the future wives of Kings. The boys often went on to the Druid college nearby on Glastonbury Tor, where they studied long years for the Priesthood.

So I was not surprised one day when she sent for me with a special request. Little did I know then into what high matters it would plunge me.

She was, as usual, in her workroom. It opened out onto a terrace above the lake, and always there was the sound of weaving waters winding round the sunken stones. It was spring and the waters were flowing strongly with the meltwater from the Mendips hills. It was a room I loved. It was beautiful – oh not in luxury – but rather in its proportions and the finish of the polished wood panelling, where the Roman craftsman had inlaid various woods. It was a room of peace, where urgency was out of place. But the Lady was walking to and fro, agitated, holding a crumpled sheet of vellum. She was wearing the full robes of the High Priestess, which was unusual at this time of day, but even its rich violet colour could not warm the pallor of her skin. She had a strange expression on her face, a combination of impatience, irritation and concern, and I saw that she had been crying. There was an air of desperation about her that I did not like.

The Lady is not young. The Priestesses have a longer life than most, the result of their magical studies, and nobody knows just how old she is, but we all tried to keep her safe and shield her from petty worries. She has many activities related to the State, advising the High King, receiving diplomatic requests, and most important, giving prophecies, which means entering into trance, and linking with the higher powers for the benefit of the land, which is very dangerous and physically demanding, so we did not like to see her distressed in any way.

I was very concerned. I said, anxiously, 'May I help you, Lady? Is there anything I can do?'

'Come in, Aella, my love,' she said, holding out her hand, 'I have a problem which I am at a loss to know how best to solve.

But it is in my mind that you might be the very one able help, if you are willing.'

'Tell me,' I said lifting her hand and kissing it. 'You know I will do anything. I am so deeply in debt to you for all you have done for me these last years.'

She shook her head, dismissively, and sat me down next to her on a couch. It concerns Ygraine,' she said, taking a deep breath. My daughter Ygraine, the High Queen... You have met her?'

I shook my head. 'I have heard of her great beauty and her reputation as a priestess of wonderful abilities, but she had long gone to her marriage with Gorlois, Duke of Cornwall before I came.'

'Ah yes.' There was a long silence. 'I have had a letter from her...' She waved the vellum, as though it was a soiled rag. 'Aella what I have to tell you is for your ears only. I am not proud of my part in the tale. It must not be known.'

'Of course, I will not speak of it.' I promised, beginning to be worried. Secrets are dangerous, especially the secrets of the great ones, and Vivienne was the among the greatest of Prydein. It was no secret that the Lady and her daughter, now wife to High King Uther, were estranged. We did not know what had caused the rift, although it was presumed to be religious.

'My daughter Ygraine was indeed an exceptional priestess, and looked to become High Priestess here after my time. She is extremely beautiful and therefore of high value in the outer world. At the time King Ambrosius, Uther's brother, was organising the first resistance to the Saxons, pushing them back gradually but lacking money and men and the support of the British nobles. The Romans, the Roman-British that is, had withdrawn to Brittany in large numbers – thousands fleeing the raids of the Saxons. It was essential that more men, money and support be raised. A matter of life or death. I had a desperate appeal for help from Ambrosius.'

She paused, and then made herself go on, but could not met my eyes. 'Gorlois, Duke of Cornwall was very rich from his tin mines and trading far overseas. He had a war band of over two hundred trained warriors, and could bring to service as overlord, many hundreds, perhaps thousands, more. He was a widower, looking for a wife and heirs. I arranged a treaty for Ambrosius, with marriage to Ygraine as the price.' She was speaking very quickly now, plucking at her gown. 'Unfortunately, Ygraine would not agree.'

She got up and went to the window, staring out at the waters. clutching the parchment angrily. 'She claimed to be desperately in love with one of the young druid priests on the Tor, It was a trivial excuse, of course, not to wed Gorlois. She has no sense of duty, that one. Instead she slipped away to the Beltane fires that year, and presented herself to me, later, smiling and triumphant, saying she was pregnant. The Archdruid acted very quickly. He despatched the young man concerned away on a long trip to Egypt. And I sent Ygraine off immediately with an escort to Gorlois, and she was married within the week. A few days later. Gorlois' warriors were on the road to London, where a great battle forced the Saxons back to the federate lands.'

Well, of course, with my history, you can guess the horror I felt. I stared at her back and said nothing. She turned and came back to the couch with a grim smile. 'Gorlois did not suspect a thing. He was well content with his new bride, and was happy when she was brought to bed with my granddaughter, Morgan.

The following year she bore another daughter, Mawgawse. Everybody, including Morgan herself, believes that Gorlois was her father.'

Once more, silence fell. I was stunned, wondering why I was being made privy to this knowledge, which should certainly have remained secret.

At length she kicked away the hem of her robe and began to walk backwards and forwards again. 'Well, all the world knows the outcome of that marriage. Ambrosius was killed – murdered they say – and Uther his brother, was chosen as the next High King. Gorlois took Ygraine to London to Uther's coronation. Goddess knows why Gorlois took a woman who looked like that into such a den of wolves. King Uther saw her and immediately wanted her, nothing would prevent him taking her. He made no secret of his obsession. Gorlois withdrew from the court. Uther pretended offence and went after him. In some way, nobody knows, Uther won his way to Ygraine in Tintagel Castle and lay with her. But that same night, Gorlois attacked Uther's men from his other castle twenty miles away and was killed.

Ygraine bore a son she calls Arthur, but Uther does not fully recognise him. He might be the son of Gorlois after all.'

I said, slowly, 'I am sorry that Queen Ygraine has had such a difficult life. But forgive me, Lady, I don't know why you have found it necessary to tell me.'

'It will become apparent,' she said, dryly. 'Old sins seldom die. You need to know the background. Our problem is with Morgan, the first-born grandchild.'

Surprised I did a quick calculation. 'She would be, what, fifteen, fourteen now?'

'Nearly fourteen.'

I felt a pang in my heart. Thirteen, as I had been.

'My daughter blames me for everything that is wrong in her life. This time it is her daughter, Morgan. She does not live with Ygraine. Uther did not want his step children around his court, a constant reminder of her previous marriage. So she sent Morgan to the Abbey which she founded in Tintagel, a novice, eventually to become the Abbess there when she takes her vows.'

'She was happy with that?' I asked, doubtfully. 'She is very young to make such an important decision. But perhaps she is a follower of the Christ?

'I have no idea. I have never met the girl. Of course, she should have been sent here for her education, but Ygraine would not allow it. She holds grudges. She has never forgiven me for her arranged marriage. And now she writes to accuse me of having interfered with Morgan's life.'

'Interfered? But how could...'

The Lady laughed bitterly. 'She is irrational. Now she writes to say that to spite her, I have infected Morgan with a devil!'

I had to smile. 'How can you infect someone with a devil? Surely she doesn't really believe you would do such a thing even if it were possible?'

'Ygraine believes I have conjured up a devil to inhabit Morgan, to ruin her Abbey or just to make things difficult for her. The nuns have written to her about Morgan. They say that they cannot do anything with her and she must be removed. Apparently, she is causing mayhem at the Abbey. Here, read Ygraine's letter.' She thrust it into my hands.

It was close written in a tiny, perfect hand. I scanned the

first paragraphs of hysterical accusations, and came to the nub of the matter: 'It is your fault that she is what she is, and you can deal with her. She is totally wild. The women there are afraid of her. They say she is a black witch, demon-possessed, and spends most of her time as a raven or cormorant.' I raised my eyebrows and glanced at Vivienne, but she was staring beyond the window into the glittering waters. 'She is able to inflict injury from a distance, and is quite mad. Can call the storm, the winds and flood. Can prophecy horrid dooms. Has knowledge of poisons and herbs, and at the full moon calls down the Goddess. They say she will no longer talk to them and sometimes seems more animal than human...'

I looked up and met Vivienne's anxious glance. 'Very talented.'

'Inheritance. Two strains of magic and psychic development combined. Mad like her father.'

I looked my question. But she shrugged. 'The Druids say one of their greatest, mage and enchanter. And my own line combined. Madness.'

Not promising. I returned to the letter: 'The holy nuns in my Abbey say they can no longer look after her, and have asked that she be taken from them. They say that despite all their efforts to expel the devils that inhabit her – they have beaten her, kept her solitary and even starved...'

I exclaimed in horror, and stared at Vivienne. 'Beaten and starved?'

'I believe that is how the 'holy' nuns of the Christos have interpreted his teachings. Ignorance. They cannot have read the Testaments. Morgan will not honour the Christ and learn the prayers, saying she is of the old religion. But Ygraine is now a convert and approves the punishment.'

I said, wonderingly, 'What kind of mother can Ygraine be?'

Vivienne shook her head. 'No kind of mother. If anyone is mad it may be Ygraine. I never knew a colder, more icy woman. No warmth. No emotion. Like marble. All her life and thought focussed on the Goddess. She was a peerless oracle. Prophecies invariably correct and usually terrible, uttered with a small cold voice, without emotion, that sent shudders down your spine. Vortigern murdered. Invading Saxons. Cantii overrun. Thousands fleeing to Brittany. The death of the Empire... She carried out the rituals exactly, without error, and woe betide anyone who made a little mistake. No forgiveness. A fanatic.'

'And she is now a Christian?'

'A fanatical Christian. She blames me. Says I ruined her life. She was meant to live spotless and virginal and I sold her into marriage for the revenues of the tin mines and an army of warriors just to enhance the power of Avalon.'

'What of the Druid? What of the advance of the Saxons?'

'She says that all resistance is futile. They will take all in the end.'

I shivered. 'What of the younger child – Mawgawse? What has become of her? Is she still with her sister?'

'Uther married her off to King Lot of Lothian and Orkney, and she has already birthed a child.'

By this time, I felt very sympathetic to Morgan who seemed to have been misused badly. Even her little sister had been taken from her. I thought Ygraine sounded like an unfeeling monster.

'What will you do?' I asked. 'About Morgan I mean?'

For a while she looked away into the blue hills, painted with brilliant sunlight today. Then she looked back at me, rather desperately, I thought. 'I think we must bring her here to Avalon, and find out more about this so-called devil. If you are willing, Aella, I would like you to look after Morgan, bring her here, see her settled. You have studied the workings of the mind and may be able to understand and help her develop her great abilities. Let her love you.'

'But surely, your own granddaughter...?'

She shook her head. 'I am too closely implicated with her mother. She will be wary and distrust me, even hate me. And you are nearer her own age.'

'She must be terribly injured psychically.'

'Yes, I think it will be too late. They will have knocked too many devils in, and she may be truly mad. Merlin has been mad sometimes.'

'I will try,' I said. 'Avalon will heal her. When must I go?'

'As soon as you can make ready. John and his two sons from the Village will go with you, and you may take one of your assistants from the healing hall to help. You will need an extra horse for Morgan, and a couple of pack horses too – but I needn't go into all that. You are so practical; you will know what to do and what healing herbs you might need. Fortunately, Cornwall is at peace at the moment. There are no reports of conflict and John and his sons will see off random thieves. Go with the Goddess. I will ask her for a safe, quick journey for you.'

And that was how I found myself on the way to Tintagel to pick up a mad girl, who might be violent. But I remembered my own coming to Avalon, and my condition when they found me, and I felt a great sympathy for her, and determined to do all I could to help her, devil or no devil. I had packed some of the poppy with the herbs, and antiseptic cleaners for cuts and bruises. The pack horses were burdened with our gear and food supplies, and John, his two burly sons and sturdy Megan from the Healing Hall and myself, set off the following morning, in bright sunlight, all of us excited to be on the road to a place we had never seen, but had heard much about.

Aella 5

We were nearly two weeks on the road to Tintagel, taking the Roman Roads as far as we could, and then the high ground, following the old trackway that had been ancient when the Romans had come to our island. The village men, Avalon called them 'the Guardians', were strong, quiet men, with their own ancient magic. I had made many journeys with John and his sons and we made good time.

We journeyed through the lands of the Dumnonii, without difficulty, a smiling land of small steep hills and red earth, but Cornwall was wild, a land of wind and dark granite, the coast deeply indented and washed with the great pounding seas of the western ocean, that flung itself against the black cliffs, rising high as the cliffs themselves, and threatening to drag us from the narrow, coastal path. I had never seen anything like it, and thought it a menacing and hostile country. We were thankful when we saw, at a distance, perched high on very edge of the cliffs, the great castle of Tintagel.

Ygraine had lived here with Duke Gorlois and her two daughters, Morgan and Mawgawse, and I did not envy her.

Surely the dark bleak winters in this solitary place must be hard to bear.

It seemed that she had established her Abbey nearby, a little inland, in a narrow valley. We came first to a small village with a few tumble-down huts, which must serve the Abbey, and I was curious to see how Ygraine and her Christians had improved on her mother's sanctuary of Avalon.

The settlement had a stone wall around it, higher than two tall men, with a thick, oaken gate. Over the wall a church glowered at us, both built of the local granite. It was clear that no expense had been spared. But it seemed that the nuns must be living in the low huts of wattle and clay we could see surrounding it. The gate was barred with iron, closed with a heavy padlock. I shivered, feeling the stone pressing down on me and its darkness seemed to draw in all the energy and joy. John dismounted and tugged at the bell to summon the porteress. We waited, but there was no response, and all was silent except for the blowing wind.

John clicked his tongue in annoyance. 'They must have seen us come along the track. They do not seem overly keen to offer hospitality.' He pulled the bell again, and again we waited.

'Perhaps they are at prayer,' I said.

'I will go and ask someone in the village.'

He was back quickly, shaking his head. 'Not friendly here. Says they will open the gate when it suits them. No welcome for thirsty travellers, apparently.' He pulled the bell again, and this time kept ringing it. When, at length, a narrow door next the gate creaked open, we were all indignant at the discourtesy shown us, and expectant of an apology but there was none forthcoming. Instead, a sullen young nun said, 'Well, what do you want, making all this noise?'

'We have come a long way...' I began, but she started to close the gate.

'We don't take in vagrants. And there is no Guest Hall here.'

John wrestled the door back and stuck his boot in the gap. 'Show some respect, young woman. Do we look like vagrants? My lady has come to speak with your Abbess.'

The young nun looked him up and down. 'And who might you be?'

I dismounted, and stepped forward, enough was enough. 'My name is Gwenaella. I bear letters from Vivienne, the Lady of the Lake.'

She sneered. 'That old witch.'

For a moment I was speechless, but the anger jolted my wits. 'At the request of Ygraine, the High Queen. Of whom you will have heard.'

This at least got a response. Her eyes widened, and she stepped back. 'You'd better come in,' she said grudgingly.

We entered into a courtyard, and John and his sons were told to take the horses to the stables and wait, while Megan and I followed the woman to the main building. If the outside had been unpleasant, the inside was even more so. Low dark rooms, smelling of lye, rotting wood and mildew. There were few windows and no grace notes such as flowers or embroidered hangings. you might have expected in a building devoted to the worship of God. Everywhere there was darkness and austerity.

We waited again while the woman disappeared into the depths. No offer of a seat or food and drink. I began to wonder about this place, and how Ygraine's daughter had been looked after. Megan, my assistant from the Healing Hall looked around and pulled an expressive face. 'Not at all like Avalon! I thought the High Queen's daughter would be living in a splendid place. There's not even a place to sit.' She leaned against the stone wall, sighing.

I continued to stand, my anger and concern growing. Ten minutes later an older woman in black robes and a white veil rustled in, full of lying smiles and condescending words. But her eyes were cold as iron.

I said, cutting her short, 'You are the Abbess here?' But already she was shaking her head. 'Mother Cecilia is indisposed, and has sent me to talk to you. I am Sister Drusila, the Prioress, and can deal with your problem.'

I said, dryly, 'As I understand it, the problem is your own. I have been sent by Vivienne, the Lady of Avalon, in the matter of Ygraine's daughter, Morgan, in response to your pleas for help. Let me give you the letters. And if we could, perhaps, sit down somewhere? We have come far today.'

'Of course, of course.' The smiles disappeared and she led us hurriedly into another small dark room empty except for a rough table, a bench and a carved armchair. She gestured at the bench, and sat herself down in the armchair at the head of the table, quickly taking the proffered letters. Clearly there were to be no offers of refreshments!

She glanced quickly over the letter from the Lady, and more intently at the letter from the High Queen. Her eyes hardened and her mouth thinned. 'Yes, the problem is set out clearly here.'

'Forgive me, what exactly is the problem with the girl that you can't deal with it?'

'Total disobedience, as it says here. We have done our best

but she will not conform.'

'You have punished her?'

'Of course, many times. She takes no notice. She is impossible'

'Perhaps you have punished her too much?'

'Too much?!' She was furious. To my astonishment, hate looked out of her eyes.

'You do not know what we have had to put up with. She pretends the Goddess has chosen her and refuses to pray to our Saviour. She will not learn the prayers even. She will not set foot in the chapel. She has run away four times... She SWEARS at us.'

I had to smile a little. 'A naughty girl.'

She stared at me, unable to speak for a moment, and then lowered her voice. 'You think it a light matter? No, she is not naughty'. Her voice dropped even lower, hissing. 'She is evil. Possessed by the Devil.'

'Evil.'

'Totally, utterly evil.' Once again, unmistakeably, unbridled hatred stared out at me.

I felt a cold shudder run down my spine. 'That is a very serious charge to bring against a small child.'

'Thirteen. Not a child. You can have no idea...She is...' She was wild with horror. 'She is a... shape changer...No don't you dare laugh! It is true. I have seen it. She changed to a cormorant one day, and then to a hedgepig. And one day, as a hound, she savaged Sister Mary Gabriel when she cornered her with a pitchfork in the stables...'

I said, dryly, 'No doubt she was defending herself. Was she injured?'

'Sister Mary Gabriel's hand was mauled – she had to drop the pitchfork!'

'I meant Morgan.'

She shuddered. 'A little blood. But the Devil looks after his own...and we did bind it up.'

So that was the reason for all this hatred. Morgan had begun to develop magical abilities, inherited from her grandmother and mother no doubt. Magic was anathema to the new religion. Had Ygraine sent her to the nuns to drive out the magic? Abruptly, I was very anxious for the girl. What had they done to her in the years she had been here? And why had no one looked after her? What a strange unmotherly mother Ygraine must be, to just dump her daughter here in this god-forsaken dark place without light or love, and forget her. No doubt, as High Queen, Ygraine must have had many things on her mind. They say the King had swept her away and married her only hours after her first husband had been killed, but all the same... And what of her grandmother? My mind questioned, inconveniently. Surely Vivienne should have taken an interest in her little granddaughter? I could not help being critical of both of them. And what of the women here, who according to the teachings of their Master, should be looking after and loving a vulnerable, orphaned child, rather than attacking her with a pitchfork?

'I must see the child,' I said.

She hesitated and looked away uncomfortably. 'Well yes, I suppose so. Sister Agnes will take you. She is in charge of her.' She hesitated again. 'You must understand that we have had to isolate Morgan to keep her from infecting us all. She breaks the furniture and tears up her bedding. Rips her clothing. We have done all we could...We have prayed for her so often... I assure you...'

'Where will I find Sister Agnes?' I said, impatiently, cutting her excuses short and standing up.

'I will ring,' she said quickly, clearly relieved to pass the problem on to someone else, and seized a brass bell on the table. 'We have tried everything...when our prayers failed again, we even reduced her food hoping to starve out the devil...'

I began to feel very cold.

If anything, Sister Agnes was even more forbidding than the Prioress. She had a stony white face, lipless and grim. Her eyes dilated strangely when she was told to take us to Morgan.

'She may be sleeping. We forced a sedative on her last night to stop her leaping on us when we tried to feed her.'

'She does not eat?' Megan said, worried.

'She smears it over the floor. Says we are poisoning her.' Sister Agnes said contemptuously. 'Such a fuss about a little Bayberry emetic and Senna for cleansing her insides. She is a wild animal. Not human. Come.' I was breathless again. They were giving her herbs to make her sick and loosen her bowels?? I could not believe I was truly hearing this.

We followed her outside across the courtyard to a row of stone cells built into the side of the cliff itself. The nun lit a small lantern and handed it to me. She collected a key from a peg in the wall and picked up a stout stick nearby, saying nothing, but her eyes glittered and I became more and more apprehensive.

She inserted the key and opened the heavy door a few inches, thrusting the stick ahead, and peering into the gloom. I waited for a wild creature to explode forward, but nothing happened, and I pushed Sister Agnes to one side and raised the lantern. I shall never forget what I saw then.

The light played dimly over the low stone walls like a pig sty, empty except for a pile of bones on a handful of straw in the corner. I caught my breath and nearly vomited at the stink. Human waste and urine, rotten food, mixed with thick mud on the floor, where the rain had run in under the door.

'What on earth?' I exploded, and then I saw that the bones were a human creature chained to the wall. It lifted its head.

'Chained?' I said, unbelieving.

Sister Agnes sneered. 'How else can we keep a shape shifter imprisoned here?' She went forward and poked at the creature with her stick. 'Up Satan's get. Up. I say!'

The creature struggled to stand, holding on to the rough stones of the wall, and received another poke. 'UP, I said.'

She was small for her age, covered in mud and filth, and bloody wounds and bruises, her hair in tufts, close to her skull, like a misshapen goblin, one eye blackened. I don't think I have ever seen such a poor little creature. My heart went out to her.

I whipped around to Sister Agnes, like an enraged dog. 'Chained in the dark, bruised, starved, beaten, made to live like a pig in filth – you all deserve to be whipped in the stocks. This is an insult to the Goddess and the White Christ both. The Archbishop shall hear of this.'

I turned to the girl. 'My Lady Morgan, I am sorry to see you in such circumstances. I am Gwenaella. I am here to take you to your grandmother, the Lady of Avalon. Will you come with me?'

She took one step towards me, her huge eyes on mine, not quite believing, her hand held out in entreaty. I felt the tears run down my cheeks. I took her hand, gently, a handful of tiny, icy, bones. Her legs folded and she slid unconscious into the shit and muck beneath our feet. I picked her up. She was without substance, unnaturally light, like holding a shadow.

'Unlock the chain.'

'Set the devil free? She'll escape and...'

'You are the only devil here. You have damn near-killed her, you diabolical creature. If she dies the Lady will see that the High King will hang and quarter you.'

She stared at me, saw my rage, and knew that I was telling the truth. She scurried forward and unlocked the iron band around Morgan's ankle releasing another stench from the festering wound there, and I carried her out into the blessed fresh air. There was another of the stone cells nearby, which was empty but clean, and I laid her on a low pallet and saw, to my relief, that she was still breathing.

'You...woman... fetch hot water, blankets and clean clothes – immediately. Megan, go with her, and see she does. and bring back my saddle-bag with the medicines. And then see if you can find the kitchens. Morgan will need warm milk with two eggs beaten into it. She has been starved.'

'She'll never be able to travel in this condition,' Megan said, worried, hurrying away.

While they were gone, I examined Morgan carefully, calling some emergency healing spells, to help the pain and her irregular breathing. I had never treated any one in this condition. Her wasted body, was covered with bruises and cuts. Her arms and legs were little more than bones. Where the iron band had been around her ankles there was a great festering sore. And when I gently tuned her, I found her back was scored with many whip marks that were oozing with blood and pus. Morgan's torture had gone on for many months. When I touched her side, I found she had two broken ribs.

Megan was right, Morgan would not be able to travel for a few days at least and we would be stuck here in this deathly place. This knowledge added to my fast-growing rage, and when the Prioress came with a cohort of her nuns bearing the hot water and clean clothing, you can be sure I made no attempt to restrain myself. I can tell you that I set that place by its ears, and soon they were all running around, like frightened hens, shocked and trying to pacify me, realising, I think, that they had gone too far and were in danger of retribution from the High King.

'We have done our best,' said the Prioress, with indignant tears on her cheeks. 'We have done everything to drive out her devils and save her from everlasting Hell, just as her mother instructed us.'

'You are the only devils she has suffered from. The White Christ himself would have driven you from these doors. Love your neighbour, he taught. And you, you have been torturing a child. Get into your chapel now, and start praying for forgiveness, and hope that we will be able to save her. The Archbishop will be here to see what kind of Christianity you are professing.'

John and his sons herded the women into their chapel and locked the doors, standing guard outside while Bethan and I set about attending to Morgan properly. The Abbey servants, came and were very helpful, providing food and sleeping places for us all, glad that they could restore order, and Cook told me that they did not like what was being done to Morgan, but of course, had no power to stop the orders of the Abbess.

Morgan was unconscious, and to my relief we were able to wash away the dirt and blood, destroy the lice, and put stitches into the two deepest slashes in her back, before her eyelids began to flutter, and she came to herself. We used woundwort and arnica for the bruises, and my own special ointment, sovereign for healing broken and poisoned skin. We put her into a clean white shift and wrapped her in a blanket. Her skin was grey and icy. John found an iron fire basket in the stables and some logs to heat the cell a little.

Morgan asked for water and we persuaded her also to drink the warm milk and eggs.

She got most of it down and some colour had begun to come back into her cheeks. She tried to smile as she gave back the cup. 'Thank you. I did not hear your name properly.'

I held her hand and smiled at her. 'Gwenaella. Call me Aella. I am a Priestess of Avalon. I am sent to fetch you to your grandmother, when you are a little better.'

'Thank you, Aella. I think I owe you my life.' She gripped my hand, the dignified politeness disappearing into the onrush of fear. 'Don't leave me. Please don't let them come near. Please... Don't let them get at me... I can't hold out against them again...'

'You are safe, Lady Morgan, completely safe. They are shut into the Chapel until we leave. Sleep now. Let your body heal you. I will be here with you through the night.'

She slept, but irregularly, frequently waking and crying out. I sat stroking her hands and, when she woke, there was herbal tea, camomile and valerian, to help her relax her tightly locked muscles to help her sleep again.

That night forged a strong link between us. A friendship

made in such circumstances is lifelong. She trusts me, perhaps the only person she does trust. Later she learned to love her grandmother dearly, but I think she could not entirely forget that she had abandoned her to the Tintagel nuns for so many years.

Early on the third day, Morgan insisted on trying to climb on to her horse for the journey back to Avalon, Shaking and fearful, she could not bear to stay another day in this house of horror, fearing that the nuns would find a way to stop her leaving. I understood only too well, but she could not sit a horse by herself, and in the end, I held her in my arms tightly while John guided us on a leading rein.

We made our way in short stretches, stopping early and starting late. But Morgan made no complaint. It was only her pale face and grim mouth that told us the truth of her suffering. I had done all I could with my herbal medicines and healing spells, and her flesh wounds had begun to heal, but I did not like the strange, blank look in her eyes, and the way she kept drifting away into a shadowy darkness. I realised with horror, that she was much nearer death than I had thought. I could feel her life spirit loosening, withdrawing, now she had no further need to fight. She was so weary, giving up and ready to sleep the long sleep. I could not bear to lose her now. But I did not know what to do.

I did my best. It seemed important to keep her consciousness with us, and as we journeyed, I kept talking to her softly. I questioned and listened to her appalling story of bullying and torture, and her determination to follow the Goddess, and the old religion as her old nurse taught her when they lived alone in Tintagel Castle, before her mother had sent her to the nuns. She was very bitter at her mother. She had known that her grandmother was Vivienne, the famous Lady of the Lake in Avalon, where young women went to study, and begged to go there, but Ygraine had told her that her grandmother did not want her, and she must go to the Abbey and learn to be a nun. She told me how she had learned to change into animals and birds to try to escape from the Abbey. and I shared my own story of my father and my escape and rescue, and it made another bond between us.

I told her about her grandmother and the wonderful people she would live among. I don't think she believed me but she said, 'Yes, tell me about Avalon,' and listened avidly to all I could tell her, as though I was telling a lovely story of Tir na nOg, or some other ancient wonderland. I didn't care. If it kept her with us until we reached the safety of the healing hall I would keep talking.

'It is a beautiful place, Morgan. You will love the wondrous library. You will be able to study magic, or whatever you want. Kings and chieftains send their daughters to learn writing and reading, Latin, and household management and herbal remedies, to fit them for them for noble marriages, so there are other young girls there. You will make friends. There are even advanced magical studies for those who wish to stay permanently. Your grandmother, Vivienne, is the third High Priestess to hold office and under her rule Avalon has become famous for its healing and wisdom throughout the land, and her advice is sought from as far away as Armorica and Rome and Constantinople...'

I tried to explain to her the magical enchantment of the place, the feeling of peace and love. Morgan said nothing. She had drifted away again, but there was a half-smile on her face and I hoped so much that she would decide to stay with us after all.

'There's a tree,' she whispered, 'A great tree with birds in it, singing, beautifully...'

Tir na nOg again, I thought, and despaired.

But Morgan, thanks be, was still alive when we finally arrived back in Avalon. We were all exhausted, even the Guardians, who went off home quickly, pleased with their generous payments, and the additional gifts, Vivienne pressed upon them with our very sincere thanks.

We went immediately to the Healing Hall, and I cried with relief when I found Sophia our finest healer and my own dear mentor, waiting for us. Morgan lay insensible. She had spoken once when we started that morning, but not since, even when we carried her to the ferry. We stared down at the broken child, and suddenly I was determined to fight for her. She should not be lost. It seemed that she was like my own little daughter returned to me.

'We must fight hard,' I said. 'She is a very special child. A future high Priestess of Avalon.' I never knew why I said that, but her eyes opened briefly, and stared into mine. They were strange fey eyes, glowing gold, like an animal or bird, and then, wonderfully, she tried to smile, before falling unconscious again.

Sophia examined her carefully, every one of the cuts, sores and bruises, then she laid her hands onto Morgan's forehead and heart, motionless for long minutes. At length she shook her head and looked at me. 'Trauma of the body, of course. She has broken ribs and internal injuries where someone has kicked her in the stomach, but worse, trauma of the mind and spirit. I do not think she wants to live.'

'Is there nothing we can do?'

'We will try the Deep Sleep.' Sophia said. 'Let her body relax and heal.' It was a treatment we sometimes used when the patient had suffered such severe trauma that his spirit was loosened from his body. The patient was deeply sedated and put into a long-lasting sleep while the body healed and the mind threw off its panic and despair. Sometimes it was successful.

I went to see Vivienne in a fine temper, describing Morgan's condition and the tortures she had undergone, making no attempt to soften the horrors. There is no doubt that the Lady was totally shocked and full of remorse at her own failure to protect her granddaughter. Letters began to fly to the High King, the Archbishop, and one to Ygraine which must have haunted her for the rest of her life. The Lady ended by forbidding her to have any further contact with Morgan, and saying she had chosen to stay in Avalon to serve the Goddess. This was news to me, but to my surprise it later proved to be true.

As for me, I went back to the Hall of the Deep Sleepers, which was located in a very quiet section of the palace at the end of the Healing Hall, and sat with Morgan day and night, using all my powers of psychic healing. Relays of healers would sit with her over the next days, surrounding her with an intense network of healing light and holding and strengthening her fluttering spirit. Occasionally when she woke briefly, she was able to drink milk and honey, and it seemed that her wounds were healing.

Gradually, as was usual, the Deep Sleep lightened, and one

afternoon she woke naturally, and lay there, bringing herself into full consciousness, and to my joy, I knew she would survive, but how deeply her injuries had affected her mind we would not know for many months. But for now, at least, she had decided to stay with us.

I bent over her. 'Good afternoon, Lady Morgan. How is it with you?'

'Am I dead?'

Tears came running down my cheeks, and she put up her hand and wiped them away.

'I think I should know you. Are you an angel?'

That made me smile. 'You are in Avalon, in the House of the Goddess, and I am a Priestess here – your mentor when you are better and your healer and protector for the time being.'

She sighed with relief. 'I am truly in the House of the Lady? They tried to make me give her up, but I would not. I have met her, you see.'

Morgan chose to stay in the Healing Hall for several more weeks, slowly gaining in strength and confidence, and then, with increased appetite and nutritious food, sitting at peace in the sunlight in the garden, making big steps to full recovery. I think it was a long time before she really believed that she was in a place of peace and safety, and I knew it would be a long time before she began to recover her mental health, and perhaps, in some ways, she never did recover completely.

Aella 6

Morgan settled into Avalon like a jewel in a gold setting, although it took her months to recover her health and spirits fully. She met and talked with her grandmother, and was, at first, wary and suspicious, but as the atmosphere of Avalon began to heal her, I could see that the old memories were set aside and she seemed to forgive her grandmother and, I think, came to love her dearly, as we all did.

Avalon suited her well. She held to the Goddess with total dedication, and was happy carrying out the rituals and her duties as an acolyte. To my delight she asked to be attached to the Healing Hall and Herbarium and we worked together happily. Her thirst for knowledge of plants and herbs was unquenchable. She was highly intelligent, and her memory extraordinary.

She loved studying, and worked very hard. She read and spoke Latin fluently and particularly enjoyed exploring the collection of ancient scrolls in the library. She soaked up knowledge astonishingly quickly, developed a great interest in history and, especially, Land Law, and it was not long before she began working with her grandmother as an assistant, writing letters and trying to promote co-operation and peace among the British warring kings, learning about the governance of the land and the diplomacy needed to achieve power to maintain the influence of the Goddess, as our religion was being constantly undermined and challenged by the Bishops, the Roman Emperor Constantine had imposed on us.

Her interest and knowledge of the ancient documents in the library became very useful in the running of the Avalon estate which was extensive. Avalon owned not only the palace and the attached farmland on the lake, but most of the surrounding properties, farms and villages. People had gratefully donated grants of land in return for Vivienne's magical help, and as it grew the estate had become tangled and largely neglected. Morgan was able to sort out the finances, bring increasing prosperity and making sure the land was properly farmed. As a result, Avalon's extra income allowed them to effect repairs for tenants, build new houses in the villages, improve the facilities of the school, and buy farming tools and sacks of seed for sewing in the drained lands. Before she was eighteen, she was handling all the land disputes for Avalon, in the law courts, and winning them too, and Vivienne had made her one of the nine Senior Priestesses, with the enthusiastic agreement of the other eight. Almost all of the Priestesses loved and respected her. She could be lively and interesting company, a witty debater, laughing, and singing her own songs to her harp.

As the years passed Morgan's magical powers developed startlingly. It was quickly apparent that she was outstandingly talented, beyond any of the other acolytes, and the oldest Priestesses said they had not seen such abilities since Ygraine herself had come to Avalon. She scryed easily and transmitted messages so accurately that Vivienne used her regularly in her communications to the Priestesses scattered all over Logres, who regularly supplied information to us. Her first prophecies began to break through spontaneously at our festivals and rituals, and it seemed that they came true. She predicted new arrivals at Avalon before they came, and she could predict the outcome of battles, and what time was auspicious, to start new projects. And gradually it seemed also that she might be able to host the Lady herself in our rituals, which few could do without danger.

Her abilities were guided carefully in the community but the old Morgan had not gone. She was settled, but not tamed. There was always a streak of wildness in her, which I could well understand. Sometimes she would grow restless, and her search for freedom would not be denied, and she would change into a sea eagle, or a deer or a wolf, and would disappear for a while to ride the dark October gales. I think in the early days it was the only thing that kept her sane. The powers which had troubled the nuns were still there, but nobody tried to stop her shape-changing. It was as necessary to her as breathing. It was her way of keeping in contact with nature, with the wild, and the creatures that lived there. It was freedom too, to be untrammelled, to fly and to soar on the wind. The danger was pointed out to her, of course, that she might want to relinquish her human soul and not come back if she stayed more than a few days in the animal host, but we were awed and envious of her powers.

I never asked what she did on these expeditions, or sought to prevent her. There were many magical happenings in Avalon, and her difference was acceptable. What we could do for her was to show her ways of controlling the dangers she laid herself open to, and over the years I was able to help her control the limits of her despair, and reach for a calmer way of living. There were failures, but I do think that Morgan was truly happy in those years, revelling in her freedom, and the opening of her mind.

Rhianna, I don't want you to think it was all sweetness and light, because it wasn't. Morgan was, and is, a difficult person. A strong personality of shifting moods, one moment in ecstasy of delight over a butterfly's wing, the next in bitter depths of despair at her perceived failures. She was always very hard on herself, a woman of sheer creative eccentricity that left you gasping and wondering. But creative? Oh yes, creative in all ways. I never knew a greater healer, until you, my dear Rhianna, started to come into your powers. She would examine a patient carefully, and then, out of the blue, suggest a combination of herbs that one would never have thought of in a thousand years, and yet which proved to be exactly what was needed. It was as though some second sense told her what was wrong. I am a good herb-wife myself, if you'll forgive my boasting, and was appointed Senior Healer when my dear Sophia stood down , but I have never owned the genius she showed.

Morgan's eccentricity did not disappear in Avalon. She would always be different from other women. Disappearing for days in a changed shape was only part of it. She slept very little and would rise past midnight to dance wildly in the moonlight with some creature attracted to her, a hare perhaps or a hind. She was able to swim like a fish, and once swam the length of our big lake out to the Sabrina Sea. She dived. She flew. It was as though these physical activities helped her to control the wildness of her nature. She was indeed like a wild cat, very loving in the house, but riding the wild wind in the night. From being an undersized twelve-year-old, Morgan grew taller and taller. She was deceptively slender but very strong, with long arms and legs, and she reminded me of a heron or some other wading bird, stepping forward lightly and agilely

Through all this, Morgan and I retained our close bond. She confided in me, explaining her fears of the strange powers that had begun to manifest in her as she grew into womanhood. She felt that her healing abilities and advanced medical knowledge were being directed from elsewhere. She hoped that it was the Goddess herself who was somehow entering into her hands and mind, but was frightened because the nuns had told her the voices and powers were from the Devil – and how could she be sure? My reassurance was not enough and I suggested she should speak to Vivienne about it. But Vivienne reacted with scornful laughter at the devils, and not understanding Morgan's very real fear, was delighted to hear about the new powers and she dismissed the problem, saying it was all entirely natural and nothing to worry about – which had not helped Morgan at all.

To me, privately, Vivienne said joyously that she thought she had at last found a successor, with all the magical abilities needed by a High Priestess, when she had virtually given up hope. She was getting old, and although the Priestesses of Avalon lived to an exceptional age, she was aware that she was getting weaker.

'When the Goddess comes through,' she said, moving the glass of water on her desk backwards and forwards, avoiding my glance. 'It is always a shock. You feel you are falling, or fainting. You lose control. Your heart pounds and your brain panics as the great power enters and possesses you. And when she departs, all your energy goes too, and you are like a rag doll, unable to think, unable to speak for several days. There's nothing left. You are empty and dying.' She moved the glass again and looked up at me, trying to smile. 'I don't know how long I can go on. The Beltane prophecy, especially...and as for the great Sovereignty rituals of the kings...Hieros Gamos, the Sacred marriage...I dread them. It takes me weeks to recover.'

I knew this to be true. She was always secluded for many days afterwards. I was surprised to hear that Vivienne was frightened too, despite her many years as High Priestess

I was appalled and worried. It had never occurred to me that the price she paid was so high. I tried to calculate her age, but beyond knowing that she had been in Avalon when King Uther's father and brother had been High Kings, I could not guess. I suspected her heart was weakening. Her last pregnancy from a Sovereignty ceremony had been four years ago and she had nearly died. She must be over seventy. Ygraine was a child of her old age. Even Atlantean magic could not put off old age for ever. Certainly, another child would kill her. No wonder she was so happy to have a possible successor. I wondered though, how Morgan felt about it. Had Vivienne ever discussed it with her?

When I asked her, Morgan was full of delight that Vivienne was thinking of her as a successor. She felt that she had been called by the Great Goddess herself as a child, and as she went through her strict, difficult, Priestess training, it became clear that she was one of the few who was strong enough to sustain the incarnation of the Goddess herself in the great Rites of the seasons. She was in no doubt herself that this was the great work she had been born for, and proudly accepted her future role, preparing herself with all the fervour of her soul.

Morgan was devout and deeply spiritual, and when, later, I heard the stories of black witchcraft and wicked sorceries, I never believed them. Morgan was incapable of using her great powers against the Law of our life-giving Goddess in whatever deviance her accusers, especially the priests of Rome, laid at her door. Many of these men were sick in their spirits and mind and must lay the evils of the world on all women, especially on women they perceived to have better knowledge and power and freedom than their own.

Morgan modelled herself on Vivienne and loved her deeply. More, she revered her, seeing Vivienne's greatness and dedication, her moral and spiritual beauty, and admired the way she had maintained the old religion against the encroachment of the new, as it spread rapidly. She remembered that Vivienne had rescued her from her hellish life in the Tintagel Abbey, and was giving her the chance of achieving her greatest dream, serving the Great Goddess as Lady of Avalon.

So when the trouble came, it devastated her, wiping away the good of the years. The very foundation of her new life was shattered and she was plunged once again into despair, bereft of love and trust.

Part Two

Aella 7

In Avalon we were careful to observe all the secret rituals, weekly and monthly of the Goddess, but we also celebrated the great Wheel of the Year Festivities, Imbolc, Beltane, Lugnasadh, and Samhain, and the solstices – Yule and Litha – and the equinoxes – Ostara and Mabon, along with everybody else. Indeed, we had a special part to play in them, singing, dancing, and calling down the Goddess to give guidance and prophesy for the following year. Each of them had its own particular feeling and purpose, but I suppose the most popular and dearly loved was the Beltane celebration in May, when we welcomed the Summer and renewed the fertility of the land, beast and man, with fire and feasting. It has always been the most joyful of occasions, and even the Christian priests have not succeeded in driving it away yet. So when Vivienne called us together to explain that this year there would be an extraordinary event for which we must prepare with the utmost effort, we were both excited and apprehensive.

This year at Beltane there was to be a Gathering. It would take place in the traditional sacred Gathering place at the centre of the land, which had not happened since the Romans had come. Its purpose was to initiate a new High King, of all Logres – the first for four hundred years. The king would undertake the sacred rites, run with the deer and kill the white stag, and swear his life to the land with the full Sovereignty ritual, the Hieros Gamos. There would be games, feasting, dancing, music and the long Prophecy, if we could draw down, and sustain the Goddess for the time necessary. It was essential that all this be accomplished without error and with the maximum power. Even getting to the Gathering would be difficult, the sacred place was on the borders of disputed territory. It must be done secretly without bloodshed or the initiation would fail.

We stared at her, stunned. The difficulty of accomplishing all this – the impossibility – was clear to all of us, and we were speechless.

The Lady of the Lake looked around at us, and attempted a smile. 'We will start the spell chanting tomorrow. With deep meditation at dawn and dusk each day from now on.'

We set off at moonrise. A large party: The Lady, all nine of the High Priestesses, and any of the other Priestesses and acolytes who chose to come, plus a company of Guardians to clear the way ahead and protect us. The stables had been emptied of horses and mules for the older women to ride, and the rest of us walked alongside. Most of the Guardians from the Village had departed a week earlier, taking the ceremonial tents and ritual regalia, and large amounts of food, water, and medical supplies in the harvest wagons. All had been armed to the teeth, warded for protection, and heavily spelled for invisibility.

Despite our excitement, we went very quietly, hardly

speaking, dressed in our ritual robes and dark hooded cloaks, slipping through the forests like shadows, travelling through the night, or through magically raised mist in the twilight and few saw us pass. We were moving in dangerous territory, country that had been fought over and ruined for years now, some settled by our enemies, Angles and Saxons. It was a fluid, disputed border. We did not know where it was this night.

On the fourth day, near dawn, as we left the deep forest behind, we were suddenly surrounded by a silent troop of warriors. They were a frightening sight, with helmets and leather breastplates, furred cloaks, spears and swords. Taken totally by surprise, we crowded together. It was too late to flee.

'Identify yourselves,' said the officer, riding forward. He spoke Brythonic but with an unfamiliar accent, and I thought we had ridden into a band of Jutes.

'We are daughters of the Great Goddess,' Vivienne spoke clearly, without even a tremor in her voice, to my admiration. 'Priestesses of Avalon in the Summer Country. I am Vivienne, Lady of the Lake.'

To my astonishment, the man slid from his horse, and kneeled, bowing his head.

'Be most welcome, Lady. We are of the Durotriges, near Dorchester. We have heard of your great wisdom and healing work. We are here patrolling the perimeter to protect the Gathering Place from intruders. You are nearly there.'

My heart slowed down. Friends, not enemies.

'We are in good time, then.' Vivienne said. 'We are tired. There will be time to rest.'

'We are honoured to form an escort for you and your party.' He mounted his horse. 'Your men arrived a few days ago and have already set up your camp.' That was good news. We would have proper beds and hot food.

All the warriors bowed respectfully from the back of their horses, and surrounding us, led us up a scarcely discernable trackway, into high hilly country, and a mile or so later we passed through a rocky defile and came out high up, into open country.

We had halted involuntarily, taking in the scene. It was a great bowl of land, a natural amphitheatre, surrounded by low hills, and those hills themselves surrounded by higher hills, broken and rocky. To the north there was a great fall of cliff, and at its base a raised terrace, treeless and flat, with a river, falling from a higher hill, flowing clear and strong alongside the valley floor. The grassy valley was, perhaps, the size of two or three fields wide. It was the most sacred of our ancestors' gathering places, protected for generations, where only the most sacred rituals took place. It had never been used during the Roman occupation, and now we were here, and would be awakening it to its old powers. I could feel the energies in the earth, swirling around certain tall stones, building up at the base of the cliff, where I could see now, the entrance to a dark cave, The scene was wonderful, full of the rich fertile green of the grass and the hills in varying shades of misty blue fading into the distance. It was so very beautiful but my stomach was gripped with tension. Would we be strong enough to hold the powers? Would we be able to call the Goddess for her Prophecies? And would the Hieros Gamos be forged so strong that we would have the great new Leader that we needed so sorely? What if we failed abjectly in front of all these people?

I had never seen so many people in my life. They were

swarming everywhere, men, women, children, of every age and degree, wearing a huge variety of traditional costumes. They must come from everywhere in the country, all the different tribes come together for the first time in hundreds of years. Some were preparing food, others were building a great bon fire, people carried buckets back and forwards to the river, and suddenly, when I looked up, I realised that all the hills had their camps too, pennants flying, drums ready. Each party had established its own territory, and seemed cautious, but here there would be no dispute. Death would come instantly to any truce breaker.

Morgan standing next to me, said suddenly, 'Oh Goddess, I feel...' and swayed, alarmingly.

'What is it?' I asked, taking my eyes from the great bowl of shimmering light, reluctantly, and just managed to catch her before she fell. 'What...?

'I don't know. I feel very strange...'

Before I could do anything, Vivienne began to ride down the track and we all followed, Morgan, gripping my cloak tightly.

The Guardians had done a wonderful job. Vivienne's Pavilion, and the Healing Hall, with several smaller tents clustered around them, had been set up between the raised terrace and the waterfall. Our pennant blew bravely in the light wind.

We were greeted jovially by our neighbours, I recognised as the Druids from Glastonbury Tor, who all seemed to be in high spirits.

Morgan sat down suddenly on the springy green turf and put her head in her hands. I gave her my water bottle. 'Drink.'

And after a while the colour came back into her skin.

'Is she all right?' asked Vivienne coming over to us. She always noticed everything.

'A little faint, I think.'

But Morgan did not bother to answer. She closed her eyes.

'Come,' said Vivienne, 'We must get settled and washed. There will be food and time to rest. The first rite takes place this night at moonrise.'

We found our small tent, Morgan and I, and after forcing down a bowl of vegetable broth, Morgan fell into a deep sleep and I did not wake her until it was time to begin the cleansing ritual in the sparkling river. We changed into our ceremonial robes of deep violet silk, with the full split sleeves which allowed our white arms to emerge when we raised them. The skirts too were split nearly to the waist, so we could move freely in the dance and ritual movements. They were a compromise, of course. In our own private rites, we were naked, open to the Goddess, but here it was thought more seemly to be covered, although later, in the Beltane celebrations the robes, no doubt, would disappear.

The sun was beginning to go down, and was painting the hills in intense shades of green-gold, outlining every leaf with a gold that that seemed to glow with extraordinary clarity. In the distance the line of very high hills was a deep blue violet.

I took a deep breath, and was suddenly flooded with a feeling of awe, and some overwhelming feeling of the sacredness of the place, a gratitude for the great beauty and a deeply welling excitement. I could not wait for the sacraments to start.

I turned then and went to the Pavilion, where we would sit in meditation to calm our minds and align our souls, the most important part of our preparations.

As the darkened sky began to lighten for Moon rise, everyone began to gather in the amphitheatre, quiet, a little apprehensive or fearful at the quivering tension and power that was rising, and could be felt now. I glanced around at the bowl of the Gathering Place and saw that the hills had quickened with watch fires. Thousands of people were there, gathered into their own clans. Each hill glowed, and I became aware of something that had been beneath my hearing for some time. A slow, deep, thrumming, an echoing, almost lazy beat.

'Drums.' I said.

'All around,' Morgan said. 'Makes you feel on edge. They seem to be beating in my stomach.'

I glanced at her. 'Are you alright now?'

'The sleeping helped. This is extraordinary. I never thought it would be like this.

Look, Aella, look there in the shadows by the giant rock, there are the little dark people, and there...' her voice faltered, 'Surely...'

'Fair Folk!' I exclaimed, shocked. 'The Fae are here!' They were unmistakeable. very tall and thin, with a pearly glow, and shining hair.

'I think,' Morgan said, her voice shaking, 'that the whole of Logres is here to welcome the new High King whoever he is. He must be somebody very special.

Something unprecedented is about to happen this Beltane. I think I am afraid.'

'So am I.'

At that point, three men in bardic robes strode forward

with their helpers carrying amazing instruments, great bronze horns, each more than eight feet in length with a wide bell shape at the end, which rested on the ground.

The Moon began to rise, golden and joyous, and the three horns sounded in unison – a great bellowing of sound, demanding attention, lifting the hair on the back of my neck, and all the people in that vast bowl instantly fell silent, waiting. The horns sounded again, and we watched the Moon raise herself above the dark hills, glorious and golden, light flooding down, like liquid honey.

'Now!' said Vivienne and led us down from our terrace, joining a like procession of Druids, from the other end of the terrace to the levelled ground. The two lines of priests and priestesses wove together and began to coil into a giant spiral, the Goddess's sign of all life and eternity.

The echoing sound of the horns died away, and the spiral voices began to chant. At first it was a little ragged, until it gathered strength, and spoke with one voice, an ancient Atlantean spell in a language no one now understood. Deep voices from the onlookers joined us, rising. And then, suddenly there was a sound you sometimes hear when there is a fierce lightening strike, a splitting, cracking, and then the whole perimeter of the Gathering Place lit up transparent silver, and burned blue.

We spiralled again, increased the tempo of the chant, linked hands, and the splitting sound, arrowed again across the sky, and then beyond the first warding you could see another, extending far out. My whole body was shaking with the power. We swayed into another circling, shouting the chant like thunder, and far out in the country a third glimmering of silver blue shone briefly.

A triple warding! I had heard of it, but had never hoped to see such an extraordinary working, let alone take part in it. It was awesome. The warding must stretch fifty miles or more into the surrounding countryside.

There was a brief silence, then the High Druid stepped forward. 'The Power is raised. The Circle is safe.' And looking up I saw, amazed, that there was a dome of silver blue stretching over all the hills and over the Gathering Place.

The procession reformed and we walked the spiral again, away from the centre, up to the raised terrace, but not to relax. Our job now was to maintain a long, night vigil. The people were dispersing, their voices low, awestruck. I do not think anybody who was there will ever forget that night, the Dome, the glorious Moon, and the whole firmament of shimmering stars. The raised energies strengthened through the night filling the whole place with quivering power, still growing. The drums were silent, but our linked minds were adding a kind of thrumming to the air.

It was the Eve of Beltane, and throughout the night, as was the ancient tradition, we prayed and gave thanks: For the safety and prosperity of the Land, the fecundity of man and beast. We gave thanks for its bounty of plants and crops. We chanted the long list of ancient laws of the Universe, so they should not be forgotten, and we thanked the Goddess for the Gift of Life, and the beauty of our World. And we prayed that she would bring us her Beltane prophecy for the coming year.

Towards dawn, the great bowl of the Gathering Place began to fill with pearly mist.

We watched silently, waiting, as the light grew. Finally, the mist parted, and a single file of deer walked, ghostlike, one at a time, down to the river to drink. At the same time four men had emerged from the cave opening, on to the terrace, as silent and ghost-like as the deer. Three were older warriors, cloaked and armed, the fourth, was a very tall man in a dark robe, some sort of mage or priest, perhaps.

Editha, next to me, caught her breath, 'That's Merlin!' she whispered.

All four bowed deeply, and from the cave came another, a young man this time, exceptionally tall, with broad shoulders, slim hips, very strong arms and leg. He was near naked, with only a short kilt and belt slung low around his hips holding a ritual knife – and he was painted head to toe in the ancient patterns of our people, the Goddess' winding spirals, for magical protection.

Editha said, 'That's the Initiate, the King to be. He must prove his courage; he must be willing to shed his blood for the Land. The King must die for the King to live.'

Her words sent a shiver down my back. What must he do? Surely, they wouldn't need to kill him?

'What a beautiful young man,' Morgan said, tranced.

'It's not fair. He isn't armed.' I said.

Editha said, 'A small athame, there in his belt.'

'Useless.'

The mist thickened, and we fell into silence, anxious for him. The deer began to thread the path away from the river, and I saw the young man look up, his body tightening, alert, and then we became aware of another presence. Above on a low hill, a huge white stag was observing us. Many antlered, he was fierce and proud, not afraid. He was staring across at the young man, challenging, arrogant. They stared at each other for several minutes unmoving. Then the young man stepped forward. The Stag lifted his hoof, tossed his head contemptuously, and bounded away after his herd.

The young man, raised his right hand to his friends and leaped lightly down the slope in pursuit. The mist closed around him. Nobody moved. I think we were all praying for his safety. After a few minutes, the three warriors walked slowly down the slope after him.

'Observers,' said Editha. 'They won't protect him. They will observe the kill, so it is known he hasn't cheated. Or if he fails, they will bring back his body.'

Merlin stared after them for a while and then returned to the cave. I thought he looked worried and tense, and why not? The Prince seemed very young to be undertaking such a dangerous trial.

Finally, it was Beltane. A fine day, sunny with a cool breeze, just the weather for all the activities. There were foot races, sword fights, spear throwing, archery contests, horse and chariot racing, sheep dog trials. There was music and dancing, and we Priestesses began the preparations for our attempt to bring down the Goddess for the Prophecy, and for the Great Rite, the Hieros Gamos, or sacred marriage.

I spent most of the day in the Healing tent, with an assortment of healers from all the different peoples, exchanging ideas, learning new things from each other, and, of course, healing all the people who came with a variety of problems.

It was a long day and in the late afternoon I retired to our tent to get some food and sleep for a few hours. We had the most demanding rites ahead of us, and would again be up all night. Morgan was already there, in a silent mood, almost fearful, I thought, but she didn't want to speak of it, and quickly fell asleep.

When I woke the sun was going down and spreading the glowing gold over the hills. The drums were beating, and adding a sense of excitement and anticipation as folk rested and ate, and the Priestesses went to the river for the Purification Rite preparatory for the Calling of the Goddess.

I asked Vivienne if the young King had returned safely, but she shook her head.

'He should have been back several hours ago. Merlin is worried. We have been scrying to see where he might be. But there is no image.'

As I returned to the tent, I called out to one of the Druids asking if there was any new information, and he said that they had been up into the hills, looking. They had found the three Observers, returning, totally exhausted. The Hunt had been wild and reckless, and they had lost track of the Prince hours ago. They had been searching for him but there was no trace.

'It will be disastrous if the Prince does not appear in time for the Sacred Marriage,' he said. 'They say that Lot, that ambitious thug, will insist on taking his place, and he is unthinkable as High King.'

As the evening came on, I noticed more people climbing up to high points in the hills, scanning the distances anxiously. Bands of warriors were setting off along the trackways, search parties sent out before it became too dark to see. The mood had changed from laughing excitement to worried uncertainty.

'What will we do if he does not come?' I asked Editha, as we prepared ourselves. 'Will we have to abandon the Hieros Gamos? Surely the Goddess will be very angry?'

'We will do what we always do at Beltane in our yearly calendar: Call down the Goddess and ask for her Prophecy, then celebrate the life and fertility of the land, human and beast. As for the Great Rite,' she shrugged. 'Who knows? It is 400 years since we have had a real High King. Not since the Romans came, have we attempted the King Rite. Perhaps we have it wrong. Perhaps the Goddess does not approve and has destroyed the Initiate. Look, it is nearly time. They are putting out the fires already.'

Indeed, the watch fires were being dowsed. Later they would be relit with magical need fire from the huge bonfires that had been built in the centre below the terrace. The drums had begun again, louder, deeper, beating with the heart rhythm, and a preparatory warning. We had bathed, changed to thin white robes, unbound our long hair, and assembled barefoot. Below on the level the people had drawn close to the terrace, now surrounded by the priests and the Druids. Everyone was looking anxiously toward the sky, waiting for Moonrise.

We could wait no longer. Vivienne began to move, slowly, reluctantly, also looking up, and we fell into place behind her, walking up the ramp two by two to the terrace in front of the cliff and cave. I thought Morgan, next to me, still looked pale, but when I raised my eyebrows in question, she shook her head and gave a half smile. It was no wonder she looked unwell, we all found the Beltane Rites fearful and awesome. We stood along the back of the terrace, waiting patiently, but trembling a little at the magnitude of what we had to do.

And then, suddenly, there was a disturbance in the crowd. People were moving apart, gasping, allowing someone through the throng, and up the ramp to the terrace. A figure, glimmering in the light of a single brand, held aloft by Merlin, walking at his side. The Prince had come after all. He was riding the great White Stag. A dream figure out of Legend.

We could see clearly that the animal was exhausted, barely standing, his head with the noble antlers, drooping, defeated. The Prince was naked, covered in blood, swaying, and I saw with concern that he was injured. His left shoulder was still bleeding. He slid off the Stag, fell, recovered himself, stood upright.

The animal staggered. His front legs folded slowly and he fell.

A great cry went up from all the many peoples gathered in that place.

But the Prince knelt down next to him and put his hand on the head of the dying animal. I was close enough to see that he was crying, the tears running down his cheeks.

I took a step forward. Surely someone should be attending to his injuries? There was something wrong with his left leg. And blood was running down from a puncture in his groin.

He was covered with cuts, bruises and welts all over. Vivienne glared at me and I stepped back, flushed. Of course, no help must be given. This was a test of strength, physical and mental.

Merlin moved to the young man's side, laid one hand on his shoulder, and put a sword into his hand. There was deep silence now throughout the Gathering Place. The Prince stood. He held the sword high for a second, impatiently shook the tears from his eyes.

'Forgive me,' he said to the animal, and with a mighty stroke, he severed the neck of the Great Stag cleanly, and watched its blood running down from the terrace into the earth below.

Another great shout went up. A dozen men came forward and took the stag away, and Merlin, looking up, saw the sky lightening with Moonrise. He dowsed his brand quickly for the beginning of the Beltane Rite, and stood next to the Prince, supporting him.

The Rite is a long one, involving praise and invocation. Ancient words are chanted which have been handed down from time immemorial. We no longer understand them completely, but we believe them to be spells of great power to charge the energies of the earth and allow a portal to open between the worlds, so that the Great Goddess can come to us. I have taken part in the Rite many times but I have never again experienced the power that we raised that night. I saw Nimue hand Vivienne a cup of water. Was she ill?

The thrumming in the air seemed to be taking my breath. My heart was banging in my chest, and it was difficult to sing the final high appeal. We waited, silent, trying to breathe normally, but the air was so thin, translucent in the moonlight.

Nothing.

Surely, she would not refuse us, not on this special night? Sometimes, if she did not come to us at Avalon, Vivienne went into trance, and spoke for her. Would she have to do it this night? I found myself passionately praying that there would be no substitution, that the Goddess herself would truly come. Vivienne gestured, and we sang again, louder and more desperate. Again, silence. A single owl hooted in the silence of the darkened arena and we waited. A third time our voices rose, breathless, breaking. The silence stretched. There was only the thrumming in the air. We gave up hope, and looked to Vivienne waiting for her to step forward. And then it happened.

The moonlight coalesced into a single beam of light which shone down full on Vivienne, and strengthened. She stepped forward, gladly, relieved.

'The goddess comes,' she cried out, then suddenly flung up her arms, and dropped to the ground, like a stone, unmoving. We were so shocked, nobody moved to go to her. We just stared at the light, enthralled. Then, to our horror and astonishment, Nimue pushed forward, clearly offering herself but the light drifted on slowly along the long line of priestesses, rejecting her. Then the light beam began to fade. The Goddess was retreating.

Morgan, next to me, groaned softly. The light stopped, settled on her. Morgan made a strange, desperate sound, and stepped forward, accepting. The light waxed in intensity, strengthening by the minute, spread outwards, hurting the eyes. For a moment, I saw Morgan there, standing upright, strong, glowing, and then she was gone, the Goddess herself, unmistakeable, was there instead. We could all see her clearly. Taller, smiling, awesome in her beauty. She had chosen Morgan.

There was a collective gasp, and all the people in that great arena, sank to their knees.

'You have called to me. I have come.' Her voice, golden, bell-like was strangely amplified, so all could hear. She lifted her hand in blessing. 'Stand.'

Merlin, visibly shaking, gathered himself, and spoke. 'Lady we are greatly honoured. Your people welcome you. We seek your guidance and help. Our Land lies shattered and torn. Our halls are burnt and lay open to the skies. Our people are sick and starving. What must we do? What do you see in the future for us?'

Her face held an expression of infinite sadness. 'Blood, oceans of blood. War and Death.' There was a subdued groan from the darkened arena. 'A time of great change. A time of struggle. Great Wars. Blood. Death. A new Land is being born. It begins here, tonight. For two thousand years change and conflict. For you, glory and victory, that will ring down the years in ways you cannot imagine. People will come – new threads to be woven into the strong braid of the Land. Stronger than a single thread. There will be wide dominion beyond the seas. Greater than Rome. Empires fall. Never forget, all is change. Follow the light bravely.'

'King Uther is dying.' The arena gasped at the news. 'The new High King will lead.'

She turned to the young Prince who was still on his knees. His head was thrown back, his fair hair shining in the light. His eyes were wide, trained on her, and his blood was still running from his numerous wounds. The Goddess seemed taller, more majestic.

'I am Sovereignty. I am the Land. I am the Law. Will you swear to me? Will you surrender your life to me?'

'I will. I will die for the Land to live. I will protect the Land and its peoples. I will die for the Land, and I will live for the Land. I surrender my life and soul, now and for ever more.'

There was an audible intake of breath. His oath had been far in excess of what had been asked. Forever. Beyond the Grave. His soul was forfeit.

The Goddess had a small chalice in her hand. She poured glistening oil on his head, and we watched it run down his face until it disappeared. She bent over him, touching his shoulder and raising him. Her voice was gentle, affectionate. 'Come my Prince.'

He stood, dazed, and we saw that all his wounds were healed. The blood was gone and he stood splendid in his young male strength.

'Come my bridegroom.' She took his hand and they walked into the cave behind them. There was an explosion of brightness that hurt our eyes.

For a few moments, nobody moved. We were utterly shaken trying to come to terms with what we had heard and seen. But it was Beltane still, and someone tossed a light onto the bonfire, and people were coming with their brands for the need fire to relight their own fires. The drums burst into a loud, triumphant rhythm. The smell of cooking meats for the feast floated delectably, and barrels of ale were being broached at the trestles. They had begun to drive the cattle over the coals for fertility and to protect them against disease and already people were dancing to the pipes and drums in the centre, celebrating, although I thought there was little reason, the Prophecy had been terrifying.

Soon couples began to disappear into the surrounding hills and countryside, honouring the fertility of the Goddess. All who were born of the Beltane rituals were thought to be children of the Goddess and honoured; those born of this Beltane would be extraordinary. A little awestruck, I wondered about Morgan, chosen so clearly by the Goddess herself. She had been strong enough to bear that great power, as only a few could. I hoped she would be all right acting out the Hieros Gamos with the young Prince. I remembered my own initiation only too well.

And what about young Nimue, putting herself forward so strangely? Didn't she know how psychically strong you had to be, with enormous magical powers? Did she really think she could replace Vivienne? Nimue had not been with us very long, but we all knew that although she had a lot of little tricks, she had very little magical ability.

And Vivienne. What had happened there? She had lain like a log through the whole prophecy, but had seemed to be breathing normally, and now she was sitting smiling and relaxed, talking to a richly dressed noble, who might be one of the High King's Council. A strangely quick recovery. Had she faked the collapse to avoid the Hieros Gamos and the risk of another pregnancy? Or perhaps she was determined to make Morgan her successor? I did not want to think ill of Vivienne. She was the centre of my world, the person who had rescued me and given me my true life. When we were back in Avalon, I would talk to her privately.

Aella 8

By the time the morning mist had burned off the hills, the day after the after the great Beltane ceremonies, many people had gone, disappearing silently through enemy lands.

The rest were packing up, saying goodbye to friends made, hoping to meet again one day. I was returning from the Healing tent with my bag and medical supplies when I saw Nimue, reluctantly folding ritual robes into a saddle pack. I pounced. 'Nimue! Just the person I want to see.'

'You too? You need not, everybody has been on at me all morning.'

'What on earth were you thinking of yesterday? Surely you realised how dangerous that step forward was?'

'I don't know what you mean.' she said, sullenly. 'The Goddess was looking for someone.'

'And you thought it might be you?'

'Why not? No one else had stepped forward.'

'Of course not. The nine Senior Priestesses were there and many long-experienced Priestesses. Didn't you ask yourself why they had not moved?'

'I just thought you were all too cowardly...'

'Cowardly!' I was angry. 'You silly little fool. We knew we weren't strong enough to carry the Goddess. She chooses. So how could you be the one? You have no knowledge, no experience, and very little magical ability. And you are too young. You have only been with us a few months.'

'And I am not Vivienne's granddaughter.' She sneered, tossing her head. 'I'm the same age as Morgan.'

So that was it. She was eaten up with jealousy. I stared at her. 'You don't know about Morgan. She has great strength of mind. She has been tested. And she is just coming into her magical powers. She could blow the rest of us out of Avalon already, if she chose.'

'I know that you're her friend, and you all think the sun shines from her. But she is no better than I. I don't know why the Goddess chose her.'

'Because the Goddess didn't want to destroy your mind and turn you into a gibbering idiot. Although to be honest it sounds as though you are not far off that already... Understand, none of the Priestesses are strong enough. We knew that.' She stared at me.

'None of us. Not even Editha.'

'Only Vivienne!' she sneered.

'Yes. Only Vivienne. Until now.'

'She's old. Time for a new Lady of the Lake.'

'You, perhaps?

'Why not?'

I laughed, and then I saw she was serious and angry.

I looked at her, and suddenly, events rearranged themselves, slotting into a new pattern. Not the charming, unworldly, scatterbrained child, we all thought, with her cap of ginger curls and infectious giggle, but a woman of determined ambition, and, it would seem, dubious morals.

'What did you put in the drink you gave Vivienne before she collapsed? Ritalfia, perhaps?' I suddenly remembered she had shown great interest in the poisons in the Herbarium.

She went pale.

'Nimue, you will never be the Lady of the Lake, no matter how ambitious you are... You are vain, ignorant and jealous. Your soul is corrupt and the Goddess chooses the Lady not us.'

'You think you will stop me?'

'Oh no,' I said, 'You will destroy yourself, because you will never learn.'

'We'll see.' She threw down the robe she was holding and walked away.

I thought again of what she had done. 'Nimue?' She looked back. 'You must find another field. You are no longer welcome in the Healing Hall and Herbarium.'

I was beginning to be worried about Morgan. Where was she? I thought that after the Sacred marriage she would return to our tent. But how long was it supposed to last? Vivienne and the other Nine were not worrying. Vivienne said it varied according to the King's wishes. Sometimes it was just a quick connection to show that the marriage had been consummated. Sometimes, if they were compatible it might last all night like a normal marriage bed. So where was she? She had been gone from the tent when I awoke, and there was no indication she had been there.

It was now mid-morning and already the big pavilions

had been taken down, and the wagons were nearly packed. But Morgan's things were still there. I packed my own bag and then Morgan's to save time and went looking for her.

I found her, at last, further downstream, where the river fell from the high cliff, which we had used for our Purification rites. The place was deserted, and Morgan was lying in the pool naked, her eyes closed, not moving.

My heart jumped into my mouth and for a moment I thought she was dead. Had it been so bad she had killed herself? Then I saw she was breathing and crying too. My heart was pounding as I hurried down to her. Something was clearly very wrong, and I thought I must act calm and normal, despite my fear.

'Morgan, sweetheart, I've been looking for you everywhere. It's time to go.' Fortunately, I had thought to bring her travelling cloak and robe with me.

'Aella.' She tried to sit up, but she was blue with cold, her skin puckered from long immersion. How long had she been in the water?

'Wait. Let me give you a hand.' I lifted her from the water, and supported her to the bank. She could barely stand. I wrapped the cloak for warmth around her, rubbing life back into her arms and back, but stopped when she winced and twisted away, and I saw raw marks on her thighs and belly where she had scoured herself with handfuls of water weed, over and over again.

'This is no good. You will need healing ointment to stop these wounds festering. Come, pull the cloak around you and let's get back to the tent, if it is still there. Can you walk now?'

Fortunately, the smaller tents had not yet been taken

down. She sat on her cot and could not stop shivering. Shock, I registered, and made her drink hot herbal tea with honey in it and aconite, and other helpful herbs, while I applied our best healing ointment. Colour came back into her face, and she got into her clothes, while I slipped out to find Vivienne, and explain that Morgan was not well and would need a horse or pony.

'She's all right?' she said. 'It is a very exhausting. The Goddess is not easy to carry.' I thought of the raw patches, Morgan's wild attempt to cleanse herself, and thought it had not been the Goddess, but the sexual encounter that had done the damage. But if Vivienne wanted to minimise the problem, I would say nothing more.

A horse was found for her and I walked by her side, asking no questions. When she was ready to talk, I would be there to listen. But it was a mainly silent journey home. Although we had been wonderfully successful in carrying out the serious rites, we all had much to ponder on. Those magical events were about to change our world – and Morgan had been at the centre of those events.

Aella 9

It was good to be back in Avalon safely, to settle back into our normal routines, enjoy the luxury of hot baths and proper beds, not to mention the quiet and good food.

At first private opportunity, I told Vivienne and Editha what had happened with Nimue, and explained why I was not willing to have her working in the Herbarium among the dangerous medicines and poisons. Editha was shocked and outraged, but Vivienne said she had suspected that her collapse had not been normal, and that someone had tried to interfere with the carrying out of the Great Rite.

'I thought it might be political,' she admitted. 'That someone did not want to see a fully initiated High King, and tried to prevent both the Prophecy and the Great Rite. To be honest, it is something of a relief to find that it was just a silly ambitious little girl.'

'It might have killed you.' said Editha. 'Do we know what was in the water?'

'Almost certainly Ritalfia. No smell, no taste, and very quick action.' I said. 'It is an old herb, very rare and valuable, coming from beyond Constantinople. Sometimes used by the Romans on the battlefield for amputations in place of poppy. We have only a small supply. Nimue could only have stolen it from us. Few people would have any.' I drew a slow breath. 'The question is where did she find out about it?'

We looked at each other. I said, 'Perhaps it was political after all. Perhaps she was paid to do it by someone else?'

Editha said, 'Have we got a spy, worse, an assassin in our community?

Vivienne said, sadly, 'We can't take a chance. Not now. I will find another place for her.' And not many weeks later, Nimue found herself on the way to the Court of King Leodagrance who had sent to request another healer for his Hall.

Vivienne seemed to be fully recovered. She was excited and jubilant about the success of the Initiation Rites with a new leader who would draw all together to deal with the shattered country. She said that she had been working towards this moment for eighteen years.

She called the Nine to a deep discussion about the way we could support the new leader, what he could do to bring proper governance to an unruly Land, for the safety of all. We needed a new High King who could work miracles in making the Land whole and undivided, who would stop the warring, greedy kings who were tearing it apart like wolves, killing trade and laying the land waste.

Letters flew out to her informants all over the country, giving news of the Great Gathering and its outcome, bringing back information about those who would accept Arthur and those who would not. It was soon apparent that many high lords would not agree and Arthur, would have to fight for his realm. So, Vivienne began to call in old favours and get promises of assistance. Money was raised and dispatched to allies to begin the recruitment and training of men-at-arms. Her tentacles were formidable. Her power as strong as Merlin's.

They were working together I soon realised, although their relationship puzzled me. They were not friends, although they respected each other. But there was something between them, a wariness, a reservation. But for the time being, differences were being buried for the sake of the greater good.

Within a few weeks, news came that High King Uther was mortally ill, as the Goddess had told us, He had been carried in a litter to a great battle against a combined force of Northern Kings, Angles and Saxons, and had accepted Arthur as his true son and heir on the battlefield. Father and son had fought side by side, and Arthur had distinguished himself as a valiant warrior, saving his father's life and killing the Saxon leader. The Saxons had been pushed back to their original land grant. It was a great victory.

In the meantime, something was wrong with Morgan. It seemed she had withdrawn herself from the community. She remained in her room most of the time and would hardly speak to me. I was at a loss to know what was wrong. There was a sense of overwhelming despair, and underneath that a simmering anger. Something was boiling up, coming to a head. There was plenty of deadly nightshade plants in the hedgerows around Avalon, and Morgan was well able to make herself a brew. I grew more and more worried, and eventually sought help.

'Vivienne, there is something very wrong with Morgan. She

will not tell me what is wrong. She hardly eats. She has lost so much weight, and looks dreadfully drawn, although I cannot detect any infection. She drifts through her work in the Healing Hall like a wraith, when she is there... I have tried, but I can do nothing for her.'

Vivienne nodded. 'We have been very busy, as you know, but I did notice she has not been helping with the letters. I thought, perhaps, that the Goddess coming to her had been a shock, and that she needed time to recover. It is a very strange sensation, Aella. Overwhelming. Someone entering your mind and controlling all your mind and body...

I thought of the raw patches on her body, new and unhealed. 'Could it have been the sexual experience, do you think?'

'Perhaps, but surely that is hardly important enough to provoke such an extreme reaction? It could have been shock, I suppose. Was she a virgin?'

'I have no idea, we have never discussed it.'

'Well, I suppose I must speak with her. It has gone on too long.' She thought, tapping the desk with her long fingernails. Suddenly she smiled, gave a joyous laugh. 'Would it be too much to hope she might be pregnant? Think, Aella, a child of the Goddess and the High King! A Beltane child!"

'It could be,' I said, 'but perhaps not welcome to Morgan.'

On returning to Avalon, I had thought of Morgan's strange purification actions, which might well have been a suicide attempt, and had thought to remove all the herbs from the Herbarium that I knew to promote abortions, along with the most popular poisons, just in case, and a few days later had indeed found Morgan poking about in that section, without any explanation.

'Bring her here to me, Aella. Let us get to the bottom of it.'

For a moment I thought Morgan was going to refuse Vivienne's summons, but in the end, she shrugged, and said, 'So be it. Stay with me.'

Vivienne said, 'Come, sit down Morgan. Thank you, Aella. I'll see you later.'

'She stays,' said Morgan. The tension in the room rose, and I could feel anger seething in her. She stood in the doorway.

'Very well,' said Vivienne, and glanced at me. I took myself off to a window seat out of the way, and wished I was back in the Healing Hall, rolling bandages.

'What nonsense is this? Why are you not doing your work? We are very worried about you, Morgan. Since we came back from the Gathering you have not been yourself. Why are you enacting this childish drama about nothing at all when we are so busy? What is wrong?'

It was not calculated to calm Morgan, who, in the last days, had had time to think on her wrongs and had built a fine head of resentment and feeling hard done by.

'You know very well what is wrong,' Morgan said, bitterly.

Vivienne eyes narrowed at Morgan's tone. She got up from her desk and moved to the couch, patting the place next to her. 'Come, sit down.'

Morgan came in, slamming the door, and sat, but in a chair against the wall.

'The Prince used you badly? Are you hurt?'

Morgan closed her eyes and clenched her hands in frustration. 'He did not. He was...kind. You are going on pretending that you don't know?'

'I don't know,' Vivienne said lightly. 'If you could condescend to tell me, it would save time. Clearly you are blaming me for something. Was it my collapse? That the Goddess selected you instead?'

'Convenient, wasn't it? That so called 'collapse'? You had it all planned, didn't you? Do you think I'm a fool?'

Vivienne was angry. 'For fifty years and longer, I have hosted the Goddess for the Sovereignty Rite for numerous petty kings. Why would I not do so for our first High King for four hundred years?'

'You nearly died of your last pregnancy.'

'The Goddess chooses, not I. She chose you. I am not to blame. How could I? The Goddess chooses.'

'She chooses from those that are there. You did not warn me. You did not ask me if I wanted to go.'

'I did not warn you…? Morgan, are you telling me that all this sulking and rebellion is because I did not ask you if you would offer yourself to the Goddess?' Vivienne sounded incredulous. 'Of course, I thought you would be overjoyed to welcome her. Even the honour of being there on that incredible night… You know very well that you chose to go, as we all did. It was not compulsory. You should be giving thanks for the honour the Goddess did you.'

'Why did you not tell me who the Initiate was?' Morgan hissed.

'It was unimportant. Not necessary.'

'Not important? Not important? Morgan's voice rose hysterically. 'You knew it was my brother Arthur. You made me lay with my brother Arthur!'

'Half-brother. You had never met him even. What has that to do with anything?'

'It was incest. Incest. You have made me commit a wicked mortal sin.' Morgan sprang to her feet and faced her grandmother, shaking with rage. She was trembling with emotion, frail from extended fasting, her face a ghastly white, eyes burning.

Vivienne gaped at her, astonished, taking in, for the first time Morgan's complaint. 'What nonsense is this? You are a Priestess of Avalon. It was your part to host the Goddess at the Sacred Marriage. It was the Goddess that lay with the Initiate.'

'And what of afterwards?'

'Whatever happened between you, it was the work of the Lady. You were in her hands.'

'And what if I am pregnant? Have you thought of that?' Morgan's voice rose again. 'Pregnant by my brother?'

'Have you forgotten it is Beltane? He will be a sacred child of the Beltane rites – a great gift of the Lady.'

'A hideous, wicked, incubus.'

Vivienne's anger thundered. 'Never let me hear you say that again! Heresy! Would you deny a child of the Lady?'

'I am black with sin. I will go to hell.' shrieked Morgan, sobbing for her breath. 'I am destroyed.'

I thought for a moment that Vivienne was going to laugh. She glanced at me and away, puzzled. I said tentatively, 'The nuns are very strong on sin.'

'Nuns. Nuns? NUNS!!'

The incomprehension, the puzzled disbelief, were suddenly gone, replaced by a towering rage, as she made the connection with Morgan's early life and training, but her understanding, far from cooling the encounter and making her more sympathetic, exploded into a towering rage. I closed my eyes. Oh Morgan!

'How dare you bring into this place their filthy, evil-minded, ideas of guilt and sin, designed to put us all into the power of their ignorant, rabid women-hating priests...?? Evil, dirty, superstitious, slavishly grovelling, ignorant as pigs! They cannot even write their own names...' She swept backwards and forwards across the mosaic floor, viciously kicking her robe away from her feet.

Morgan stared at her wildly, perhaps understanding for the first time where her own feelings of repulsion had come from, and then, at last, reached the bedrock of her true agony.

'You betrayed me!' It was a cry from her soul. Vivienne's face hardened, but Morgan was beyond restraint. 'You did not warn me, you did not tell me. Why didn't you choose another Priestess? You sold me. Why did you do it? Why?'

Vivienne went over to her couch near the brazier, her face grim. 'Sit down and listen.'

'Answer me! Why did you betray me?'

'Here you are, the chosen of the Great Goddess herself, the bearer of the Sovereignty of the Land to the new High King – the first High King to be properly initiated since before the Romans, a man destined for glory, and you – you are obsessed with your own petty concerns, whining trivialities. You should be overwhelmed with wonder and awe about the success of the great ritual which has ensured a true High King, willing to save all our people.

'Have you not yet understood that we are not here to serve our own interests? There are greater things at stake. There is an immense struggle going on for the souls and future of our people. There is a war, a war not just against the Saxons or the Picts or the sea raiders. Have you not understood that our whole culture and lives are being undermined and infiltrated? I am not talking of the simple, holy gospel of the prophet Jesus, but the religion which these priests from Rome are developing. Have you not heard that that good holy man Pelagius has been overthrown by the new religion that Augustine has been imposing? A true heresy against Christ's ideas, but accepted. Accepted!

'Understand that our people, all the peoples of Logres are dying. Dying, you stupid girl. We are being slowly destroyed. Our culture, our language, our religion is disappearing under the waves of invading peoples, while our greedy, warring nobles do nothing.'

Morgan stared at her, her face like a sheet of ice. I willed her to listen and understand, but she leaped to her feet and strode about the room. 'What has all this to do with...'

'Arthur will be crowned High King, Morgan. High King of all Britannia. Do you understand? What he believes, the country will believe. The Archbishop, the Church will try to take him over. Impose their deathly, sin-infested religion on us all. The Goddess will be driven out. Outlawed. Our people will be made into demons and witches. That is what they are beginning to call us now.'

Morgan, struck, stopped and stared at her.

'Arthur had to be bound to the Great Goddess, and bound to the land as strongly as we know how. Life and death for the ancient teachings our ancestors brought from Atlantis.

'And now, at last there is a chance. We have a champion, a new leader, as the Goddess promised, a man to lead us to glory and a new world. A King who will gather all our peoples, all the clans and bind them together with the new people. This is what we achieved in the Gathering Place. You must have seen they came from one end of the land to the other, the tribes from the North, the West, the East, and the South. The small dark people from the forests, the elven people, the travelling people, the painted peoples of the Far North, even the Attacotti were there. Did you not see the Goddess spirals swirling across their cheeks? Morgan, through the new High King there is a chance for us to go forward, to build a land such as we have never seen before, a blended people who will build a new peaceful world.'

Her eyes were shining with dedication. 'We did it! We did the ritual, spoke the words, set the spells, the man gave his body to Sovereignty, and offered his life.'

Morgan said, 'Why me?'

'Blood calls to blood. It made the bond stronger.'

Morgan said, bitterly, hardly moving her lips, 'And so you betrayed me. That's all it meant to you.' I was just a little pawn moved across the board to destruction.'

It stopped Vivienne. It seemed for a second that she had lost her breathe. Before she could explode again into speech, Morgan said, 'It may be so, what you have said, the importance of it all, but you didn't think or care about my feelings. I really thought you loved me, as I loved you. I thought you were different from my mother. I thought I could trust you. You said she is icy and unloving, but you know you are worse, because you took my love and devotion and used them to control me and the High King too. You are obsessed with power. You are like the Roman priests you complain of. Your Goddess is Power. You knew that you would not bear the Goddess. You did not tell me that the Initiate was to be was my brother, Arthur. You should not have sent me to the Ritual. Incest is a black sin.

You betrayed me. I thought you loved me, but you only needed me to use in your intrigues. You did not have my consent. You betrayed me.'

The low, judging voice stopped, and the two stared at each other. Irrevocable judgement. I felt the tears running down my cheeks. Morgan had lived with the Tintagel nuns too long. She had unconsciously accepted many of their beliefs. The harm was done and could not be undone. Morgan, unloved and forgotten, her grandmother was the first person she had ever given her trust and love to, and her betrayal was unendurable.

Vivienne's rage and grief were terrible.

'How could the Goddess have made such a mistake? How could the Goddess have chosen such a useless lump of selfish conceit? You and your life mean nothing, are nothing. You are not fit to have been in her presence. I should never have brought you here. You should be scrubbing the nuns' latrine. You are no child of my line. You are like your mother. Get out of my sight. I don't want to set eyes on you again.'

Morgan, ashen, staggered under the diatribe, nearly fell, regained her balance and utterly destroyed, rushed from the room.

I turned to follow, but Vivienne, clutching her chest, had sunk down on her couch, and was struggling to breath, her skin pale grey, eyes closed. I rang frantically for help before going to her aid.

Aella 10

It was a long night. I thought we had lost her several times. My dearest Sophia, my teacher and mentor, the very finest of all our healers, now in her ninety-third year, climbed from her bed to come join the healing team, and we worked so hard. Infusions of digitalis, and willow steadied the leaping of the Lady's heart. Agnetha, so good with her knowing hands, massaged her heart, and Carwyn, her assistant, worked on Vivienne's ankles, for so much tension is held there. She was able to sip the calming and sleeping draughts we held to her lips, while the Spell Healers, called the air energies for oxygen, and the life energies of the Earth and the Sun, and spoke the words for extra strength. Towards dawn, when so many souls leave on their final journey, she sank into a deep, restorative sleep, her heart steady.

For ten days we kept her in her bed, tiptoeing around her, while Birith played her harp, soothing her into rest. She hardly spoke, and slept most of the time, I think, determined to recover as quickly as she could. I was too busy and too worried to think of Morgan, and I am afraid I blamed her for her stupidity in confronting her grandmother at such a time. I didn't understand her anguish at laying with Arthur, And what if we lost Vivienne? What would we do, when the whole future of our people depended on her helping the High King to his throne?

When she was well enough to get up for a few hours, the first thing she did was send Editha for Morgan! When I heard I could not believe it. Another quarrel like the last would definitely kill her. I hurried to her room. But I need not have bothered. Morgan was not there. She had gone, packed and left Avalon the morning after the quarrel telling no one, leaving no message.

Of course, enquiries were made. The boatmen were questioned. The Guardians sent to track her. At length information came back. Morgan was making her way north, with three ponies she had taken from the stables, together with a Guardian from the Village, who had had the good sense to go with her.

Vivienne sent for me. She was lying on her couch, looking so very old and worried that I wanted to cry.

'Aella, my love, you have heard?' She beckoned me to her.

'I have,' I said, grimly. 'Where does she think she is going?'

She hesitated, 'I think, to her younger sister, Mawgawse. You know she is married to King Lot of Orkney and Lothian. Uther married her off to Lot when she was not yet thirteen, to get her away from his Court. She was a handful, making scandals. They say she was pregnant before she even reached the Court. It may have been Uther.'

'Mawgawse is the younger of Ygraine's daughters?'

'Morgan was the elder by a year and not much liked by Uther. Too clever, and she loved Gorlois. When Uther married

Ygraine, Morgan was left behind at Tintagel Castle, then eventually sent to Ygraine's nunnery, as you know. Mawgawse was very insinuating, an overly-sexually mature girl. And Uther took her with them to his Court in London. I don't know how many children she has now, three, or is it four or even five? She breeds like a rabbit. She will be at Lot's Castle near Edinburgh.'

Vivienne picked at the woollen rug, covering her legs. 'Aella, I have done very wrong. You know how I mishandled Morgan. I am to blame. I lost my temper... I was so pleased and proud that the Goddess had chosen her, and that she might have conceived a child by the High King...that she might one day follow me... and then she... was so rude and scornful, accusing me...And I drove her off with such terrible words...

'I am well punished. Now I am afraid she will destroy herself. If she tries to abort the child she may be carrying, I do not know what the Goddess will do to her. She was the chosen. The child belongs to the Goddess. I am dreadfully to blame.'

I shook my head, 'Morgan is damaged. But I don't think she would harm a child.'

'I have lost my ability to understand young women. She is alone and vulnerable; she might do anything. Aella, will you go to her, and explain, and persuade her to come back?

She loves and respects you. I am asking you to go after her. We can hardly spare you from the Healing Hall, and I know well that you saved my life, but will you try to save Morgan's?'

Aella 11

We caught up with them a week later, John, one of the Guardians from the Village, his son, Bana, and myself. We were old friends, having made more than one journey together, including the very first, that had brought Morgan to Avalon and they were very concerned about her safety. Morgan had already persuaded his grandson, Peilla, to accompany her as guide and protector in her flight.

They had been moving leisurely along the great Roman Road north, not expecting pursuit, and failed to notice that they were riding straight into an ambush, set by three masterless men at the river crossing in a grove of trees. I felt rather sorry for the robbers. They were no match for our combined skills. John, moving swiftly, swung a mighty blurred fist and knocked two of the men off their feet. The third found that, unaccountably, his ankles felt as though they had been roped together tightly. As the two struggled to their feet, all three found they were suddenly stark naked, lifting into the air, upside down, flying out over the middle of the river, and being dunked like oatcakes in a barley broth. Up, down, up down, up, down.

'Witches!' shrieked the men, terrified, and half drowned.

John let out a great guffaw, Bana and Peilla were bent double, roaring with laughter. 'Did you see their faces?' Even Morgan was smiling. For a moment we watched them being borne away down river, trying to keep their heads above water.

'That'll teach them,' said Peilla.

'Will they drown?' I said, worried.

'Nay, m'lady.'

John said, laughing still, 'There's an island, about a mile downstream. They might be a bit embarrassed like, seeing it's an Abbey with fifty nuns.'

We went on our way, still enjoying the joke.

I think Morgan was pleased to see me, although she made a great fuss about being followed. But she would not be turned from her intention to go to Mawgawse, no matter how much I begged and pleaded, and gave her all the Lady's messages of love. She had decided to go on, and that was that. 'Mawgawse will understand,' she said. 'I'm sure she will help me. And I will be free.'

John and his sons began to set up camp by a huge oak tree, apart from us, understanding that the argument would not be quickly solved and uncomfortable with overhearing Avalon's private business.

'I thought you loved Avalon well.'

'So I do, but after what Vivienne said...I could not stay. I cannot serve the Goddess there. I am black with sin. Avalon would be poisoned, no matter what Vivienne says. I will not let that happen. Maybe, one day, I will go back to see her, but now we move on. You may tell her, that despite everything – her fake collapse, her betrayal, I still love her.'

'I can't tell her anything,' I said sadly, 'I will not be going back, I will be coming with you. She would expect that.'

She stared at me. I made another effort. 'Morgan, your grandmother did not betray you. She did not fake her collapse. It was Nimue.'

'Nimue? Are you mad?'

'Nimue gave her a draught of Ritalfia in the cup of water she gave her during the Rite. It renders people unconscious almost immediately.'

'But why?'

'She intended to host the Goddess herself.'

Morgan laughed scornfully. 'Never. She is just a silly little nitwit. She wouldn't have the courage.'

'Or, more likely, someone paid her to do it. Someone who did not want the Initiation ceremony to take place. Someone who would be High King himself, perhaps?'

Morgan was shocked. 'But that's sacrilege. That's interfering with the Goddess' will... She will kill her.'

'Morgan, the Druids say the most likely replacement would have been ambitious King Lot.'

'King...' She went pale, her eyes dilated. There was a long moment of silence then she recovered herself. 'It seems we wade in deep waters.'

'Deeper even than we may think. Morgan, Editha spoke to me of your sister before I left Avalon. She says there are stories circulating about Mawgawse. It seems she believes herself to be an enchantress. Apparently magical powers run strongly in your family, but Mawgawse is using them wrongly. These stories say she has turned to the dark side in pursuit of power. They say she is behind Lot, guiding him. She wants to be High

Queen.'

'Surely that can't be true,' Morgan was horrified. 'I remember her as a little girl. She was so bright and cheerful and laughing, a real care-for-nought. She always joked me out of my black moods, and stood up for me when Ygraine, blamed me for everything. We got on so well.'

'She is not a little girl now. She is a Queen. She lived at Uther's corrupt court. She has three children and much time has passed. You do not know her now.'

She thought about it, then slowly straightened her shoulders. 'It doesn't matter, after all. My soul is black too, no matter how many cleansing rites. I have lain with my brother. The nuns say it is the blackest sin. Unforgivable. I have nowhere else to go, until the King gives me back my Tintagel inheritance. The Castle there is mine. From my father Gorlois. I will go back to Tintagel.'

I thought of the black granite and the rough seas, and shuddered. 'I thought it would be the last place you would want to go.'

'Of course, not to my mother's nunnery! To the Castle. I love Cornwall. It is beautiful. I was always happy there with my old nurse. It is so wild and free. I could live like the sea eagles...'

'Aella, why did she do it? My grandmother knew who the Initiate was. Why didn't she tell me? I thought she loved me, but she did not take care of me. We know how many strange, unpredictable things happen at the Rituals. The Goddess has spoken through me several times. Vivienne must have thought about the possibility.'

I remembered the conversation I had with Vivienne when she had said she thought she was not strong enough to bear the

Goddess again, but Morgan might be chosen in her place. It was indeed strange behaviour for a loving grandparent not to warn Morgan that Arthur was the Initiate.

Morgan said, drearily, 'In the end I suppose it doesn't matter. I cannot go back to Avalon. Black with sin, I would sow poison and corruption, and I will not have that, Aella, I think his seed has lodged. I know I am with child. Vivienne cares nothing for me and I will not let her use me and my child like pawns.'

I said nothing, but I could understand Morgan's conclusion. We sat silently for a while. The moon had risen, and a nightingale above us in the great oak was pouring out a waterfall of silver sound.

'She does care for you, Morgan, I know she does. She has been so pleased and proud of your gifts.'

'Only so she can use them. All she cares about is power.'

'For a great purpose,' I said severely. 'To save the Land and the Goddess.'

She shrugged. 'Perhaps. Whatever you say, Aella, I am not going back to Avalon.'

'Then I am coming with you, and you need not bother to argue.'

'Aella, you will say I am wrong, but I really think she hoped the Goddess would come to me and not to her. She didn't want to risk another pregnancy...'

And I remembered Vivienne's long white fingers, stroking the back of the little Goddess sculpture on her desk as she spoke, and I suddenly knew that Morgan was right. Vivienne had planned all. She had not even been surprised that she had been attacked by Nimue.

'Morgan,' I said slowly, 'Say nothing of all this to your sister. Nothing of the Hieros Gamos, Nothing of the Initiation, Nothing of Arthur. Nothing of carrying the Goddess.

We must be careful, Morgan. We must not give them information they can use against us or Avalon, or particularly, Arthur.'

'But she will want to know who the father is...why I have left Avalon."

'A simple story. All true: You quarrelled with Vivienne.. You went to the Beltane fires and lay with a stranger. You did not know his name. And now you are pregnant. Vivienne is very angry. She told you to leave. Morgan, never let Mawgawse know that it was Arthur.'

'Do you think I am mad? Would I spread that around?'

'I don't know. She may trap you, persuade you... Knowledge is power."

'But why would she want to hurt us? Aella, she is my blood sister. I can't condemn her on gossiping stories...'

'Morgan,' I said impatiently, 'Have you scrambled your very clever brains? Your sister is Lot's wife. Anything she knows, Lot will know too, especially if it relates to the governance of the Land. Don't you realise that any child you birth will be the High King's heir? Sister's child is our law. Lot is ambitious. Ruthless they say. And he strives to become High King. He would not hesitate to remove such a small barrier. Don't throw away your child's life and inheritance.'

Morgan drew in a long deep breath, and I realised she had not thought so far.

'And here's another reason for silence. We are of Avalon. Priestesses with secret advanced magical knowledge. If the stories are true, Mawgawse will be jealous, she will try to prize the knowledge from us to enlarge her skills. Please think! Will you let her destroy Avalon and Arthur?

For a long moment she looked at me, then drew another breath. 'I will be very careful and silent. I had not realised...'

'And don't tell her about me. I am merely Aella, a servant. A lowly friend of no importance.'

Morgan was outraged. 'But you are Head of the Healing Hall. One of the Nine. I can't treat you like a servant!'

'I must go unnoticed. Unremarkable. We must be close and secret. They are very dangerous people.'

In two days, we would be at Lot's Castle, and in his power.

Aella 12

The next day the party split up. John and Bana his son, went back to Avalon, to report to the Lady of the Lake, while Peilla, decided to go on with us and see if he could find work as a man at arms in Lot's service, but in secret, he would look to our protection and help us if need be. We decided he should ride ahead, so that he would not be known as our man.

Morgan looked dreadful; it was as though the departure of our friends had shown her clearly the choice she was making. She was sick several times, could not eat, and sat huddled in her cloak, weak and shivering, the tears running down her cheeks. It seemed as though her strong spirit had been broken. For the moment, travelling was out of the question.

We drank warm camomile tea. I sat down next to her and put my arm around her shoulders. 'What is it, Morgan, my love? Have you changed your mind? Do you want to go back to Avalon after all?

'Aella, all I ever wanted was to live in Avalon. To study, explore my gifts, serve the Goddess, and perhaps one day, become the Lady of the Lake myself. When you came for me at the nunnery, I could not believe my dreams were coming true. And now, after only a very few years, it is all over. My life is in ruins. My soul is splintered and black...And you ask what is it?'

'Do you want to tell me what happened at the Hieros Gamos? It seems that this is the key to what has driven you into this terrible state of despair. It isn't like you, Morgan. You survived the hell on earth of the nunnery. You never gave up. But now, suddenly, you are broken, near to taking your own life. Do you think I don't know that?'

She looked away, plucking at the embroidered braid on her dark violet Priestess's cloak. Clearly, she was desperate and lost, but I managed to hold my tongue and clasp her hand for support, and let her tell me what had to be told.

'How could she do that to me, Aella?' She sounded like a lost child. 'I trusted her. We were all so happy and excited...' And then the words broke out in a torrent. 'That night...it was all so awesome and strange as we stood there. Do you remember? It seemed the drums were beating into my blood and mind. There was a kind of heaviness over me.'

'A dark shadow?'

'No, no. Not dark at all. A kind of power. An intensification of the air, of the light, of the blood running in my veins, of the movement of my brain. Reality was changing, expanding, and I was a tiny part, pressed away safely. I could not move. Then the drums again, pounding in my brain, shaking me apart. I had no arms or legs or body. Just, for a while, my consciousness. And a voice, whispering, like a mother. 'Don't fear. Safe.'

There were horns in the far hills, summoning, calling, calling again for something. Begging for something to come alive... It seemed to me that the earth was moving, expanding slowly outwards, upwards into the shining sky, and there was light coming, and colours I had never seen before. Great waves of coloured light, and then there was nothing except light and a feeling of huge power, strength, love. I was huge. I could do anything. A voice was coming from my mouth, speaking, to a great assembly of people, crowding, spreading out beyond the light into the darkness of the hills... And there was an awe-inspiring love for them all. Love and concern. Love overwhelming...Too strong for me, and I fainted, I think. I don't know how long the Goddess was with me. When I came to myself, I was aware, first, with a great grief, that she had gone. I could move my arms and legs again. It was dark. Not a gleam of light. No drums.

Then a young, male voice, saying, 'Are you all right? My Lady...are you awake? My Lady, please wake up... Please speak...' The voice was panicking. 'Lady, Wife...?'

I realised then, that I was awake, naked, and in a bed, with another human body next to mine. And I could see a lighter area, some sort of cave entrance, and it all began to come back to me. The Hieros Gamos. The Sacred Marriage.'

'It's all right,' I said. 'I'm alive.'

'Thank the Gods!' The tension went out of his body, and he held me close, shaking. 'I thought you had died.'

'The Goddess?'

'Gone now.' His voice trembled. 'I think. Are you human?'

'Yes.'

He did not speak for a while, but held me closer, as though he would never let me go. 'You are mine. My wife. Mine.'

'I am a Priestess of Avalon. I am Morgan.'

His body went rigid. For a moment he was utterly still, and

then he gave a strange laugh, and his grip tightened. 'So be it, Morgan. My wife. My love.' He was touching me, stroking me, kissing me, and soon we joined and moved together. We did not speak.

Beyond his shoulder the sky was lighter, the false dawn.

'It's getting light.'

'They will come.'

'Yes.'

We kissed and made love again. He was stronger, more demanding. 'Mine. Mine Mine.' He was impressing his body into mine. Claiming me. 'My woman. My wife. Always. The Goddess' gift.'

I realised then that he did not see our congress as symbolic. For him it was a true marriage – a sacred marriage, dissolvable only on his death.' She stopped, and her voice trembled. 'And, Aella. I felt the same. Do you hear me? I felt it was a sacred marriage dissolvable only by my death. An oath to the Goddess.

'They will come,' I said. And a terrible desolation filled me. All the wonder, all the love, and the Goddess, all gone.

'It's finished,' I said.

'No. My love, my wife, always and forever. I will come for you.'

But I knew that would never happen.

Outside there was the sound of cautious footsteps crunching on stones and a low voice. 'Sire, it is time to go.'

And another voice. 'Are you awake, Sire?'

His grip on me tightened. 'Remember. I will come.'

'Sire, please. We have to go.' The voice was beginning to panic. 'There's danger.'

'A moment,' he said to them. He pulled me into his arms

and kissed me deeply.

'Arthur! We have to go now, Please. I have your cloak.'

He kissed me again, and said three words in farewell, 'Mine. Remember. Wait.'

I saw his black silhouette against the lighter sky, as he took the cloak and flung it around his shoulders, and then he was gone.

Arthur. I knew the name. Of course, I did. Arthur, my brother. The brother I had never met, never seen even and knew virtually nothing about. He had been born to my mother when she went away with King Uther, and I was left behind. Arthur was the Initiate, the High King to be, anointed by the Goddess. My lover. My husband. I could not move, rigid with horror. Someone had played a terrible trick on us. Why had my grandmother not told me? And then I heard the horn in the far hills calling again, challenging, calling something into life.

'Aella, he was my brother!' She had torn the braid on her cloak. Her fingers were white and rigid.

I said, practically, 'Yes...well... half-brother. You have different fathers,'

'My brother! Don't you understand. It was incest. The blackest sin. Forbidden. What if there is a child?'

'Not a sin. Not forbidden in our religion,' I said, admonitory. 'It was the Sacred Marriage, the Hieros Gamos. And at Beltane. All life is sacred. All are Children of the Goddess.'

She shook her head, the tears glinting on her cheeks. 'You don't understand.'

'I understand well enough,' I said. 'It's you who don't understand. You don't know your history. It was not forbidden to the Cretans, the Egyptians, or the Atlanteans. Not to those who follow the Goddess anywhere. It is sometimes inadvisable, perhaps, because of the genes...'

'What are you talking about? What are genes?'

I sighed. 'We are talking secret Atlantean lore. You won't have studied it yet. When there is time I will explain. But for now believe it is not a deadly sin as the Christians believe. We do not ask people to wallow like pigs in imaginary guilt, so our masters can keep us under control. The Goddess leaves us free to devise our own ethics of good and bad action. These we have to learn ourselves, and not allow others to impose their own ideas, especially if those ideas are merely superstitions, or devised to keep dominion over us.'

I said severely, 'Morgan, are you for the Goddess? Or did the nuns brand you with their evil ideas? Will you let them go on torturing you for no reason?'

She stared at me, and then walked away, but I knew she had listened. We would see if the words had any effect.

That night, I could not sleep. I wrapped my blanket around me, and thought of how we humans make our own cruel prisons and tortures for no good reasons. Above me the great bowl of the heavens blazed with stars, and the night bird's liquid song purified the darkness in my mind. Beauty and goodness are everywhere. We must look for and hold to them. For a while I felt confident and overwhelmingly happy, sure it would be all right.

Part Three

Aella 13

Our time in Lot's court was miserable, uncomfortable, and dangerous. It was such a violent place that sometimes I despaired of surviving. We were there four years. It was the worst time of my life, and it seemed to go on forever. There was nowhere else to go and nothing we could do about it.

Uther Pendragon, on marriage to Ygraine, wanting to be rid of his scandalous, inconveniently pregnant, step daughter, had quickly traded her off to King Lot of Orkney and Lothian, for a treaty promising non-aggression, thus securing his southern border, while he fought the Saxons and Picts, forever encroaching in the east and north. Lot thought that marrying Mawgawse would put him strongly in line for election to the High Kingship when Uther died, especially as he appeared at that time to have no legitimate son. Arthur's appearance had shocked and infuriated him.

Mawgawse was very tall, taller than her husband, with a ripe, full body, a mass of red hair, and a high colour, inherited from her father, Gorlois of Cornwall. At first, she professed herself delighted to see her sister again, but quickly the novelty wore off, and when she found we had little information to trade, she became bored and impatient with us, pecking at us and quarrelling. There was no sign of the delightful, lively girl, Morgan remembered.

Mawgawse, was not happy. Married at thirteen, she had already borne three sons, and was heavily pregnant with a fourth. She was fretful, demanding and imperious, her moods erratic, her temper uncertain. Husband and wife spent their time quarrelling.

Lot was a sot and a lecher, and his men followed his example. His Hall was a huge, grim, stone-built castle, chaotic and barbaric, that squatted in the landscape like a toad blighting all the land around it, ruled by violence and fear. Around the walls of the Great Hall were the shields and weapons of the Chieftains. The men slept in the Hall, ate in the Hall, and lounged there all day, when the weather was bad. At night, when they were drunk, they frequently fought each other, and no woman dared set foot in the place.

And it stank. No one ever cleaned or replaced the strewing herbs on the floor, inundated with offal and rotting food, mixed with the droppings of the dogs and pigs and chickens, which were allowed to roam at will. The servants were sullen and terrified, captured into slavery from raids into Ierne, or from other tribes. The women scullions were beaten into grovelling submission and sexual availability. The food was appalling – half-cooked stews with floating bloody meat of indeterminate animals, and rough bread full of unground seeds that you could hardly swallow.

Mawgawse made no effort to take charge of the Court. Her own servants did her bidding, cooked her rich foods and made sure that Lot himself had plentiful roasted meats and the best brewed ales and wine imported from Gaul, which they both drank copiously.

You might imagine from the state of the Court that Lot was a poor man, but that was not true. His treasure room was filled with the spoils of many raids on neighbouring kingdoms, south of Emperor Hadrian's wall, and coin extracted from his over-taxed people. His riches allowed Mawgawse to dress in silks, furnish her rooms with costly tapestries and furniture looted from Roman palaces.

As far as I could see, she spent most of her time in her rooms, threatening her servants and conducting doubtful magical experiments. Working with an crone from the local village, she fancied herself an enchantress, but when I saw the dried blood and parts of dead animals, I realised she was indeed following a dark path, to what end I could not guess at the time, but which turned out to be directed at the acquisition of power. Like all Ygraine's line she had inherited some magical powers, but Mawgawse was limited and untrained, and I think she made little progress. Nevertheless, everyone was terrified of her.

In the meantime, her children, without nurse or teacher, ran riot, unchecked, unloved and neglected, like little wild beasts, rolling with the dogs in the mire, never washed, fighting with each other and the other children for any food available.

At first, she had thought that Morgan would reveal the priestess secrets of Avalon, and pestered her to know who had fathered her child, but when Morgan insisted that he was a child of the Beltane fires, and that what she had learned on Avalon related only to healing, Mawgawse retreated, angry and disappointed, and tried to draw Morgan into her black schemes, but Morgan was ill, and increasingly so.

It was good that we had decided to conceal my real identity. I had cut my hair into a fringe to conceal the crescent tattoo we Priestesses wore, and Mawgawse believed that I was Morgan's old nurse, now acting as her maid, and this suited me well. At first we had been crammed into a small room near her own, so she could spy on us, and I slept on the floor, but eventually, when I suggested we would need more space for the birthing of the babe, or risk disturbing her and Lot, with all the screaming and crying, Mawgawse had waved her hand bored, and said we should find other rooms.

By this time we had begun to know what kind of a place this was and I found a few small rooms at the top of one of the more distant towers, which led directly down to a small, enclosed yard by a kitchen, and persuaded a blacksmith in the stables, a decent man, to fit a strong lock to the door to our rooms, to protect us from the drunken sell swords and discourage visitors. The rooms were filthy of course, and after sweeping out the straw and all kinds of rubbish I bullied two of the poor wretches in the kitchen to bring up pails of hot lye water to scrub them clean. In Avalon it was well taught that cleanliness was essential in bringing babes into the world healthily and saving the mother too.

Then I went on a hunt for essential furniture so that we should be as comfortable as possible in our exile for however long it should be necessary. I admit that if I had known how long we would be there, I would have sunk into hopeless despair.

The Castle was a rambling labyrinth of corridors and chambers and like a ghost I moved silently and quietly, throwing up a displacement spell so I should not be noticed. Eventually, I struck gold. My blacksmith friend in the stables, who I had treated with one of my sovereign remedies for a festering burn, told me of stored furniture that Lot's first wife had used, thrown out by Mawgawse, and long forgotten. It was a treasure trove. Two wooden beds of the kind the local people used, low and solid, with wool stuffed mattresses and feather beds, which I have to say were the best things I ever found in that benighted place, and they only needed shaking and airing. There was a long wooden table for our food and work, a smaller table, a few stools and two chairs with arms which needed only a cushion or two to make them comfortable for a pregnant lady with a back ache. The rooms already had enormous wooden chests for our few clothes.

I found a brazier broken at the back of the stables, and my friend very kindly repaired it for us, for I could see that in this climate, we would need warmth in the coming winter, and the stable lad carried it up our stair, together with a store of cut logs, which should keep us warm for many days. And so, we moved in feeling a little safer.

Although she tried hard to be enthusiastic about our better accommodation, Morgan could no long hide that she was very ill. Her pregnancy was not going well. In fact, it was the worst pregnancy I had ever known. She could not eat properly. Right from the start she was sick every morning and not only in the morning. The sickness did not wear off, instead it got worse and I was at my wits end to know how to treat her. I have no doubt that much of it was a mental reaction and aversion to carrying what she still regarded as the fruit of great sin. I brewed relaxing herbs, stomach soothing herbs like camomile, herbs to help the cramps of the pregnancy and finally, vervain to allow her to sleep. I tried everything. Very little helped.

Her ankles swelled and her belly was bigger than it should be for a mere four months foetus. Her heart beat was irregular. I watched her closely, and one day examined her, and was sure.

'Morgan, my love,' I said carefully. 'I am afraid that you are carrying not one child, but two.'

She closed her eyes and tears seeped from the lids and slid down her thin cheeks. I held her hand, sitting next to her on her bed, stroking it soothingly.

'Aella, I don't think I can go on. Not with two. Even the thought sickens me.'

'If you could see them as gifts from the Lady...'

'Aella, I don't want them. They have no future. I am not right for a mother. You know that. There are months to go, and I can't do it. I really can't...'

I stiffened then, knowing what was coming next, and knowing that I couldn't do what she wanted.

'Let me go. I want to die. I am in agony all the time. I ought to have turned into a bird immediately after the Sacred Marriage. I could have drowned at sea. I am a better bird than a human being. Please. You know you have taken the oath to give release to any who genuinely ask.'

By this time, I was crying too, because I knew that I was going to have to break my oath – the most solemn of our Priestess oaths. 'No.'

'You must. I have asked. I am deathly ill.'

'Then you will have to die naturally, Morgan, for I cannot do it. You are carrying the Lady's gifts, doubly sacred, and I cannot kill them too.'

'So, you too are betraying me, Aella. Even you.'

She turned away and lay on the bed burying her face in the pillow. I put my hand on her should imploringly, but she shrugged it off.

I hesitated, 'Will you drink your milk?'

'No. No milk. No water. Nothing more.' And I knew she intended to starve herself to death.

I left our rooms and went down to the small wood near the castle, to walk in the quiet and peace. It was September and the dew was shining on the spider webs, glistening in the sunlight between the bushes. The leaves were already beginning to turn. In another month the branches would be brilliant reds and golds and Morgan would be long dead and would never see them again, and would never fly as a cormorant out to the wild autumn sea. I think it was the darkest hour in my whole life. I knew that I too had betrayed her like all the rest of the people in her life.

And then, suddenly, I was angry. Why was I left to look after her in this dreadful place? Her family, powerful people all, should be looking after her, not an ordinary plain woman like myself, out of my depth, with insufficient skills. Her mother Ygraine was High Queen of Britain; her grandmother, the Lady of Lake, the most powerful Priestess who ever lived. And Merlin, the greatest mage ever known in this land, both of them responsible for the Initiation and the Sacred Marriage. Merlin should do something. He was a healer.

There was a pool at the centre of the wood, and I stared at it. I had kept in touch with Vivienne, though it was difficult as the distance increased. But Vivienne should know that her granddaughter was dying, as a direct result of her machinations.

Staring at the still water I opened my mind fully and sent out the call, powerfully strengthened by my anger. A cloud slid over the pool, and then Vivienne's face appeared surprised and anxious.

'She's dying,' I said abruptly. 'Starving herself. She is very ill from the pregnancy. She has evoked the Priestess's Oath. The long sleep. I cannot do it. I have been forced to break my oath and I am very angry. I have done all I can but I cannot help her. I cannot give her the great rest. You had better tell Merlin. He might be able to heal her, if any of you care about her, and can be bothered.' I broke the connection, shaking with fury and emotion, letting the pool clear, refusing to respond to the call to reconnect.

Aella 14

Unbelievably, Merlin came on the third day. Where he came from, or how he covered the distance, I never knew. He strode into the gatehouse leading a white mule, laden with leather bags of all shapes and sizes. There were expensive jewelled presents for Mawgawse and Lot, a threaded, holed stone, beautifully carved with runes, which changed into a strange sea-green when poison was present, for me, but his first call was to Morgan. He took her hand and I saw the powerful healing coursing through her whole body, surrounding her with a blue light, which turned white, then gold. She sat up and stared at him. 'Merlin?'

'Well, daughter, have you regained your courage?'

She was very angry. 'I don't lack courage. I have lost myself. I am filled with black sin and cannot see the light.'

'You are cleansed. I have taken the darkness upon myself. It was necessary that Arthur must make the Sacred Marriage, necessary that the Priestess selected to host the Goddess must be the most powerful.'

Morgan stared at him with hatred. 'You have taken

everything from me. The Goddess called me and all I ever wanted was to prepare myself so that I could serve as the Lady of Avalon. Work there as a healer and live a virgin life. You have taken that away from me, to no purpose.'

'You have served the Lady well. Go back to Avalon. Live as you wish.'

'Never. Never will I go to Vivienne. She betrayed me.'

'She did what she had to do, and you are punishing yourself for no reason. Your children are important – they must be born.'

She lay down and turned her back on him and he went away.

But after Merlin's visit, despite herself, Morgan's health improved and she was able to eat and sleep properly. Merlin had left with me some rare herbs which helped the pregnancy and slowly the months went by. He had left books for Morgan, irresistible books on herbs and healing, which we read together, and, surprisingly, a small harp, which she taught herself to play and which gave balm to her soul.

The Court bard, unappreciated in that violent place, came to sit with her for hours, teaching her new songs.

I don't think she ever forgave me for withholding the long sleep, but over time our old trust reasserted itself and we became close again.

Despite the defeat of the Northern Lords, Lot continued to plot. Envoys from surrounding Chiefs and Kings came and went, some, surprisingly, from the new settlements in the east. Lot's war band grew. The Hall filled with sell-swords and archers, drilling relentlessly all through the autumn and winter, and it was clear that he was planning some new uprising. Word came that the Kings and great lords were again assembling in

Winchester, to attempt to elect a new High King and Lot rode off in haste, taking his war band with him to reinforce his claim.

A month later he returned in even worse temper. Uther was dead, but Lot had failed in his attempt to seize power. The assembly of Kings had failed to elect a new High King, certainly not King Lot, but they had elected Arthur as Dux Bellorum, in charge of all the armies of the Britons. Arthur had been fighting battle after battle and had never been defeated. He was a great hero, a fighting fury, dressed all in white on a white horse, acclaimed Battle Duke by the army. Lot, swore viciously, and stamped about the Court and Mawgawse was furious and berated him for stupidity and tardiness, until he slapped her mouth closed. No one spoke for a week, and we made sure to keep to our rooms.

At the end of the most bitter winter I had ever experienced, Morgan was brought to the birthing stool. I attended her, with the help of a little maid from the kitchen who said she had birthed most of her brothers and sisters. It took longer than I thought it should, but at first, all was well. The Bard played for Morgan for hours and she was patient and serene.

Our dear Rhianna came first, a pretty little girl, as neat and easy as you please, golden hair already framing her tiny head and happy, after her first indignant protest at the cold of the world, to be quickly cuddled in soft warm wrappings where she went to sleep without more ado.

But Medraut fought us. It turned into a truly frightful birthing. He would not be born. Hours went past, with Morgan straining and getting weaker and weaker and all our Avalon knowledge of midwifery was of no use. I tried everything I knew, every position advised, and still the child resisted us.

'Strange,' Morgan gasped at one point. 'It's trying to kill me, and I was asking for death. But now I want to live...' This ended with an involuntary scream, longer than before, and she fell unconscious. I thought she had gone, but after some anxious minutes I managed to revive her.

The next morning, early, after all the hellish hours of the night had reduced us to total exhaustion and black despair, Mawgawse came, tall and stately, her red hair spread over her rich breasts, displayed in a green velvet gown slashed with cloth of gold. She herself had birthed her babe, yet another boy, only two weeks before. She stood over Morgan, looking at her poor white sweating face, and erratic breathing, and laughed.

'What a pother you are making of this birthing, sister. You haven't the knack of it like I have. All this screaming is upsetting the slaves.'

Morgan closed her eyes.

I said, 'Lady, we are at the end of our knowledge. We have tried all, but the babe will not be born.'

'The birth cord is trapped? He comes feet first?'

I was furious. What level of skill did she think I had? I said coldly, 'He has been turned. The birth cord released. He continues to fight us.'

She looked at Morgan again and laughed. 'Well, for all your wonderful Avalon knowledge it has not been able to help you, has it? Let us see what I can do. Perhaps my skill is greater than yours after all.'

She swept out, followed by her frightened women, who returned a few minutes later, with a draught in a golden goblet, thick and black and viscous.

'I don't like the look of it. It is from the dark side.' I said.

'Give it to me,' Morgan said. 'What matter if it sends me into the nether world? It is only a matter of time.' She gulped it in one go, glad, I think to be at the end of the affair. She retched twice, but managed to hold it down, and minutes later, writhing, a male child came, expelled violently from her womb, screaming and fighting, dark as night. With him came great quantities of blood and black mucus, and then, eventually, the afterbirth, and more blood. I had much ado to stem the blood, and once again, I despaired and thought I would lose her. The chamber looked more like a battlefield full of gore than a high birthing.

But if I say it myself, I am usually, an excellent midwife, and using all my Priestess arts, I sent Morgan into a deep sleep and worked on her with needle and hair suture, stitching, repairing, with the smallest stitches while the little maid from the kitchen, who was pale as a ghost herself, helped to staunch the still-flowing blood. I was very afraid that Morgan would die from blood loss, or be permanently injured, and I thought it unlikely that she would ever bear another child.

The boy child lay wrapped, but bloody and screaming still, but we could not spare the time to deal with him while we saved the mother, and to be honest, I felt a strange reluctance to lift him, and I did not care if he lived or died.

It would have been better for all if he had died then.

In the next months, as Morgan slowly recovered her health, it began it seem that a devil had indeed come with the child. He was a screamer, bellowing with fury, if his will was crossed in any way and if his demands were not instantly met. He was greedy and violent, kicking and punching everybody around, including poor little Rhianna, and I had to keep her away from him.

By the time of their first birthday, it became obvious to our uneasy understanding that he was sly and cruel, crawling after insects and butterflies and if he caught them, tearing them to pieces. Rhianna was gouged with his fingers and was often black and blue with bruises as he kicked and hit her.

Morgan disliked him and had refused to breast feed him, and could not bring herself to hold him.

But if Medraut was a devil, little Rhianna was an angel. Always smiling and intent, studying the flowers and one day I found her in the little garden surrounded by birds. Medraut had moved on from killing creatures to torturing them, and just as often I found Rhianna rescuing them and trying to put them back together, or just simply holding them, and yes, even healing them. I could not believe this at first, at so young an age, but the blue aura was unmistakeable and some of the creatures, the ones not too far gone, emerged from her gentle hands, whole and healed. I said nothing to Morgan, but I began to watch the child and was convinced she was developing extraordinary powers.

'You must stand up for yourself, Rhianna,' I said crossly, bathing the latest bruises on her arms, but it was clear that Rhianna could not injure another living creature and was no match for Medraut's rage. But when he found sharp edged flints and learned to cut, I became seriously alarmed. I could not be around every moment, and he was sly, watching and waiting his chance.

I need not have worried. One day I found Rhianna playing with a furred creature I thought was a large cat from the kitchen, but when I approached it rolled over and onto its sturdy legs in front of her and snarled viciously at me. It was as big as a dog, and I saw, horrified, that it was one of the dangerous mountain wild cats, common to the northern mountains, which had never been tamed in the land's history. It had black fur, with a white patch on its chest and amber eyes.

Rhianna laughed and plunged her fingers into its thick fur, and my heart nearly gave out, thinking to see it spin around and claw out her eyes.

'Silly,' she said to the cat, chuckling. 'Only Granny Aella.' She said to me 'Cat Sith come.'

'Welcome, Cat Sith,' I said, feebly, giving the creature a wide berth, and receiving a slit-eyed snarl for my pains. How on earth did she know its name? Wait, wasn't there some myth about a Cat Sith?

But it was soon obvious why it had come, or been sent. The next time Medraut attempted to beat Rhianna, he received a scratch from his elbow to his wrist, and a bad bite on his hand – and a fine fuss he made about it! Medraut was clever and sly, but the cat was too quick for him, and within a week, Medraut had sullenly decided that hurting Rhianna was no fun when the animal was by. Cat Sith seemed to have an unnatural ability to know when Rhianna was threatened, and Medraut got his retribution. He hated the cat, but feared it, and finally turned his vicious attention elsewhere, to little Gareth.

I think it was this incident that finally made me understand that Rhianna was no ordinary child and was divinely protected. After that I watched with even greater care and attention as her powers blossomed, helping in all the ways I knew to expand and develop her understanding. She trotted at my heels the day long, watching and copying, and soaking up learning as the earth absorbs the rainfall after a drought. She began to learn her letters, and to play a pipe, and to sew and embroider. She loved the coloured threads and would spend hours playing with them, plaiting them into different combinations.

Predictably, Mawgawse found Medraut's ways amusing, and made much of him, spoiling him with sweetmeats and kisses, encouraging him in his killing, and to fight with his cousins, a pack of wolf children who ran wild without hindrance or education, except for the Sergeant at Arms who began, at Mawgawse suggestion to beat his skills of sword and lance into their lice-ridden heads.

Aella 15

Cat Sith was with us for a year and a day, frightening the slaves and the local people who claimed she was a supernatural being. She would not come into the building, but lived outside, mostly atop the tall, courtyard wall, except at night when she crouched at the base of our tower, hidden in the shadows by the door, on guard. Very effective she was too – no one dared to enter after dark. We fed her well and Rhianna loved her, speaking with her nose to nose lying on the cobles, but she left us anyway.

The next day the ravens arrived– a big mob, noisy and quarrelsome we thought at first, but they settled down on the walls, shouting out to Rhianna and making her laugh but taunting Medraut whenever he showed his face. He hated them and tried to catch them, but they were too clever and clearly enjoyed the contest, attacking unexpectedly, pecking his head, pouncing on his back and tripping him, and generally making him look a clumsy fool.

As they grew older, the difference between the two children was extraordinary. We had thought, given they were twins, that they would be alike, but they were poles apart, not only physically. Medraut looked very like his mother. He had her very pale skin, and straight, shiny, black hair that looked almost irridescent. His eyes made you uncomfortable; darker than hers, they seemed to accuse, and glower. Rhianna was altogether different – amber eyed, with curly, true gold hair, always laughing, interested in everything with a big thirst for learning. I wondered about her colouring, but Morgan exclaimed over her, a little fearfully, I thought, and said she was the image of her mother, Ygraine. I realised this was not a compliment, although Ygraine was generally acknowledged to be the most beautiful woman in Logres, but Vivienne had told me that she was an icy woman with enormous and very strange powers. She was certainly not motherly and had treated Morgan very badly.

I said, 'She may look like her, but she is a very loving and happy child.'

But Morgan was not to be won over so easily. 'It will be interesting to see if she has any of her witchy gifts.'

I laughed, 'Witchy? Morgan, you are the last person to talk of witchy gifts. Shape shifter, healer, Goddess bearer...'

Her eyes shone with amusement, acknowledging a hit. 'My mother was a very strange woman, always talking to people with funny names, who weren't there. At least I could not see them. Strange things happened. People in the village wouldn't work for her.'

I grinned. 'I'll let you know when Rhianna starts talking to people who aren't there!'

We both watched the little child, sitting on the cobbles, burbling away happily, holding out her hand to one of the ravens with one of her oat cakes in it. There were many ravens about Lot's Castle now and it seemed they had come to stay. They were fearless, took little or no account of the humans and completely ruled our courtyard. Rhianna, of course, loved them almost as much as she had loved Cat Sith. The bird walked nearer and very carefully, it seemed, pecked the edge of the cake, lifting it away, so that it didn't peck her skin.

'There,' I said, triumphantly, 'She's so good at making friends with birds and animals. Did your mother do that?'

'No,' she said, soberly, 'She turned them into something else...things.'

'Oh,' I said, silenced, feeling cold.

Rhianna, looked up at us, grinning. 'Big Wing eat.'

Morgan raised an eyebrow. 'Big Wing?'

'She has names for all the ravens. Rhianna, who?' I said pointing at a second raven walking nearby, obviously hoping there was another oatcake on offer.

'Rip Eye.'

'What?' Morgan and I said together.

'Rip Eye.' She pointed at other Ravens sitting on the Keep Wall. 'Finder. Hard Claw. Big Tail...And Blue Beak,' she pointed again as another bird flew down.

'Where did she learn these words?' Morgan said to me. 'How does she know which is which?'

'Rhianna, my love, how do you know their names?'

Rhianna looked surprised, bemused. 'They tell me.'

We looked at each other. Morgan said, grimly, 'You were saying?'

Rhianna was certainly an unusual child, right from the start. She must have been barely walking when she came and tugged at my skirt. 'Come see.' She was very excited, and her meaning was plain. I followed her across the courtyard, where we spent bright days, and the children played. She was bent over a tiny plant which had forced its way up between the cobbles, not two fingers high.

'A weed?' I queried, puzzled.

She looked at me, her eyes shining.

'A weed. It's just a weed, Rhianna.'

She squatted down and cupped the tiny plant in her hand, so gently, so lovingly, it brought tears to me eyes. 'Flow'r.'

And I saw that the tiny plant had an even tinier flower.

'Flow'r.' she said again, with reverence, looking at me with such joy. And staring at it, I saw that it was indeed, very beautiful. White, silky, delicately coloured pink at the edges of the minute petals. A miracle. I had never looked at it before, but Rhianna had found it, and shared its beauty with me.

Sometimes I saw her sitting in the dirt, unmoving for minutes at a time, and when I queried her, she said she was watching the ants. 'See. Egg too big.' and together, entranced, we watched two ants struggling to move the too-large egg to its new home under another cobble. She was always finding new and wonderful things. So I began to take her on my brief expeditions outside the Keep when I went looking for healing herbs, and taught her their names and benefits. She learned astonishingly quickly, and accurately.

She was so different from her brother who seemed only interested in destruction. He delighted in killing anything he found – birds, animals, worms and insects, even plants and soon he was pulling wings off bees, and birds, watching with delight when they tried to fly. When I punished him for these crimes, he became sly, and killed them behind my back, sneering and laughing. He was outside our control, took no heed of us and refused to do anything we said. He began to take his dead things to his Aunt Mawgawse as presents, who, far from punishing him, laughed and praised him, and perhaps used them for her experiments. We had realised, that Mawgawse was now moving further into the rituals and spells of black witchcraft, and when babies from the surrounding villages began to disappear, I was horrified and sure. Medraut clearly preferred being with his aunt and running with his pack of cousins. I hoped she was not teaching him her black arts, but to be honest, I was more than glad to see him gone from us.

The months passed slowly. With little to do, Morgan was bored and dejected, and as her health returned, she began again to slip away at night, in changed form, returning with the dawn to sleep through the day.

Mawgawse and Lot were both preoccupied, and I guessed that once again, they were plotting rebellion and treason, bargaining with the Saxons and Angles to provide land in exchange for men and weapons.

Mawgawse was now anxious to be rid of us. She tried on several occasions to persuade Morgan to take one or other of Lot's banner men to husband, but Morgan reacted with such horror and fury, that she had to abandon her plans.

She said, petulantly, 'Well, I don't know what else you are going to do. You can't stay here for ever.'

Morgan's mouth tightened and it was clear she was trying to keep from making an angry reply. 'You know I have written several times to our brother Arthur about my Cornish lands, and Tintagel Castle. Small wonder that I have not had a reply when he is fighting battles all over the land to achieve a lasting peace and protect us from our enemies. When he has time, I know he will settle the matter.'

'In the meantime, we have the expense of your upkeep and your children, and your servants!' said Mawgawse glaring at me. There was no love lost between us, as she believed, wrongly, that it was my fault that Morgan would not consider marriage with her low-born reavers.

'Never fear,' said Morgan, contemptuously, 'I will repay all the money you have spent on the luxurious hospitality you have given us.' As we walked away, she said to me bitterly, and to my disquiet, 'How can I marry? The Goddess knows I am married already.'

After that we kept even more close and quiet, seldom appearing in the great hall. We used the small courtyard at the foot of our tower on good days, where Rhianna played at finding small plants in the walls and replanting them in the unpaved mud against the wall, and where to my surprise, they flourished and bloomed, softening the dark granite of that fell place.

We heard nothing from Avalon, nothing from Merlin. But another Great Council was called in Winchester, and this time, to Lot's rage, it seemed likely that Arthur would be chosen as High King.

So, the time passed. The children grew, and we endured.

However, I was not entirely inactive. I had made it my secret business to find a possible way of escape should the necessity arise. I never lost sight of the fact that Mawgawse and Lot were dangerous enemies.

Aella 16

In March, when our fourth winter at Lot's Court was finally gone, and the clear melt waters from the hills were tumbling down their stony pathways, we had visitors. Early one morning a huge concourse of knights and men-at-arms came riding through the mist from the South, as the alarm brayed from the Gate House. When they were nearer, we could read their banner.

'The Pendragon, by God,' said Lot, 'Arthur's men, in force.' He was sheet white. Since his second defeated return from the Great Council in Winchester when Arthur had been finally elected High King, he had spent all his time setting up alliances with the Northern chiefs and plotting a great Northern uprising along with the Saxons and Angles. I think he was planning to seize the crown by force at the Coronation, planned for May and his plans were well advanced, judging by the increasing size of his war band. Had Arthur, who had been fighting continuously since appointment as Dux Bellorum got wind of this new threat?

They rode closer, their banners flying their weapons

glinting, and hailed the Guard at the lower gate.

'Prince Bedwyr, on behalf of the Dux Bellorum, Arthur Pendragon. We would speak with King Lot.' Lot's colour came slowly back, as he understood that there was to be no immediate attack.

We crowded into the Great Hall, curious to see Arthur's first knight, who was almost as famous as Arthur, for his prowess as a swordsman, if the tales drifting from the South spoke true.

He was a young man above middle height, very strong seeming, with a powerful width across the shoulders. A muscular body, but not fat and he moved lightly and smoothly like a dancer. He was a good-looking man, clean shaven in the Roman style with a courteous, easy manner. He had a lazy and friendly charm, appearing very relaxed but his dark eyes were wary, concealing a sharp intellect. Formidable, I thought. It was said Arthur used him in diplomatic missions. But what did he want with Lot?

As it happened, nothing.

Despite the profusion of gifts and letters, nothing. Bedwyr had come for Morgan, bringing three hundred men with him.

'My Lord Arthur, sends his greetings and would have the pleasure of your company and your lady wife at his Coronation in May at Winchester.'

Lot said smoothly that he was honoured by the invitation, and would make every effort to come south when his current campaign against the Pictish tribes on his northern frontier had been concluded. And although highly honoured, had it been necessary to provide such a princely escort?

Bedwyr smiled and said that indeed, an escort was not necessary when it was known that Lot's own men were so highly trained and... numerous, but the princely escort was thought appropriate to conduct the King's sister, the Lady Morgan, back to Arthur's Court.

I heard Morgan draw a long deep breathe, just as Lot said, even more smoothly, that they must consult the Lady Morgan's wishes in the matter, and Mawgawse, smiling, said that, of course, her dear sister, Morgan would come too, when they all rode south together for dear Arthur's coronation. Together with his immense war band, I thought. No way could we be part of that rabble. In the meantime, Mawgawse said, Sir Bedwyr and his men would be made most welcome here until their return.

Bedwyr bowed politely and thanked her for her generous hospitality, but said that they hoped to leave with the Lady Morgan at first light tomorrow.

Mawgawse looked at Lot and laughed lightly. 'I am afraid that the Lady Morgan could not possibly be ready at such rough notice. She must have time to prepare. She has been ill. It will be much better for her to come with us...'

Bedwyr managed to look both troubled and sad. 'Lady, I am afraid that we have been instructed by the High King not to return without her. He has great need, he says, for her help in the preparations for his Coronation. He feels the need for his family about him at such an auspicious time, and has fond memories of their previous meeting.'

I looked at Morgan, stunned at the audacity of the message. Colour flooded her normally pale cheeks, her eyes flashed and I expected a furious outburst any moment. But instead, she said 'How did he know where to find me?'

Bedwyr looked confused. 'Of course, he has always known where you were, Lady, and has always been most concerned about your welfare.'

Fortunately, at this point Lot intervened. 'Well, well,' he said genially, 'We will talk about it later. In the meantime, you must allow me to offer the hospitality of my board to you and your officers. The servitors are waiting to set out the tables. You must be sharp set for fresh food.' And he summoned his own body servants, instructing them to conduct Bedwyr and his officers to guest chambers where baths and changes of clothing would be offered.

Bedwyr bowed gracefully, and gave swift orders to an officer to see his men encamped close outside the walls of the Castle, an order not lost on Lot, and followed the servant out. Morgan, seething, swept out too, but I stayed to help set up the trestles to find out what was going on.

Mawgawse looked around and seeing the place emptying, drew Lot privily, to one side of high table. I ducked behind the kitchen screen nearby. Fortunately, my hearing is sharp.

Mawgawse hissed at Lot, 'You must not let her go. She must not gain Arthur's favour. She will promote Medraut as his heir. He is Sister's Son.'

'Sister's Son?'

Mawgauze snarled impatiently. 'Arthur has more than one sister. Gawain, our son must be his heir.'

Lot said, 'You are merely the younger sister. Besides, Arthur is young. He will get his own heir, his son, according to Roman Law.'

'Are we Romans? Do I need to remind you that always before the Roman's came, and still for us, inheritance is through the female line? Sister's Son inherits, as all tribes know. All can be sure of the Mother. What man can be sure of his fatherhood?'

'Indeed.' Lot's voice was suddenly knife-like and dangerous.

Mawgawse took no notice. 'Arthur is a soldier, in constant battle. His life hangs on a thread. Our son Gawain, my Lord, is Arthur's true heir. Medraut is a child of the Beltane fires, with no known father.'

'And Morgan's next son?'

'There will be none. She is barren.'

'You hope.'

'Medraut's birthing was very hard. Her body was torn, and then there was a small helpful draught I gave her, which settled the matter.'

I had to press my hand against my mouth to stop the cry escaping. That black viscous fluid. I knew it was from the dark side. I knew Morgan should not have accepted it. Mawgawse was cruel and wicked, and now her motives became clear.

'Fear not, my Lord, Gawain is secure.'

'Except for Medraut.

'Except for Medraut.'

'A small accident, perhaps?'

'A pity to destroy so useful a tool. He has great possibilities. He is full of hate and anger. We must keep him in our power for a while.

'What do you suggest?'

'Hide him in Orkney with our brood, for the time being. The cliffs are dangerous there, it is easy to fall if need be. Arthur must not get to know him.'

'And what of Morgan's girl?'

'Rhianna? A fatal accident. Her line will die. She is an unnecessary complication. Remember she too, is a sister and her sons could claim the crown if Medraut won power. Safer to eliminate them both.'

'With the nurse,' said Lot. 'She knows too much and I mislike her eyes.'

Mawgawse laughed harshly. 'She is certainly no ordinary nurse, but I haven't been able to find out her history. Avalon surely, but beyond that, the mind link is closed to me. Even Ellen could find out nothing.'

So, the little kitchen maid was a spy after all. Suddenly I felt very cold. We were all in immediate danger – and much more danger than I had thought.

Lot said, 'When?'

Mawgauze considered. 'Soon. Before we go south for the Coronation. Before the Northern rising. Perhaps during the confusion of leaving and packing up the court?'

Lot grunted. 'Make it soon and simple.'

I smiled grimly, and when they went away, I moved rapidly to put my escape plan into action.

'I can't go!' Morgan pounced on me, when I reached our chambers. 'I won't be Arthur's paramour. I won't. Prince Bedwyr says that Merlin has married Arthur off to little Gwenifer, the King of Gwynedd's daughter and she is already pregnant! He says it's necessary for Arthur to produce an heir quickly for his own safety, and in case he gets killed.' She was crying with fury. 'What does Arthur want with me? I have the children; I can't leave them. I don't trust Lot.'

'It's Mawgawse,' I said. 'She's trying to keep you from Arthur's favour. She intends Gawain as his heir, not Medraut.'

She stared at me. 'What nonsense is this? You know why Medraut cannot inherit. The Archbishop would never allow it.'

'Mawgawse does not think in this way. She thinks Sister's

Son, and there are two sisters. If the elder were to...disappear, have an accident, Gawain could become Arthur's heir.' I chuckled, 'Although it sounds as though Merlin has already put a spoke in that wheel!'

'I don't believe it...'

'I heard her, just now. Do you think I lie?'

'Of course not! But...You must have misunderstood. It's Lot...'

'Lot is a pawn,' I said impatiently. 'Mawgawse is your enemy, our enemy. You and the children are all in danger. Me too. Don't you see?'

She was silent, thinking, her eyes getting darker and darker, tear-filled.

'You will have to go, without the children' I said. 'You will have to leave them here with me and I will try to get them away as quickly as I can and come south after you. It's your only protection. In any case I don't think that young man, Prince Bedwyr will give you a choice. He will carry out Arthur's instructions to the letter, even if it means occupying this castle, or riding back with you in chains. And Lot will have to agree. The garrison is at half strength here. His main warband is concealed on the Wall, training in secret. He cannot stand here against Pendragon's picked men, three hundred of them. He is frightened, too, they will discover his plans for the Northern rising.'

'Aella, why does he send for me?'

'Bedwyr gave an explanation, but I think Arthur is trying to save your life. He must know about the Rising. He might even have suspected Mawgawse' and Lot's plans.'

She stared at me. 'But what of the children. What are we to

do with Medraut and Rhianna?'

I said, 'They will be safer at Arthur's Court.'

'I can't,' she said. 'I cannot do it, Aella. I can't do that to him. The truth will come out and his enemies will tear him apart. The Church will excommunicate him. He will lose the throne. We committed a mortal sin, don't you see? The children must remain hidden, until I can get to my own lands in Cornwall.'

I thought she was living in a dream world. Lot would decide.

I was proved correct. Lot said Morgan must go. He could not afford to offend Arthur, with his plots only half secured, and he could not afford to lose a valuable castle to Bedwyr's men. He said Morgan must make ready to ride out in the morning, and leave the children in his care.

Mawgawse, of course, said she would be delighted to look after the children safely until Morgan could send for them and Morgan was persuaded to agree however uneasily. I should remain here and take charge of them, Mawgawse said. She loved Medraut so much, she said, that she would bring him up as her own second son, until Morgan's circumstances changed. Morgan was at her wits end, torn every which-way, and not happy, but she could see no other solution.

And so, at last, with a scramble we crammed her clothes and her books and her little harp into the too-small panniers, and half-distracted, Morgan made ready to ride, in tears, clutching convulsively at me and begging me to keep well until we met again. The bright column rode off, the pennants flying bravely and I wondered if I would ever see her again.

Aella 17

As I watched them ride off, I can't pretend that I didn't feel deserted. Of course, I had said I would remain, willingly, but I knew now how great the danger was and I knew the time had come to put my secret plan of escape into action.

I had never trusted Mawgawse and believed that one day we might need to leave the Castle quickly and over the months I had already taken steps to make sure we would be ready. I had explored possible ways of escape. Go by road, or perhaps even, sea. They would not expect that. Getting out of the Castle itself would be the most difficult. I watched, waited, and made friends.

Peilla from Avalon, John's son who been hired as a guard for the main gate, watched carefully the comings and goings of the Castle and he introduced me to Cleland, a farmer who daily brought produce to the Castle in season. Cleland suffered from excruciating headaches and I was able to provide him with bark of willow, for which he was profusely grateful. He detested Lot, and when I told him that we were in danger of our lives, he said that I had only to let him know, and he would take us out in his cart. It was a handsome offer and I kept it in my mind.

We would need extra money. Morgan had money, of course, but Mawgawse was not generous. We might need to hire horses, buy food, pay for sea passages maybe, or rent rooms for overnight stays. To my surprise it was not difficult. At night, when the men were drunk and insensible, I helped the servants clear the tankards and trestles. Where they had been gambling there was always scattered coins. I became adept at sliding them into the little pocket I had sewn into my gown. There was money too, fallen among the rushes of the floor, gold as well as bronze. It was surprising how quickly my little hoard grew.

I gathered food, long lasting waybread, cheeses and sausages. I lined our cloaks with warm brychans, and from a strong bed cover I made a bag with straps, such as the shepherds carried on their backs. I had to look after Rhianna, and would not be able to carry much.

And now the time had indeed come. I found Cleland unloading sacks in the stable yard, and made arrangements for him to pick us up on the morrow. Myself and one, possibly two, children, I said.

Medraut, was the problem. I did not think he would want to go with us, leaving his cousins, and he would tell Mawgawse – but I could not just leave him. I must somehow find out his feelings, without letting him guess we were leaving immediately. I went to look for him, but could not find him, or, indeed, any of Lot's sons.

Mawgawse, smiling, complacently, said that because of the gathering danger of war with the Pictish tribes, they had sent all the boys to safety in Lot's Dun in his Kingdom of Orkney. They had left immediately after Bedwyr, to catch the evening tide.

My heart jumped wildly and I felt sick. 'They have gone already?'

'What need for delay?' she said, smoothly.

'But you said that I should look after Medraut. You told Morgan so.'

'They will be quite safe, I promise you. Ellen has gone with them, and the Sergeant at Arms, and an armed guard of thirty men. They will sail around the coast and spend a wonderful spring and summer in Orkney, while we prepare to go south... To Arthur's Coronation, of course.' Her mouth smiled again. 'If I'd known you wanted to go with them, I would have made arrangements...'

I said, sourly, 'I wonder he did not come to say goodbye.'

'I'm afraid that he has not learned his manners well.'

'Or not at all,' I said, shrugging. I would not let her think she had scored a point against me. 'I am not one of his favourites.'

There was nothing I could do for Medraut now, and remembered with some relief, that they were proposing to keep him alive as some sort of tool or hostage and I must concentrate on getting Rhianna and myself out of this woman's clutches as soon as possible. She had moved more quickly than I had anticipated, and I had underrated her. I would not make that mistake again. So, I curtseyed, smiled back amiably, and took myself off apparently unworried, to my place among the servitors for the evening meal, until I could unobtrusively get to my frantic preparations for the morrow.

When the Castle gates were flung open in the early morning next day, we went, Rhianna and I, in Cleland's cart, hidden under his piled empty sacks, smelling of corn, cheese and honey, with Peilla saluting and saying quietly in my ear, that he would see me back in Avalon one day soon.

Well, we were safely out of Lot's Castle, but I was still fearful of hearing the sound of horses ridden at speed behind us.

I had planned on making my way westward, to the coast by easy stages where I hoped to find a ship trading south. But Cleland had a better idea. He said that the road from Edinburgh to the west was much travelled and likely to be one of the roads searched by Lot's men, along with the great Roman road, leading directly south to the border. He said he knew of a better way, if I would trust him, which of course I did. He was clearly taking a great deal of pleasure in outwitting Lot.

Very soon afterwards we turned off from the main road, into ancient trackways, heading south west, and by the afternoon we crossed the border at Luguvallium which had been one of the Forts on the Emperor Hadrian's Wall. We drove on westward, and reached Cleland's objective, a busy little trading town, with a harbour, where several larger ships were loading cargoes of hides, fleece and salt among a smaller fishing fleet, unloading their catch.

Within an hour, Cleland had secured passages for us on the Sea Eagle, which was taking grain and fleeces southwards to Glevum along the Sabrina sea. It couldn't have chanced better, and I thanked the Goddess for sending Cleland to help us. When we parted from him, I pressed two gold coins into his hand. He was astonished and reluctant to take them, but I insisted in case he should be implicated in our escape and lose his castle trade. He assured me that we had covered our tracks well. We had seen few people in all that long day, and tomorrow he would be back carting as usual. He said he would bet a rabbit to a pig that they would be still be searching down the road to Eboracum and Deva.

All the same, I spent an anxious night on board the Sea Eagle, before, in the dawn light, the ropes were cast off, and we rode the strong tide into the Western Sea. Mawgawse was finally left behind. A brisk wind caught the sails, and the Sun rose warm and bright. A heavy weight fell off my shoulders. Freedom after all the long years.

'A fine day, I'm thinking, Mistress.' said Captain Bowness, as he passed.

'A fine day, indeed, Captain Bowness, Thanks be.'

Rhianna climbed up next to me as I sat on a locker, out of the way, revelling in the sun's warmth. She cuddled into my skirts, chuckling.

'Aunt Mawg looking,' she said.

I thought my heart had stopped. 'What? What did you say, Rhianna?'

She chuckled again. 'Aunt Mawg look in mirror and call me.'

I swallowed. 'She came into your mind, love?'

'Oh no, I in her. She looking for us.' She laughed. 'I hide in attics. Play hide and seek.'

I breathed again. She was just imagining.

'She shouting, and send the men. Shouting more when they came back without me. Then I hide below in the smelly cells and caves.'

'What caves?'

'Down under the cellars, under cells. Big caves.'

I stared at her. Was it possible? Were there really caves under Lot's Castle?

'Aunt Mawg send men again. They cursing and get lost. Uncle Lot beat her. Say she is mad. But she keep looking in the mirror. I make it blank.' She looked at me, suddenly worried. 'Just play hide and seek.'

I could barely speak. What was I hearing?

Mawgawse was scrying, searching for us, trying to take over Rhianna's mind? That seemed obvious. But Rhianna had taken over Mawgawse's mind instead? 'Rhianna, love, are you able to go into people's minds? Make them do things?'

'Some,' she said, 'If I want.'

'Do you come into my mind?' I held my breath.

She shook her head, and looked at me shyly, wriggling. 'No. Secret. Animals more interesting. Aella will you teach me knots?'

'Knots? My mind was still trying to take in the implications of what I had heard. That such a young child had this power and also the wisdom and feeling to know that it could be wrong was astonishing. And what was this about animals?

'The sailors are using special knots.'

Ah Goddess! I don't think I have ever felt so out of my depth before.

'Rhianna,' I said, 'Make sure that you don't let Aunt Mawg into your mind. She is dangerous. It would be better, too, if you didn't go into hers. We must remain hidden and secret. Do you understand?'

'Dangerous,' agreed Rhianna, clearly, nodding. 'She wants to kill us if she can.'

And I lost my breath again.

Part Four

Aella 18

I well remember that sea voyage from the north. For the most part the weather was fine with a fresh, brisk wind and the huge waves of the western sea were rising and rolling in long heavy swells. I remained on deck as much as possible, watching Ierne, low and misty along the horizon on the right, feeling a little seasick for awhile, until I became accustomed to the rhythm. Rhianna, of course, ran around the deck sure footed as a squirrel, and quickly became a favourite with all the sailors, begging for stories and listening, rapt, to their tales of far places, and practicing, with surprising dexterity, the complicated knots they showed her, with threads she had pulled from the braid on her best cloak.

It was hard to believe that we had truly escaped from Queen Mawgawse, that black witch of power. who had intended to kill us both and would surely do so if she caught us. Several times during the voyage I had been aware of her searching, scrying in her great black mirror, but I had managed to throw up an invisibility spell around the vessel long enough to conceal us from her random searches. I was reasonably sure that she had not managed to locate us. And now, here we were in the wild western sea, sailing at last up the estuary of the Sabrina river. I stood on the deck, holding Rhianna tight against my skirts and took a deep, relieved breath, of the smell of the vegetation, of the trees crowding down to the water, pleased to be back in the warm and kindly south again. There were few tall trees in King Lot's demesne and those few, twisted and bent from the winds howling around the great stone walls of the Castle. I had missed the trees, and much else too.

The Sea Eagle was bound for Glevum, but when I told the Captain that I was going to Avalon, taking my daughter's daughter to be educated there, he suggested that he might put me down at the fishing village of Stillwell, on the River Brever, a tributary of the Sabrina River, where I could travel inland across the Summer country in only a few days, direct to Avalon, saving several days travel, I was delighted. Not only would it bring me quicker to my destination but I would be avoiding Glevum. I knew that Glevum, an important port and town, might be dangerous for us. I was sure Mawgawse would have salted Glevum well with her spies. People would notice us, a woman and a child, travelling alone without servants, and I did not want to fall into her hands again when we were so near safety.

I had told the Captain, Avalon, but, in truth, I had intended to go to Arthur's capital of Caerleon, where Morgan had gone, but the more I thought about it, the more I was convinced that Avalon would be the better option. I knew that Morgan would be furious, that she would blame me for putting her daughter into Vivienne's power, but where else would she be safer, from Mawgawze' malice? And Mawgawze and Lot would be coming south to the Court for Arthur's coronation in only a few weeks, bringing an army with them.

So here we were, standing hand in hand on Stillwell's narrow landing stage, with only my shepherd's bag, at my feet, waving goodbye and thanks to the Sea Eagle, as the wind blowing our cloaks about, freshened the sails too, and the ship turned away up river.

I looked around. It was a small village with only three or four roundhouses, along the river inlet where there were a couple of ancient fishermen mending a coracle, and watching our arrival with interest. But when I asked for the Inn, they shook their heads and gestured me up the single rising track I could see now at the end. I realised then that most of the village lay hidden inland in the trees as, after a few minutes steep climb, the ground levelled.

A good number of trim roundhouses clustered along the winding track, and a woman came from one of the larger houses, smiling and curious to meet someone new.

'Welcome to Upper Stillwell, lady. I am Rhoswen, Head woman of the village.'

'Greetings, Rhoswen. I am Aella, travelling with my daughter's daughter, Rhianna...' Rhianna held out her skirts and curtseyed gravely, like a great lady, which made Rhoswen laugh. But she grew concerned when I said I was looking for an inn and to hire a horse. I explained that the Captain of the Sea Eagle had said we could travel quickly across the Summer country to Avalon, where Rhianna was going to school. Before I was finished, she was shaking her head. No, there was no village inn in Stillwell, and no, I could not hire a horse, or even buy one. In fact, there were no horses. As usual the men had all gone to the Spring muster of Arthur's war band, and had taken their few horses with them. In any case, there was only one trackway from the village but it ran through the Perilous Forest, and there was no way a single woman and a child could make their way through the Forest, without a guide and guard, and no villager would set foot there now.

I was astonished. 'Why not?'

'Fierce animals. Wolves, bears, and...worse. You cannot journey there alone, lady.'

She stared at the half moon mark on my forehead, which I had tried to conceal beneath my hood. 'We couldn't allow it. It would be suicide.'

She looked at the mark again, and lowered her voice. 'In recent years there have been ...things...there, that nobody has ever seen before, and from where they come nobody can guess. Strange things.'

I wanted to laugh, but she was a practical, sensible woman, I could see. Fair- haired, blue-eyed and plump, she stood tall, with an open honest face. A woman of my own age, not some shivering ninny. 'Some have seen the dead passing on a Ghost road...And there are masterless men, robbers, and mad hermits there too. Those who go in, seldom come out. Something strange is happening there. Truly you must not do it, lady.'

'And there is no inn, where we could stay?'

'Nought but fifty families or so.'

I cursed under my breath. I was a fool. I should not have been so hasty. I should have made better enquiries. I thought furiously. I would have to wait for another boat and go to Glevum after all. What on earth had Captain Bowness been thinking of?

'I came by boat. Will there be another soon?'

She shook her head. 'Nothing regular – maybe once a month. We are just a small trading village. A village of women and children when most of the men are away at the war.'

'I am a fool. I am stuck.' I groaned. Rhianna tugged at my skirts. 'Aella...I hungry.'

We both looked at her, and the Head Woman smiled at me sympathetically. 'No inn, but...well, I don't know... there's a widow... perhaps you might consider that. It is not what you would want, I think, but. perhaps, in an emergency... Brigitta, is our ale wife, and sometimes she puts up travelling packmen. The village men go there to drink at the end of the day, when they are home. So it is sometimes noisy... She is famous for her brewing. I know she is always glad of a helping hand...'

I sighed with relief. I was not proud – a roof over our heads is all we needed, and it would not be for long. 'Will you show me where she lives? And introduce me? I can pay well. I am wroth with my stupidity!'

We climbed up the trackway, where more round houses stood back a little from the path, and climbed again until there were only two houses left in the shadow of the great forest. The ale wife lived in the first.

Rhoswen introduced me, and we stared at each other. I liked her on sight. Brigitta was a rosy, bustling woman, straight forward and direct with fists as large as a man's. I thought we might get on well.

'I'm Brigitta,' she said. 'And what's your name, my little lovey?'

'I'm Rhianna, and this is my grandmother, Aella.' Rhianna repeated her curtsey, which she had learned from Ellen at

Lot's Court, smiled up at her, and clasped her hand. 'I'm very hungry,' she confided, to my mortification.

Brigitta guffawed and swung Rhianna up into her arms. 'Then we'll have to find some bread and milk for you, won't we, sweetheart?'

'Thank you,' said Rhianna sunnily, 'I like bread and milk.'

'Why, you little love,' said Brigitta kissing her.

She bore her off into the house, and I followed, thanking the Head Woman for her help, and she left us, laughing, down the trackway. It seemed to me that by luck and chance I had arrived in a friendly, happy place.

I was not mistaken. As Rhoswen had said, it was a village of women and children, with a few old men who were too old or too ill to go off to fight for Arthur and who scraped a living by coracle fishing in the Sabrina. The village was built on the high bank of the River Brever, a tributary, where it met the great River. A huge, dense forest behind. closed it off from the country inland, making it seem secret and remote.

The Alewife, Brigitta, my first friend there, was delighted to have a visitor. She was a strong, big-boned woman, sociable and cheerful, with a loud, gusty laugh that made you want to laugh with her. Her husband had died two years previously, fighting with Arthur at the battle of the river Dubglas in Linnuis, leaving her childless and penniless, but her ale was the best for many miles around, and she had survived, to achieve her present state of modest prosperity, and was content. She said she might remarry whenever she chose, but having tasted freedom, she said she preferred to go on as she was and choose whether or not she shared her bed and with whom, with which I wholeheartedly agreed. She was childless, but a woman who adored children, so she was glad of the company, she said, and spoiled Rhianna shockingly.

We settled in comfortably. The house was bigger than some of the others, with a wooden shed outside where the ales were brewed. The warm beds were screened around the inner walls for privacy, with a fire and cooking hearth in the centre, so the smoke could escape through the roof.

Brigitta and I got on surprisingly well, for women whose background, education and interests were at opposite poles. I was able to help with the cooking and with preparations for the brewing of the ale and fermenting honey, for the mead. The place smelled sweetly of the hops and honey. We ate together and shared many a joke.

By this time, I had time to think more coolly about my plans, and it seemed that it might be a better idea to let Morgan know where we were, and what she wanted us to do. I had not seen her since she had gone with Bedwyr and did not know her current circumstances. Could she protect Rhianna from Mawgawse in the High King's Court? Or would it be better for us to remain hidden? And did Arthur want it known that he had a daughter? I must try to find a way of getting a message to Morgan first, with a warning about Mawgawse, before I moved. It was not a good time to take chances.

In the end it was a nearly a month before one of the old fishermen, who was taking casks of Brigitta's ale down to Glevum, offered to take a message for me. I wrote very carefully, on a piece of parchment cut from one of Morgan's books, in Latin, so if it was intercepted it could not easily be read, of the treachery of Mawgawze and Lot and their planned revolt against Arthur, and their intended murder of Rhianna. I used only initials, not names. I told her we had escaped, and were safe for the time being, I asked what I should do now. And last I inscribed my name and the name of the village, waved a line of candle smoke over all, whereupon the letters faded back into the parchment – an old Avalon trick –   I hoped that Morgan would notice the small shadowing and remember what to do. I rolled it, and sealed it, addressed it to Lady Morgan at Arthur's castle of Caerleon.

So we stayed in Stillwell, temporarily, I thought. It was a big decision, bigger than I knew at the time, and so we settled and began our new lives, but I was ever discreet, mindful that we would be on our way soon enough and must leave no clues behind us, of our history and identity.

May came and went, and June. I heard nothing from Morgan.

The Coronation had been postponed we heard. Arthur had refortified the old Roman city of Viroconium, waiting for Lot and his horde to come south, and had fallen on them at the City of the Legions, destroying the host, driving the Bernicians and Anglians back to the north east coast. Lot was sore wounded and like to die. A glorious victory! Then shortly after, we heard that Arthur had, at last, been crowned High King at Winchester.

It seemed obvious to me that my message had never reached Morgan, as she moved around with the Court, from stronghold to stronghold. I wrote again and then again, although by this time we were established in the village, and I did not want to give up this quiet, comfortable life where Rhianna was growing up safe and happy, to return to the dangers and intrigues of Court life. So, we stayed, living discreetly, keeping our business to ourselves so that no hint of our whereabouts could reach

Mawgawse' ears.

The memory of the sea voyage and Lot's Court had quickly faded for Rhianna and under the questioning of the village children, she had identified me as her grandmother. When she asked about her mother, I told her she was at King Arthur's Court and couldn't be with us and she concluded that her mother worked there as a servant to earn our living, as her father was dead. I let these assumptions stand, and this helped to establish us in the village as ordinary, respectable people with relatives elsewhere.

Aella 19

It is easy to destroy. I have always loved those who repair, remake, reforge, weave old into new, to create something stronger, so that nothing is lost, if it can be saved.

My mind now links to that birth, where I saw utter destruction, parts rent asunder, remade impossibly whole again, against all natural laws, and believed for the first time that there was a greater power, in a way I had never truly believed before, and I knew that my beloved Rhianna was – what? Something more than human.

We had been in the village less than a month when Rhoswen, the Head Woman came to me one afternoon, grave and very worried.

'Rhoswen, good afternoon. Can I help?'

She hesitated. 'Forgive me Lady,' I had insisted that she call me Aella, but quite often she forgot and reverted to her old habit.

'What is the matter, Rhoswen? You are looking quite desperate.'

'Lady, I feel this is an intrusion, and I wouldn't do it but

I'm that worried about my dead sister's daughter, Gena. She lives with me, and she has been in labour these last two days and nights. There is something wrong. I know it. Old Maeve says not, but she hasn't much real knowledge. And Gena is weakening. I wouldn't ask, but I love that girl so much...I think she is near death and the babe still unborn. We have done all we can. Lady, I know...I mean I noticed the crescent on your forehead, although you dress your hair to cover it, and I see it is faded, but I was wondering, hoping... Lady are you Avalon trained? Would you be willing for the Goddess' sake, to look at Gena? I would be so grateful...' She was crying now. Of course, I could not refuse such a request. I checked my healer's bag for herbs and instrument case. 'Come, show me where she is. Let me see if I can do anything.'

When we had chased out the half a dozen arguing crones crowding her cot, I was able to examine her. The girl was indeed far gone, near death, she was white, sweating, and agonised and I thought she was beyond saving. The babe, half born was mangled and looked dead already, both bodies were bloodied. So much blood, soaking the cot and floor, it looked like a battlefield.

I said, 'It is very bad. I don't think...Shall I try to save the girl or the babe?'

Rhoswen said, immediately, 'The girl. My only one. Besides...' There was no need to say more.

Rhianna said nothing, she looked carefully at the horror, pale and grim like an old woman rather than a child, and began to strip away the bloodied cloths, mopping the blood from the girl so that I could see to work. I had not realised she had followed me; I would not have brought her if I had thought about it, but she had run at my heels for so long I hardly remembered she was there, but this was far from normal.

I dropped my special knife, thin and impossibly sharp, into the pot of boiling water that Rhoswen had prepared for me, and asked her to tear some clean binding strips, while Rhianna took out the cleansing and healing herbs she knew I always used.

I cut and eased the babe carefully from the girl's body, and without thinking, gave it to Rhoswen. She stared, horror struck, at the child, blood covered, who slid out of her nerveless hands, on to the bench. She bolted for the door, and I heard her being sick outside. I could not stop to attend the dead babe now, and concentrated on the girl, carefully easing her inner parts back to their correct position, bathing away more blood. I gave her my special brew of strengthening herbs with a draught of poppy, and she slid further into unconsciousness, while I set about sewing up the torn flesh with my smallest stitches, flooding all with an antiseptic infusion, in the hope that infection would not take hold, and that if she survived, she might bear again.

Time passed and I concentrated, not aware of what was going on around me. When the last stitch was in place and I had again used the lavender and birthwort ointment, we bound her up tightly in the clean bands her mother handed me, and I sat on the stool to draw my breath. Gena opened her eyes, tried to smile, and slid immediately back into deep sleep.

Rhoswen stared at her. 'She still lives,' she said wonderingly. 'You have saved her.'

'It is not decided,' I warned, 'But she is breathing better. She is fighting. A strong girl.' I looked around for the babe. It must be washed and readied for the burial. Best get it out of the house before the Gena saw it.

But it was already done. Rhianna had bathed it. There was a bowl of bloodied water and the babe, wrapped warmly and loosely was lying on a thick blanket. 'Thank you, child,' I said wearily. 'Rhoswen, your daughter should not see it. What would you have us do?'

'The baby is not dead, Grandmother. She is breathing.'

'Ahh!' I said, relieved for a moment, hoping. I lifted the wrappings, and examined the child and my heart sank like a stone. Rhoswen, next to me, made a choking noise and pressed her fist to her mouth.

The child was badly deformed. Her spine was twisted, forcing the neck and head awry, all four limbs were twisted and bent wrongly, her face was purple, swollen out of recognition, and her mouth was open, screaming if she could but make a sound. Rhianna made a crooning noise, and carefully stroked her back with one gentle finger and the child's eyelids lifted a little, eyes fixed on her. She stared back.

Rhoswen said hoarsely, 'She will never walk or use her hands...' and covered her mouth, while the tears ran down her cheeks. 'It is wrong to let her live like that. Aella, must we...?'

'I am afraid her inner parts may be wrong too,' I said. She would likely die anyway, very soon. Such children were usually smothered or left on the sacred hill to release their souls, so that they should be born again quickly.

Rhianna said, shortly, decided. 'I will stay with her. I will make her well.'

Well, of course, we argued with her, tired as we were, explained again what it would mean if she was left to grow up so terribly deformed, but Rhianna insisted that she could heal her and would not be persuaded differently. I remembered her sitting on the cobbles of Lot's courtyard healing a rabbit that Medraut had tortured. Well why not? I thought, Wait for the dawn?

In the end, exhausted from the long hours, we gave up for the time being. Rhoswen made a sweet drink for us of rosehips and mint with honey, and unable to keep our eyes open any longer we fell asleep upright in the chairs where we sat.

When I woke, disorientated, it was early morning. Mother and daughter still slept.

Rhianna sat on a stool at the table, awake. Strangely she seemed to be surrounded by a blue light. Sleepily, I wondered what kind of lantern made that kind of light, but then realised that there was no lantern, just the light surrounding her, and the babe on the table before her. She was crooning softly, slow healing spells, and stroking the babe's neck and back, then her arms, legs and feet, over and over again. I could smell comfrey and arnica and lavender, and something else unidentifiable which she must have had from my healer's bag. I had taught her the healing spells used in Avalon, but these I did not know, not even the language. Still half asleep, I listened and watched the blue light, comforted. Everything seemed well.

Then suddenly, I started up quickly. The Head Woman must not see this. At all costs we must remain quiet and hidden. Rhianna must not be tainted with rumours of witchcraft, and all for a poor dead child who couldn't be allowed to live so badly disabled. I was glad to see that Rhoswen and Gena still showed no sign of waking. Gena was breathing normally, and had colour in her cheeks, so we had likely saved one, at least.

I put my feet on the floor and stood up slowly, stretched, and with a heavy heart turned to the table.

Rhianna came to an end of her spell. She turned the child on to her belly and started again, stroking, stroking, more comfrey, more salve, across the body, across the shoulders, down the arms and hands, down the legs and feet. More crooning spells, I did not know. I watched from the shadows, hardly believing. Rhianna stopped, turned the babe again, crooned her spells comfortingly, softly, and the babe made not a sound.

Of course not. It must be dead now. I stepped forward, and my breath hissed away.

Her spine had straightened. Her head sat square on her neck, the swollen dark demon's face was gone. Her skin was smooth and pink and she looked like a human child! Her arms and legs had unbent, and lengthened into normality, and her tiny fingers curled into fists, happily, as she watched Rhianna, never taking her eyes from her.

I stared and stared and still could not believe what I saw. At last I said, 'Rhianna, love?'

She looked up and smiled at me. 'I think she all right now.'

I said, trying to keep my voice normal, 'You have done a wonderful thing, love. Wrap her closely now and put her in the cradle there.'

'She is hungry. We must wake Gena.' She got up creakily like an old lady, rubbing her eyes. 'I am so tired, Grandmother.'

I put my arms around her, and held her close. 'And no wonder. Why don't you lie down on the cot there and sleep for a while?' I put a blanket over her, kissing her forehead. 'We had best say nothing of this to Rhoswen, love. We will just say that you rubbed arnica and comfrey into her bones, and they have healed. She will think witchcraft else.'

She nodded, understanding, and was asleep instantly, and

I was left, trembling and awed. Rhianna was no ordinary child. I had always known that, given her lineage, but this was more. This was of the Goddess herself, a sacred mystery, I could not understand. What I did know was that Rhianna was infinitely precious with more abilities than I ever dreamed. What could she not do? I would have to watch her closely and keep her very safe.

Aella 20

Of course, the saving of the mother and the baby was a nine-day wonder. Rhoswen and Gena, overwhelmed with gratitude, told everyone what a wonderful healer I was, and how helpful Rhianna had been. Gena climbed slowly back to health, and the baby grew brown and bonny, with no sign of disabled limbs. So I suppose it shouldn't have surprised me, when later that month I found old Gareth, the shepherd, waiting outside for me with a long festering cut on his right arm.

Suddenly there were many new patients, not only from Upper Stillwell, but also Lower Stillwell and West Stillwell and other neighbouring villages. I always get enormous pleasure in using my skills, and I felt I had returned to the Lady's service at last. The villagers were absurdly grateful and paid me with whatever they had – six eggs, a dish of mushrooms, a basket of firewood. I had been accepted.

I increased Rhianna's studies to keep her busy, away from the prying eyes of the village gossips. They knew she was made to study, and not run free, and that I was training her to become a healer. I think they felt sorry for her, that I was so strict, but I could not let her special abilities become known, when, perhaps, the rumours would reach beyond the villages. We must continue to hide. Mawgawse was still scrying for us, but we were well warded.

That summer the trading ships did not call at Stillwell's landing stage. There was war in Gaul we were told, and not to expect them, so it seemed that I must make up my mind to stay in the village until the following spring. There were the coracles, of course, but they were so dangerous, and Sabrina was a treacherous river with surges and fierce currents, and I did not feel I could trust Rhianna's life to a flimsy coracle made of skins. Many people were drowned every year in the estuary.

A few weeks later, Rhoswen, the Head Woman, came to see me again. The villagers she said, would like me to stay in the village. As I knew, they had no healer of their own, and the nearest was many miles away beyond the Perilous Forest. They were grateful and impressed with my abilities. There was a house next to the Alewife's, here at the end of the village at the edge of the Forest, an old roundhouse, empty and decaying, but they would repair it, and I could have it for my own, if I agreed to stay.

It was a handsome offer. I knew the house next door, of course, but I went to see it again. The roof needed rethatching, and some of the posts needed strengthening, but it was commodious and large enough to hold our living and sleeping spaces. There was room to treat patients, and for the drying of herbs on a little broken platform built into the roof. Outside there was a plot of land at the very edge of the Forest where once vegetables had been grown, and I found an apple tree, struggling with ivy.

Even though the rain had got in and the place was full of leaves and insects, and, no doubt, other creatures, it had a good feeling about it, and I could picture it warm and dry with the hearth pit glowing with fire. I sat there a long time on an old log, staring and thinking.

I had never in my life lived permanently in a roundhouse, and most would say it was a come down. It was far from my father's maenol, even further from the Roman palace of Avalon, and yet it had that wonderfully safe and friendly feeling, and it would be my own house, my first real home. And I began to see the advantages of living there permanently. The village was not a bad place to live. We had been accepted, and I was able to make a living plying my trade. I knew that I was truly needed. The village was hidden by the great Forest and Rhianna would be safe. No one at all knew where she was or who she was. No one suspected that she was not my grandchild. Visitors were few and unlikely to think us other than normal villagers. We were part of the village community. We would be invisible to anybody passing through and making enquiries for strangers or visitors. The village would protect us. I could serve the Goddess. I was free. The idea that I should return to Court life made me shudder.

Rhianna was growing sturdily, running with the village children, and I was able at this stage to teach her myself. Later it might be a problem. I had to remember that Rhianna was no ordinary child, and was the daughter of the High King himself, and would one day have to take her place in the world as an educated lady at his Court. In the meantime, we were safe from Mawgawse' malice and plotting, safe from all, even Avalon.

Ah Avalon! While I often dreamed of and longed for

the comfort of my sisters and my Healing Hall, I found I did not trust Vivienne. Would she use Rhianna as a pawn in her schemes, as she had used Morgan and Ygraine? I did not want Rhianna hurt as Morgan had been. While I dearly loved Morgan, Rhianna was the child of my heart, birthed into my hands, and I would protect her with my life.

I told Rhoswen that I would stay in the village for the foreseeable future.

Aella 21

The foreseeable future! I can hardly believe that it is nine years to the day that I sat on that old log there and decided to stay. The years have passed so quickly and I have never regretted that decision.

The repairs were done quickly by Titus and Julius, brothers, small and wiry, and their grandson, Tegus. They were the village thatchers and woodworkers, too ancient and too skilled to be allowed to go off to fight the Saxons, and Tegus, to his disgust, was too young. A thick, warm, thatch swept down from the central post to the circular stone wall a few feet high, to the surrounding ditch outside the wall that carried off the rain water. They renewed some of the internal posts, built box beds for us against the wall, renewed the benches in the deep porch, where people could wait, and partitioned off a section of the floor space, where my patients might have a little privacy when I treated them, and began making a stout oak door.

'A leather door is enough Master Titus,' I said 'I could make do...'

He looked at his brother, and together they both shook

their heads, gravely. 'You are here near the Forest, best be careful. There be beasts here. Strange beasts.'

'I haven't seen any.'

'Oh yes. I seen a big cat one time, big as a cow, with stripes.'

'And one with a great long neck, eating the leaves off a tree,' said Julius, 'Strange unchancy beasts.'

I wanted to laugh, but they were quite serious, and I remembered Rhoswen had also warned me, so perhaps I should take care.

'I would rather have you repair the small platform in the roof, Master Titus. Somewhere I can dry my herbs.' So, they put two planks across the supporting timbers, but still insisted on a wooden outer door, with a five-inch bar, and hung a leather door on the inner entrance.

I scrubbed the paved floor, and dragged in stones for a bigger hearth pit. I paid Isarnos, the metal worker, to make me a tripod for my cauldron. The villagers found us a table and a bench, and a few stools, and more cooking pots that we could possibly need. I stuffed the box beds with clean dry fleeces covered with bed furs I had off a packman who came by coracle one day, and finally we moved in and shared our first meal with Brigitta who was sad that we were leaving her.

Not long after we moved in, one fine evening, when I was digging in the garden patch next the house, a short, sturdy man came striding along the track from the Forest. He was carrying a heavy pack on his back. When he saw me, he stopped.

I was alarmed to tell truth. I had never seen any traveller on that shadowed track, the sun had gone and it was getting dark.

'Good evening. Mistress Aella?' His voice was quiet,

educated.

I was astonished. 'That's my name.'

He smiled and set down his pack in my porch. 'Tomas of Caerleon. I come from one you know well and will be glad to hear from. Can you give me a name?'

'Morgan? Surely not Morgan?'

'Aye. That's the magic word.' He had begun to unstrap the pack. 'I have a letter for you, and supplies.'

My heart was bounding with excitement and joy. 'Go in,' I said quietly. 'Best be unseen. How did you find us?'

'She said to look for a guard of ravens.' He laughed and glanced up, and of course, the ravens had appeared, a blanket of gleaming feathers in the twilight. 'They have been tracking me for the last hour.'

I gave him ale, and a bowl of broth with cheese and fresh bread and butter and while he ate, I read Morgan's letter, with foolish tears running down my cheeks.

Morgan's letter was full of joyful relief, excitement and overwhelming gratitude. Two of my letters had finally caught up with her and she was overjoyed that we were both well and safe. Mawgawse had written to her, very angry that we had disappeared, apparently under the impression that we were living with Morgan at Arthur's stronghold, only to find she was being blamed for the loss of Morgan's daughter. She had told Morgan that she thought we must be dead.

Morgan was writing from Winchester. 'Arthur is Dux Bellorum, in charge of all the warbands of Logres, to deal with the Saxon threat, but many Kings continue to war against each other and will not come to an agreement about how to handle the invaders who come from all directions –many from Ierne, from the West, the Picts in the North, the Dalriadan Celts, The Saxons, the Angles, and the Jutes, and they will not give him the money or resources to allow him to organise a proper army. The Kings in the North say that the Saxons are in the South and why should they spend money when it is not their problem? So Arthur has been forced to make a levy on the rich Abbeys and churches to protect them against the sea raiders, but you will guess how unpopular that has made him with the Archbishop and the Christian churches, which seem to be acquiring a great deal of power. The whole country is in disarray. The harvests are lost. There is famine and plague.

All the same, he has done wonders. He has a superb band of young warriors, highly trained and fast moving on big horses. They are brave and daring and idolise Arthur and would die for him. He sweeps up and down the country very quickly falling on the enemy unexpectedly, and so far, he has not been beaten.

Merlin and I have been pressed into service, setting up a new administration, to restore law and order and town councils, and to help with food supplies. Arthur was married quickly on Merlin's advice, to a Princess of the Cymry, to secure the succession. Little Gwyneth is lovely. She has birthed a son, Prince Lachau, who is strong and healthy. She is pregnant again. Too soon I fear, and she is not well.

Aella, my dearest, I am so thankful that you and Rhianna have found sanctuary – you have done exactly what I would have wanted you to do, and I must ask you to continue there, until I can regain my lands in Cornwall. It seems that you are living in safety and peace, unlike the rest of the country. My mind at rest, I can get on with my much-needed work. Arthur urges me to bring you to his Court, but I need not explain why this is unacceptable, and too dangerous.'

'Tomas,' I said. 'Will you wait while I write a quick reply?' I was anxious that he be gone before Rhianna came back from the weavers shed. I cannot tell you how relieved I felt to have Morgan's letter, to know she was well and approved of how I had looked after her daughter. There was much to think about in this letter. Undoubtedly, we were better off where we were. Morgan said that she was fixed at Court on Arthur's orders. She had been made a member of his Council and the King would not give her leave to go to her own estate while the country was being rebuilt.

And would not, I thought. He would keep her by his side as long as he could, if I was any judge, a comfort and delight between his campaigns, and a trusted councillor to bring into being his new laws and justice. Morgan was brilliant at anything she turned her hand to, educated beyond the norm, and I remembered how successfully she had run the finances of Avalon. With Merlin and Morgan at his back, Arthur could go off to his wars, safe from the plotting of his enemies. I stopped thinking about the possibility of going to Morgan.

I began to take out the gifts she had sent in the large pack: Two lengths of very fine white linen to make shifts, a pile of beautifully finished parchment sheets, book size, a box of reed pens, a small box with six cakes of black-brown colour to mix with water to make ink.

Gold arm rings. Some Roman coins, much too many. (What did Morgan imagine I might do with such fantastic wealth, enough to buy the village many times over!) A glass flagon of rich rose perfume. Two Roman combs, with lovely gold decoration along the tops. Three Latin medical texts. A stoppered and heavily sealed vial of white powder, accompanied by another of black seeds – surely not what I thought? Tentatively I dipped my finger in the powder and tested it on my tongue. I gasped. Made from the poppies grown beyond Byzantium in the East, it was worth more than the gold. It was sovereign for all acute and terrible pain. but must be used with utmost care because it could kill too. Typically, she had sent the seeds too so that we could grow them

As I unpacked the bag, I was laughing and crying at the same time. Morgan's idea of the necessities of life in a tiny village on the edge of the world was so typical of her. Whatever else, it showed that she was not wanting for money. All this must have cost the earth.

After this first visit, I heard regularly from Morgan. Tom slipped through the Forest unseen, with letters and gifts. He was, a woodsman born, and fearless. I never knew where Morgan had found him. I wrote long letters back describing Rhianna's progress and education and interests. Every one of Morgan's letters finished with the words 'Let me know whatever it is you need.'

Aella 22

So, finally we were settled and happy, having everything we needed, and no more, and seemingly, well-hidden and in safety. By Avalon's standards it was primitive, but I found contentment here, with the respect and friendship of my neighbours and the good work I had.

Now, at last, I was able to turn my attention to the most important of my problems – Rhianna's education. By rights she should be studying at the Avalon school with other noble children – but Morgan would never allow that, so I would have to teach her the basic subjects that Avalon taught, which presented few problems. Rhianna was already well advanced in speaking Latin and Saxon, as well as our native Brythonic, household management, mathematics and accounts, household medicines and herbs, embroidery and sewing... My heart sank a little. Avalon trained maidens were much in demand for brides. A noble maiden was expected to be able to provide entertainment for her lord and his court, which meant music, playing an instrument and singing, and knowing the latest dances. It was many years since I had danced, and I did not play an instrument or sing. Perhaps someone in the village might be able to help?

But Rhianna was no ordinary maiden. There was her inheritance and her lineage. The High King, so far, had two children: Amir, dead before he was three years old, and Lachau, son of a Gwynedd princess, who was the legitimate heir under both Roman and Celtic law, Rhianna and Medraut qualified under the 'Sister's child,' Celtic law, where illegitimacy was accepted. Rhianna, the oldest twin, might one day be High Queen of all Prydain., which was, of course, the reason for Mawgawse' implacable enmity, Gawain, her eldest son was also 'Sister's Son.' But Mawgawse was younger than Morgan.

So Rhianna must be educated for her possible high destiny. She would need a knowledge of the laws of the land, excellent written Latin and Saxon, geography, history of the tribes. She would need to be able to converse cleverly with Kings and Ambassadors, understand the workings of their minds, strategic thinking and how to address large groups of people – what did the Romans call it? Ah yes, rhetoric. The list went on, getting longer, and longer, to my dismay. I had little knowledge of most of them.

And then there was, most important of all, Rhianna's lineage, which could not be ignored. She was the daughter of a family where the high magic had run strongly for generations. I counted them on my fingers. Vivienne, the Lady of Avalon, her grandmother, the very centre of magical development throughout the land. I did not know her origins, but she might well be the daughter of the first Priestess of Avalon, and her husband, the so-called scholar sage who had set up the School of magical healing in the first place,

Her daughter, Ygraine, acknowledged by all to be the greatest of the Avalon Priestesses, who could host the Goddess, shape change herself and others, and prophecy with unnerving accuracy. And there was Morgan's father – not Gorlois for sure. Ygraine had been pregnant from the Beltane fires and in love, when she was married to him. I wondered about Merlin. The dates were right. He would have been studying on the Tor – a young Druid priest, with amazing magical powers of his own. Two such powerful streams combining to produce Morgan Le Fay was almost unimaginable. No wonder she was so extraordinary.

And now, here was Rhianna, inheriting from her mother Morgan's line, and what of her father, Arthur himself? What had he inherited from his mother Ygraine? And he had been brought up by Merlin of all people. I had never heard any whispers about magical abilities. If he had any, they had kept it very secret. But he was certainly abnormally lucky – no wounds from so many battles, and he was known for his ability to predict the actions of his enemies with startling accuracy.

I had carefully observed Rhianna from her birth, and I knew without any doubt, that she had unparalleled magical powers, which I had never dreamed possible. There was her healing ability, far surpassing Morgan's, even as a little child and I remembered the miracle of Gena's baby. Rhianna could shape change, talk with all manner of creatures, she had taken to the craft of Atlantean magic with ease and delight, and had learned from the little dark people the alternative earth magic. But there was also much she knew that had come from elsewhere, perhaps from the Goddess herself?

Rhianna was clearly more than a witch or sorceress or

enchanter, and it came to me with a shock, that she was a Mage. I was to be responsible for the education of a mage! An awesome responsibility. I confess, I nearly gave up there and then. The burden was too great. I had not the power or the ability that would be needed.

She must grow in knowledge, wisdom and truth. Spiritual growth was as important as magical knowledge. How was it possible to teach such lessons?

But there was no alternative. I had to try. I started to plan a programme of studies and then a timetable for Rhianna, giving plenty of change of subject so she should not get bored, heavily biased to the subjects I knew she enjoyed most, and not forgetting time off for her forest adventures. It seemed to work and a comfortable routine was established that suited us both, and Rhianna began to learn with extraordinary rapidity.

I could only do my best. If that was not good enough, the Goddess must provide an alternative.

Aella 23

The months and the years slide past. Rhianna thrives. She is a quick child, full of intelligence and curiosity, full of ideas, absorbed in learning everything new. I could not keep her away from the great Forest. The big trees have advanced as far as the space around our house and no further. She had only to step between their trunks to be away and I could not catch her.

The Villagers called it the Perilous Forest, for good reason. It runs for many miles in all directions. Villages and houses are built along its edges, where the trees grow less thickly and the people are able to harvest its bounty. But in the deeper Forest, the great trees grow huge, dark and crowded. Generations of fallen trees clog the rides and house many creatures – foxes, badgers, dangerous bears, boars and wolves and, the villagers insist, strange creatures that do not belong here, and nobody can give them a name. There are dangerous humans too, masterless men, runaway slaves, bands of robbers, mad men and women. At first, I was terrified that Rhianna would come to harm until I realised that she is never alone. Her Raven Guard is always there. They follow wherever she goes, and sometimes one will come and drop a feather in my porch, to reassure me that all is well.

I blamed myself that Rhianna found the Forest so wonderful. Of course, I had to go there myself, foraging for all kinds of herbs for my medicines and salves, and Rhianna came with me. Already she knew the names and habits of the most common of the herbs, and was a real help to me. When she went by herself, she would bring back whatever herbs she found. As she grew older, she began to bring back other herbs which she insisted were healing plants, and then we would try to find them in the herbal Morgan had sent, and what they could be used for. When I asked how she knew these were healing plants she said that they had a faint blue aura around them, if you looked carefully, and some the little dark people had shown her. Again, I was alarmed. The little dark people were the most ancient people of the land, but they had withdrawn to the forests and high mountains when the great ice came and now they lived deep in caves or underground in burrows. They used a strong magic, not Atlantean, based it was said, on the energies of the earth. They rarely showed themselves to ordinary humans, but it seemed that Rhianna had made friends with them and they were teaching her their healing and magic. I was not above learning anything new that could help my patients, so we both benefitted.

I was getting very busy, as time went by and the word went out that I was a good healer. Finding and drying the herbs took a long time, even with Rhianna's help, and then she had a brilliant idea. She thought that it would save time if we could grow the herbs we used most, instead of going out looking for them. They would be absolutely fresh, too. We could take just what we needed and not waste any. There was plenty of room along the sides and back of the house, where once someone had tried to grow vegetables so it might be worth trying.

She borrowed a spade from Brigitta, our friend and neighbour, and dug over the earth, clearing the stones and weeds as she went. It was heavy going for a nine year old, and gave her blisters, but she persevered, and began to bring herbs from the Forest, planting them carefully, watering them, and speaking to them every day. I have never seen anything like it.

They grew strongly, wildly almost, bigger and looking healthier than they did in their natural home, and it was not my imagination that their healing qualities were more powerful. Soon she had begged seeds of vegetables from people in the village and they too, flourished. It was clear that she had, as the saying goes, green fingers. She couldn't resist the flowers, of course, and lavender and marigold joined our ointments, as well as others, less obviously practical, but which soothed the spirit, and gave happiness and joy to our patients as they waited in our porch.

Rhianna loved her garden, and as time went by there was an apple tree, and a plum tree blooming beautifully in the spring and laden with fruit in the autumn. Foxgloves towered over the smaller plants (digitalis, sovereign for heart problems) and many kinds of flowers found in the Forest, were climbing over the roof and burgeoning, especially one I loved with big blue tassels, its colour and perfume concealing the actual house, which pleased me greatly. The villagers watched and exclaimed and looked sideways at Rhianna, who took no notice and went about her busy life.

As she got older, Rhianna developed more and more of

her powers. Her healing abilities were very strong, almost as strong as her magical abilities. I had made very sure that she learned magic thoroughly and I knew that it was her favourite subject. But her magic was not like mine. It was exploratory and inventive. Once she had acquired the principles and governance of natural forces, and understood how they could be adapted, she revelled in combining and extending their uses in surprising and amazing ways. Not just a spell to move a pot of soup across the table but to make it rise in the air, toss is contents higher, while it turned joyous arabesques, before catching its contents and sliding it into place in front of me.

Indeed, much of her early magic was playful and amusing as if she revelled in her new-found powers, and many times she had me gasping and crying with laughter. But I had to keep warning her of the need to conceal these abilities outside our home for the fear they would cause in the village, but Rhianna did not fully understand the danger, and longed to be able to use them for the benefit of the villagers.

'Aella, that big stone in the barley field they are trying to move, I could...'

'No.'

'I could do it at night.'

'And if they saw you?'

'Well, I suppose they would be grateful.'

'They would not. They would call you witch, or sorceress, and drive you from the village. I have told you before – they are terrified of those with unusual abilities. We have dangerous enemies Rhianna. Rumour would spread beyond the village, and it would not be long before your Aunt Mawgawse heard them. Do you want to destroy our life here?'

Reluctantly she kept quiet, but I knew she thought I was being unnecessarily cautious, until the trouble with Warrior made all plain to her and she was forced to change her mind.

Part Five

Rhianna 1

Hello. My name is Rhianna. Well, that's what they call me, or Rhia, if they want to be friendly.

My grandmother, Aella, who is also my teacher, is worried about my written Latin. She said that it is as barbarous, as a Sarmatian.

'What's a Sarmatian?'

'A soldier from Sarmatia, stationed on the Emperor Hadrian's Wall. Nomadic...'

'I don't understand...' I said, grinning. 'My writing is like a Samartian?'

She clicked her tongue, irritated. 'Never mind Sarmartians! It's just a saying from my childhood. The point is, we are civilised people and your written Latin is very poor.'

'Barbarous,' I agreed, cheerfully.

'Very poor. You need more practice'

It is true that I do not write it well, or fluently, mainly because I don't see the point of it. Of course, I speak it, as well as our common Brythonic tongue, I speak it very well, even Aella agrees. But when would I ever need to write it? I'm just a village girl, and nobody in the village can write, Latin or anything else.

'If you wish to be an apothecary...' Aella said.

What was this? 'An apothecary?'

'Making medicines.'

'You know I want to be a healer, like you. Not an apothecary. I've been your helper a long time! If only you would...'

'In that case you will need to make notes, lists, things to remember, like medicines.'

She had caught me, of course. I laughed. 'Oh, very well.'

'I suggest you write a journal or a diary, as I do. A Chronicle! Just to give you practice.'

'But I am so busy...'

'You don't need to write every day.'

'But what would I write about? Nothing ever happens here.'

'Daily activities. Ideas. The village. The people. Your thoughts about things.'

So here I am, starting my new journal. I have a small pile of waxed wooden tablets which can be scraped down and remade later, so I am not wasting valuable parchment of which we have only a small quantity. And I have a new stylus. I will begin at the beginning again

Latin Practice 1

My name is Rhianna. My real name is Rhiannon, after the great Goddess, but Aella says that it is better to shorten it in these times when our religion is under threat. Many people have converted to the White Christ, and because their priests are frightened of women, they believe we are all evil witches. I don't think I am a witch, but I do study magic and can do some things.

I am fourteen years old – well, I will be, in few weeks' time. I live with my grandmother, Aella, in the village of Stillwell, which is in the lands of the Dumnonii, the Summer country, in the great island, which the Romans called Britannia, but which we call Logres, or Prydain.

Well, that's quite enough for today – boring! I am going out to find some rosemary to wash my hair. We didn't dry enough this year. I must pay more attention to the garden – it tends to get neglected now I have so much to do.

Latin Practice 2

Aella is still worried about my written Latin. She keeps harping on about it, and says I need a proper teacher, and she is not good enough now. This is not unusual. Aella is always worried about one or other of my studies, and thinking she is not a good enough teacher. I think she is an excellent teacher, and has taught me everything I know. I have got into the habit of doing my written Latin practice and rather enjoy it, so I shall go on with it, as it helps me think.

Mind you, the whole of my education is a mystery – not just the Latin but all the other subjects I am studying. Why should I, an ordinary village girl, be studying at all? Normally, I speak the Brythonic language like everyone else in the Village, and I speak the language of the little dark people, my friends in the Forest. I can even speak to the Saxon family who settled along the river long before I can remember. But enjoyable as they are I see no reason to be learning mathematics, history, geography, rhetoric, or, especially, writing Latin.

Aella says that it is the language of well-educated people, in use in the religious houses of the White Christ, in Law, in Government, and in the King's Court, and in books. And when I laughed at the idea that I would ever have anything to do with these places, she said, crossly, that it was the language of Avalon, and everyone there learned it properly.

Oh Avalon! That settled the matter, of course. Aella's loyalty to the House of the Priestesses there, where she did her own studies, is absolute. What Avalon does must be right, and my education has more or less followed it, but with quite a lot of additions, which Aella knows nothing about.

When I was small, I did not question this at all. I have always enjoyed learning new things, and Avalon teaches the old Atlantean magic, which is my favourite subject, but as I got older, I began to wonder why I had to learn all the rest. We had always spoken Latin, at home, of course, and Aella said that my spoken language was elegant and subtle and I could read it well enough. When I continued to grumble that writing it down being a waste of time, when I had so much to do in the garden, and looking for new healing plants in the Forest, and finding out what they could do, she said, exasperated, 'Your mother would expect it.'

I stared at her, startled. She hardly ever spoke of my mother.

'My mother would expect it?'

'Of course. She is an educated lady herself.'

I thought, if she is an educated lady why is she working as a servant at the King's Court? Another of Aella's mysteries. I realised suddenly that I was very angry. 'I don't think she would care. I don't think she cares about us at all. Why does she never come to see us? All these years and not once has she come.'

'You know she writes and sends gifts.' Aella said severely. 'There are problems.'

'What "problems"?' I scoffed.

'Danger.'

I laughed. 'Yes, of course, it's very dangerous here in the Village.'

Aella flushed, she was annoyed now, unused to me questioning her. 'Rhianna, you know that we are in the middle of a war. It may be quiet here, but it is not like that everywhere. Every year the men go off to fight, and are killed or wounded – you know that. The King, Goddess protect him, has fought battle after battle to protect our lands from the invaders. There is disruption everywhere. The fields are not planted, there are robber band on the roads, the traders do not come...'

'All right,' I said, ashamed. 'I know there are dangers, that she has enemies, but surely she could have come just once, or -' the thought struck me suddenly like an arrow in the back 'Why does she not send for us? Why haven't we gone to see her?'

Aella stared at me, silenced.

'We could take a boat to Glevum, and then take horses or a carriage to Caerleon, or wherever the Court is...'

'Nonsense.' Aella turned away, and I knew she would hear no more. 'Get on with your Latin and see if you can keep trying to make it better. We need a proper tutor.'

'I would rather learn Greek,' I said grumpily. 'There is that text by Galen with wonderful drawings of parts of the body, that my mother sent. I am sure it would help our healing, if only we could understand it.'

I knew she was curious too. 'Perhaps the new hermit will be a scholar, when he comes,' she said, wistfully. Father Drustus, our gentle old hermit, who had taught me to sing and play the harp, name the stars, and tell me of the great philosophers, had died earlier in this hard winter, despite our medicines and care.

You see? This was a typical conversation with my grandmother. Full of unexplained mysteries. When I need to ask questions. I get no real answers. Mysteries swirl around her like soft moths in the summer twilight, hardly seen.

Where did she get that fine white scar on her cheek.? You can hardly see it now but it must have been a very bad wound once. She is lucky that she didn't lose an eye. Why does she hide the crescent moon on her forehead under her hair? Everybody in the village knows that she is a healer Priestess from Avalon.

I would have begun to doubt this absent 'Mother', except for the messenger who comes silently at the day's end, stepping through the Forest like a shadow, bringing with him letters and wonderful gifts – clothes, expensive medicines, vellum, ink, and most astonishing of all, books, which must cost the earth. There are gold pieces too. We are secretly richer than anybody in the Village. My mother must be rich too. 'An educated lady'. This was new, something to add to my meagre hoard of information about her.

I never saw her letters. Aella destroyed them as soon as she had read them, but she did tell me the news they contained, and gave me messages from my Mother, about my health and well-being, with exhortations to be dutiful and learn well.

As though I could do anything else. You do not go against a Priestess of Avalon, too much unpleasantness can befall you. Besides the truth is I love her dearly, mysteries and all. I do not like to see her sad and upset. She is such a good kind person, and everything she does is for my own happiness and wellbeing. She worries about me constantly, though I don't know why.

Sometimes I seem to remember another place. A stony courtyard with pebbles and a big stone house. And I think I have been on a ship, not a little boat like the fishermen here use, but one that goes down to the Western Sea. I remember the big waves and the bright white sails shining in the sun. And learning all the knots, I still use. But Aella turns my queries. 'That sounds like a nice dream, my love.' But I know it is not a dream.

One day, we were weeding in the garden, and I said to her suddenly, 'There was another child, a boy, I think, what happened to him?'

She carefully loosened the roots of a dandelion. 'A baby?'

I shook my head. 'No bigger. My age.' I did not want to think about the boy, because it made me feel uncomfortable and sad. 'He hurt me.'

'Hurt you?'

'Cut me with the edge of a flintstone he dug from the wall. Why did he hate me?'

'A nightmare! I'm sure no one here has ever hated you, my chick.' She pulled me to her and gave me a hug, to drive away the memory. But when I readied myself for bed that night, I looked at the small scar on the underside of my left arm. So that was how I had got the scar. I had totally forgotten. Almost certainly Aella would have put stitches in it and bound it. She must know the boy too. So why not tell me?

At first, I didn't know that I hadn't got a father. The village is one of women, children and old men. The fathers are only there in the winter, disappearing in the spring when the Branch comes from the Lord to go fighting in Arthur's wars, and they do not return until the days grow short and darker. Or do not return at all. There are many children without fathers in the village, so it was nothing special.

'Is my father dead?' I asked Aella.

She stared at me, as she chopped dried herbs and swept them into a wooden mixing bowl. She hesitated and I knew she wanted to lie to me. But Aella never lies. I think she finds it impossible

'He's not dead but far away.'

'With my mother in Winchester or Caerleon?'

'They are not together.'

I took this in and understood. 'They're not married, I'm a bastard?'

There was no stigma attached to that in our village, but Aella looked surprised and then amused. 'You are very special, Rhianna. You are a child of the Goddess. A Beltane child begot at the Beltane fires.'

This was indeed special. Children begot at the Beltane rituals when people lay together in praise of the Goddess, and to make the land fruitful, are regarded as being blessed. Holy, even.

'And you have no idea who my father is?'

'It's not important. Beltane babes are gifts of the Goddess.'

'You know, don't you?'

'He is far away in the furthest North.'

Of course, that started me wondering. If he lived in the North, why had he been at the Beltane rituals in the Summer country, thirteen years ago?

Rhianna 2

Latin Journal

As I said before, Aella and I live in Upper Stillwell village, which is really strange when you think about it. Another of my grandmother's mysteries. I mean, I was not born here, that much my grandmother has told me and neither was she, so it is a mystery why we are here. I know that although we have lived here a long time, we are regarded as foreigners, and different by the people of the village. In the country, most people go on living where they were born and do not move elsewhere. Even townspeople do not generally go to live in another town, unless they are soldiers, or serve some great lord, as my mother does. There is absolutely nothing here that people would come to see, like a Mid-Summer Fair, or a sacred shrine or even a market with stalls. like Glevum market. It is not the kind of place you would expect to find a highly educated lady, a Healer-Priestess of Avalon, but Aella just says, 'It is a safe place,' which is really no explanation at all, and only provokes more questions. which go unanswered. of course.

Sometimes I think I can remember this other place, and a big scary woman, but my grandmother does not welcome questions about the time before and I have learned to contain my curiosity... sometimes. 'Silent and Private,' she says. 'Do not draw attention to yourself.'

Back to the village. There is Lower Stillwell, where there is a landing stage along the river Brever, where it meets the great Sabrina River. There are only four roundhouses here owned by the coracle fishers, that often get flooded. A track rises to the main village, Stillwell, where most of the houses cluster together on level land. A path to the right leads to West Stillwell, but the main track climbs again to Upper Stillwell, where there are another four roundhouses before the Perilous Forest closes in and there is only the track through the forest, which nobody uses. Stillwell is really all one village, with about forty houses in all, so quite large for a village. In truth the village is oddly named because there is not one well in the whole place. We get our water from the little stream that leaps out of the green forest and gallops down a rocky bed next to the track, vaulting over the stones and swirling around them.

This is getting boring again! Aella suggests I should imagine I am writing a letter to a new friend who has never been here, and I will try this. What I really want to do is write about our neighbours and my friends.

If you were climbing up the track, the first roundhouse in Upper Stillwell you would see on the left is where my friend Gwyri lives. It is set well back from the track in its own little field because his father, Isarnos, is a bronze and iron smith, and there is danger from the flying sparks when he hammers on the glowing metal. I love to stand and watch as he takes the red-hot bar from the fire, hammers, folds it again and again, plunging it into the water trough, sending up clouds of hissing steam and then, miraculously, there, is a beautifully shaped blade.

It is a noisy process, but nobody worries about that. It is the noisiest family you can imagine. Except for Gwyri, they are all very tall and broad, even the women. Gwyri's father, Isarnos, is the biggest man in the village, towering over everybody, and his two older sons, Tauros and Rata, who work the bronze and iron with him, are only a few inches shorter. There was another brother but he was killed fighting with the Bear three years ago, I don't remember him very well, but his wife and little boy live with the family too.

Gwyri's mother, Lania, is a very tall, robust, woman always laughing and shouting, who is likely to sweep you off your feet without warning, and plonk you down with a great platter of food in front of you, hugging and kissing you. He has three older unmarried sisters, fifteen, sixteen and nineteen, Ena, Ardra, and Lavena, always arguing and shrieking with laughter, but who can sing together most beautifully. There is an old grandmother and two Aunties, all with big voices. The whole family is always shouting, screaming, shrieking, calling, singing, swearing, banging but above all laughing. I don't know what they find to laugh about all the time but they do. They are all lovely people who will do anything to help you.

Gwyri is the youngest of the family, very thin and whippy, with straight black hair and dark eyes. He is a little older than me, but is quite a bit shorter, so that I can pat him on the head and say 'Come along little fellow!' when I want to tease him. He is goodnatured though, and just grins. The strange thing is, coming from such a roaring family, he is remarkably quiet, and doesn't talk much at all. Like me he is interested in the animals and birds, and when he can slip away from the bellows we go adventuring in the Forest, but mostly I go alone.

The next house is on the right, across the track and the stream, is Egan's house. It is much smaller and falling down. Egan works in Glevum, repairing burned shops and houses he says, and does not come home very often. You can't blame him because his wife, Gitta, is a real misery, always crying and complaining, always hard done by, and never helping anyone. She says that Senomamma, her mother in law, who is the fattest woman in the village, makes her do all the work and threatens to throw her out if she does not do as she is told, which may be true. Aine, her daughter, and my friend, is always covered in bruises, and does not seem to get enough to eat. Gitta hates us, especially, because we are foreigners, and Aella gives Aine arnica ointment to help the pain of her bruises, and bowls of pottage to feed her up when she comes to see me.

Next, on the left again, is the house of our dear friend Brigitta. We used to live with her until we got our present house, and she is lovely, like a second grandmamma, warm and loving. She dotes on all children, but does not have any of her own. I love her dearly. She is a widow, the finest alewife in the whole area, and her mead is in demand too at the Midwinter Fair in Glevum. She is a very good woman and looks after Conn, an orphan, who is lame and can't speak. He stumbled out of the Forest one day, broken and starving, and Brigitta fed him and gave him a bed in the byre, and now he helps her with the heavy barrels. He is not quite right in the head and I think he must have had head wounds, but it is too late to heal him, although I do try.

Next to Brigitta, a little further along, my grandmother and I live in the last round house, on the very edge of the Forest, which peers over into our garden. Every year more little saplings appear around our patch of ground and grow swiftly, until they are as tall as I. It is strange that they do not come into the garden I have made, but I think that one day the village will be buried in the Forest's green groves, or pushed down into the waters of the Sabrina, swift, silent and very dangerous, like the Goddess herself.

I have been writing about Stillwell and some of my friends and neighbours. Of course, there are lots of other people who live here. Some are very interesting, particularly the old people who have often done extraordinary things, or been to wonderful places.

There's Gladius, for instance who was a Centurion with the Legions, and fought the barbarians across the Danube, and in Gaul. He came home to spend the last years of his life in the village where he was born, only to find that the country was being invaded by Saxons, and he had to go off to war again. He is very old now, with severe bone pain, and we can do little for him. He has admitted, with reluctance, that he is no longer capable of long marches, and I do not think he will go with the next muster. He tells us wonderful stories of the daring of the soldiers on the Danube and the raiding parties, when Gwyri and I persuade him to sit with us. Gwyri says that one day he will be a soldier and I tell him he is a fool.

Then there is Dacia, the Cow woman. We have a few small fields by the village where we keep cows and lot of sheep for their fleeces. She knows everything there is to know about cows and sheep, and I learn from her all their diseases, and how to treat them. She knows what makes them happy or when they are miserable. They all love her, but I do not think she can speak with them as I do

One woman who I think is really mysterious and exciting is Ailidh. She runs the Weaving Hall. Stillwell is a prosperous village because we join together and sell our products as a co-operative, sharing the proceeds. Once or twice a year all our products are collected together and Rhoswen, the Head Woman. and a few of the other women who are good at bargaining, take them off to Glevum or Caerleon to sell and bring back all the things we can't make ourselves. Brigitta's ale and mead sell very well, and so do the bolts of cloth our women weave. They are of fine quality in the checks and stripes which are popular with the Cymry.

We weave braided edges, too, to trim cloaks or skirts, and Isarnos sells his swords and knives and spears, and also, when he takes a fancy to do so, he makes delightful brooches, with the Goddess spiral curling around little animal heads, which are much sort sought after. Aella and I make ointments for infected wounds and medicines for winter coughs and these always sell quickly.

Ailidh it was who persuaded the women to work together in a separate building for weaving and spinning rather than in their own homes. She said they would have more space and light, enjoy it more, and inspire each other, and this is true. The atmosphere in the Weaving Hall is lovely, joyous and full of laughter. The women share new ideas and the designs improve and hard, boring jobs are somehow easier to do and more interesting when working with others.

I love to spend time in the Weaving Hall, watching and helping when I can. I want very much to learn to weave, but Aella is not keen. She says it is not necessary, and not fitting. I don't know what she means, but I gather she thinks it is a waste of time, or somehow beneath us. But I still try to learn.

Ailidh is a strange woman. She is tall, with long dark shining hair which she wears loose down her back, unlike the other matrons who plait their hair. She has dark green, luminous eyes, and sometimes she goes away in her mind and does not hear what you say to her. When this happens, she goes to her own loom in the corner, not speaking, and tries out a new idea which none of us have ever thought of before. She invents different knots and new combinations of colours which make them glow and come alive. I think she is a genius, and I wish I could ask her to teach me, but I know that Aella disapproves and doesn't understand my interest in weaving. I wonder sometimes if Ailidh is like Aella and I, with special powers which she keeps hidden.

I must not forget to include Father Drusus, our hermit, who lived in the old bear cave, high up further along the river. He was a lovely, gentle person, and we all miss him very much. He died at the end of the year, although Aella and I tried to save him, taking up food and medicines, but he was old and frail and his chest rustled like trees, and he would not come down to the village for shelter when the heavy snow came.

He was my teacher too. He had studied Theology, Music and Astronomy at the University of Leiden, and once he had been the Court Bard of Powys, and knew how to play and sing the ancient songs. and tell the old stories of our land. Then he converted to the White Christ, and decided to become a hermit. We spent many evenings studying the wonders of the heavens from his collection of old star charts he had rolled in his wooden box, and which he had bequeathed to me along with his harp. He taught me to sing and play the harp, and we used to sing together before he got ill and could not breathe well. We talked together too, of the great philosophers and holy men, and the many religions and beliefs in the world. Just before he became seriously ill, he became very melancholy.

'My God says 'Thou shalt not kill,' he said. 'But I have ridden with the Powys War Band and have killed again and again.'

'But that was before you knew it was wrong, wasn't it? And you are always telling me that the Christ forgives sin if truly repented.'

He stared at me until I became uneasy.

'You did say that, didn't you?'

He said slowly. 'I did indeed. But I had forgot it included me. Thank you, dear child. You are a great comfort. Do you know that?'

I grinned. 'Well, Aella doesn't mention it much!'

He went on staring at me. 'You have an understanding of people well beyond your years.'

'I like animals better.'

He smiled. 'Nevertheless, I think you have a great destiny ahead of you.'

And that closed my mouth, because I remembered the Lady telling me the same thing.

Father Drusus said, 'When I go you must have my star charts and my harp. Remember, do not let them be taken. They are yours.'

I thanked him, but of course, I thought that would be many

years ahead. It was only a few weeks. And now I am crying again.

I have not mentioned the children. There are a lot of them in the village. They run freely and invent all sorts of games, as well as helping when they are needed, but they do not like me very much. After all I am a foreigner, and strange, and they know that Aella makes me learn things and is training me to be a healer. I am not allowed to run and play all the time. It was all right when I was little, but as I got older, they found me very strange that I would spend so much time in the forest by myself, which they find frightening. And then there was the business of Warrior.

Rhianna 3

I have not yet written much about my Grandmother, Aella, which is strange, because she is the centre of my life, and I love her dearly. We have always lived together, and as far back as I can remember she has always been there. I would not know what to do without her.

It is difficult to describe her, because she is... she is... shadowy. Secret somehow. And she changes. She is quite tall for a woman, very thin and you can see her bones. I don't think she eats enough. She looks fragile but this is deceiving, because she is strong, very strong indeed, and I have seen her lift a big, unconscious warrior to reach a wound in his back, and once, she withdrew a dagger that had been driven so far into the spinal bones that it was totally jammed. The man was dead, anyway, but she was the only one who managed to get it out.

She often works long hours into the night, birthing reluctant babies, and never seems to tire. She seldom loses her temper, and I have never seen her panicking, however urgent or dire the problem. She is always kind and smiling, and likes a good joke, yet she is dignified and there is a feeling that you would not like to cross her. It is difficult to describe, but she has a great authority, without making you feel small and useless.

You would not find her physically remarkable in any way. She is not beautiful, but she has a fine, kindly face, and her eyes have seen many things, good and bad. They are a silver grey, luminous, as though her clear spirit is showing through from inside. She is frighteningly intelligent and you do not need to explain things to her. She seems to understand everything, but doesn't judge at all. You feel safe, with her.

But to describe her properly... Now I think of it, she is difficult to actually see, unless she wishes to be seen. She has a way of drawing the shadows around her that makes her insubstantial somehow. You do not notice she is there, unless she wishes it. It is a trick I think she learned at a young age and found useful. She has a small crescent moon on her forehead, which she hides behind her hair, the mark of a Healer Priestess of Avalon and of the Goddess, which she does not talk about, and across her right cheek there is a very fine silver line, almost lost now, but alarming when you notice it, because it is from a wound that once must have nearly taken her eye and disfigured her when she was young – but she doesn't talk about that either. In fact, there is a lot she will not talk about

She always wears dark, plain, robes, without border patterns or decoration, scrupulously clean, with no marks or stains, washed every day, and she has a tiny, beautiful knife glowing with rubies, suspended from a plain girdle, which I have never seen her use. Her cloak is ancient, snagged and ragged at the hem. I think it was once a dark violet colour, but now it is so patched and faded that it is just a rag. This cloak annoys me so much that I tell her she looks like a beggar woman, but she just laughs and says it is an old friend, and it will last another year. I have great fun turning this cloak into all manner of sumptuous furs, like the creatures I see sometimes in the Forest, which would knock the villagers flat if they ever saw them, but Aella laughs and turns them back to the old rag.

Aella has been my teacher since I was a little child. She knows so much! Several languages, spoken and written. We have studied the history and geography of the whole land of Britannia; and she knows many things you would not expect a Healer Priestess to know, practical things like how to cook and clean, and run a house. She can draw and embroider, write poetry. She knows all about herbs and she has taught me how to recognise them, and how to use them, plus all my healing skills. And then there's the magic. Ancient magic and spells from Atlantis...well, everything! Even how to behave and speak to people. She says that she has tried to teach me what I would have learned at the school in Avalon, like Maths and Rhetoric and Logic and all that the Romans thought necessary for a basic education – but did not teach them to girls! How strange they were, but, I suppose, clever. We still can't make roads and houses and baths as good as theirs. But our music and design are much better, I think. But I would dearly like to get more of their books on healing.

Rhianna 4

It is February.

It is raining again today, heavy rain, and the water is bounding away down the track taking with it most of the stones we had laid to try to keep the mud from the houses. I wish I knew how the Romans kept their cobbles stationary in the roads for so long. A spell might help, I suppose, but water is very powerful.

It is too wet to do my garden. It is too wet and too cold to plant my babies. They must live in their boxes by the door in the porch for a few more days, although I know they are anxious to get into the deep earth to stretch their roots and grow strong in the sunlight. But plants aren't fish and they can't swim so they must be patient.

Wouldn't it be funny if all the plants could swim and spent their time swimming around the garden instead of living in rows? Perhaps they would like that. They could swim away when you went to dig them up, and dive under the big stones or get all mixed up and splash you until you were soaked... I wonder... would it be better to be a plant or a fish?

Anyway, I am neither. I am just a girl sitting here on the floor, using a cushion to keep my bottom warm. I have dragged the bench nearer to the door to catch better light, so I may use it as a table to do my Latin writing practice. My 'Chronicle', as Aella grandly calls it.

Why is she so worried about my written Latin? Why would I ever need to write it? The mysteries circle around my grandmother, Aella, like fish. (Why do I keep thinking about fish today?) But I suppose that is only to be expected because she is a Priestess of Avalon. A wise woman, as they say here in the village.

Well, back to my 'Chronicle'. It is February and for once I have something to write about. Everyone is gloomy and not just because it hasn't stopped raining. The men went away this morning, marching down the path to the landing, to join the men from West Stillwell and Lower Stillwell, and others from further along the river and the big boat picked them all up to take them to Caerleon to join the Bear, for the Spring campaign.

The Call, the Red Branch, came early this year, and the officer in the boat was really harassed, red faced, shouting and swearing, urging them to get a move on. Other years he has been hearty and full of jokes. So, there must be something special happening, something not good, everybody realised.

But, as usual, our men were excited, happy to be on their way, in their shining helmets and black armour, which is only thickened leather, and not proper metal like the officer wears, and their most treasured possessions went with them – the wickedly sharpened spears and swords, and even axes, most of which they had got from the enemy in previous battles. They sat around all winter, cleaning, repairing, polishing and sharpening their gear, telling each other how brave they had been, swapping dirty jokes, and complaining when their wives asked them to mend the roof. It seems that war makes men lazy. The only thing important is the war and killing people. All the daily things become trivial. That is why they like war, it makes them feel important, their lives significant.

I think they are glad to get away from the women and children, and the comfortable fire, and, of course, the work – caring for the animals, working in the fields. They come alive, and are glad to join that bawdy, brawny, swaggering male life, where they can pretend they are heroes.

This time old Gladius was left behind. I saw the tears in his eyes as he watched them climbing into the boat. He took a bad wound in his leg a couple of years ago, and is crippled with the bone pain in his hips, knees and shoulders as well, and our ointment does little to help him. But they took Gwyri, my village best friend, his eyes shining brightly, so excited he could hardly bother to say goodbye to me or kiss his mother. He is nearly fifteen, and has been begging to go since he was ten.

Men are strange. Why do they want to kill each other? But it is the women who suffer most. Less food, more work. More pain, more babies. In truth, it is better without the men. The village is calmer. The women get on with their planting and spinning, and there are fewer quarrels. There is less shouting and floggings.

The men will come back in the autumn, stinking, filthy and exhausted, with suppurating wounds or without an arm, or hand, which we will have to treat. Or they will not return at all and there will be more orphans and widows in the village. More misery. I know that I will not greet Gwyri again. I have seen his death – on a steep hillside, his throat cut wide open with a Saxon axe, the rain dripping on his face. He was a fool. He would not listen to me.

I spoke to Gladius. He says that there are rumours that the Saxons are coming in force this year, and they have made treaty with the Jutes and Angles who will come too. They are moving along the Thamesis Gap, and are trying to cut off the Cymry from the Summer country and they are already far inland, marching for Badon, where the hot springs are, not so far from here.

I wonder what difference it would make to us, if the Saxons won. Aella says they would burn the village and rape all the women or make us into slaves.

I have decided that if they come, I will run away and live in the Forest.

The men might be back in time for the harvest, but probably not – they don't hurry. And the women and all of us children will work together to bring the harvest in. If the harvest is lost there will be starvation in the winter, so it is a desperate effort and if there is a moon we work into the night.

Our fields, held jointly, are small and narrow, running along the higher ground on the bank of the river where the Forest thins and leaves a narrow margin. Over the years we have cut back the trees, reclaiming more land for cultivation and for the keeping of sheep and a small herd of cows. Our wealth is not in the crops but in the fleece of our sheep and the fabrics our women weave from them. We have splendid spinners who spin the fine yarn, and weavers who are noted as far as Glevum for their high-quality woollen cloth, and this, in a county known for its cloth, even in Brittany.

I am a fair spinner myself. I learned very early from Gwyri's sister, Ena, who is a champion. It is fun, but I really want to learn how to weave, but Aella does not weave herself and says, 'Not necessary.'

I have not seen my Forest friends for weeks. Winter is quiet. They sleep, hide in their warm burrows, but now things will be stirring. The bears will be waking up, surly and best avoided, but the birds will be busy, and soon all the new animals will be jumping and laughing and snuffling into their mothers. I love the new animals, love to hold and stroke and cuddle them, with their little bodies wriggling under my fingers, trying to kiss me...

'Rhianna? Are you dreaming, my love? Here is the new herbal your Mother has sent. Commit this page to your memory, to recite to me tonight.'

I sigh and put away my 'Chronicle'.

Rhianna 5

When I am not studying, or working with Aella or making medicines, or working in the garden, I go to my most favourite place on earth – the Perilous Forest. I wish I could describe properly what the Forest has meant to me since I was a tiny child. It has been my mother, my father, my teacher, my university, my dearest friend, along with all the plants, animals and creatures that live there.

It is not like the forests where the kings hunt, neat and tidy with pollarded trees and the underbrush cleared to make wide rides suitable for horses, a tamed forest.

My forest is wild, untouched, untamed by the foresters. Over immeasurable time trees have seeded, grown to immense size, crashed in the lightning strikes, and are, in time, covered by yet more generations of fallen trees in their turn, so that it is clogged and entangled, virtually impassable with fallen upon fallen trees, impenetrable thorn, and flowering shrubs, and moss hanging from the low branches. It is old, old beyond time, and more beautiful than you can imagine. The trees are wide and towering, ancient, draped in ivies and flowering climbers, hanging like tapestries from the low twisting branches and I saw that each great tree was like a huge city, supporting whole populations of creatures who lived in its roots and branches. And deeper in the forest are the wonderful creatures who make their homes here in safety, far from the greedy, dangerous men.

Oh yes, there are occasional humans. Wild men, mad and wandering, living like the animals, or hermits and old wise women, living alone, becoming part of nature themselves. But they do not live in the deepest parts of the forest. There, the big animals rule: the bears, the wolves, the boars and the big cats, and the strange creatures that are like no others in our land, and have no names here.

I did not, at first, understand that they had wandered through from other worlds and other times, and when I told Aella of them, she smiled and kissed me and said what a wonderful imagination I had, but they are as real as my ravens who follow me everywhere, scolding and guiding me and warning me of dangers, like the deep gullies where serpents sleep and bogs where one false step can send you struggling under the false, green, inviting surface. I go everywhere, staring and smelling. One day I will climb the trees to play with the great blue butterflies as big as platters that live high up, never coming down to earth. Another day I will crawl into the foxes' burrows, tumbling with the fox cubs. Everywhere I am welcomed and I never guessed how extraordinary that is.

As I grew older, I went deeper into the forest taking a pouch of food and strapping a blanket to my shoulders so that I could stay away overnight, and Aella never complained or questioned, only cautioning me to listen to the ravens and do as they advised. It was a wonderful time and all the days I was learning, learning so much. My forest is full of marvellous and magical things. There are the stands of trees which move slowly, almost imperceptibly, but if you watch carefully and long enough you will see a branch twitch here, another there, and if you come back in a day or two, the trees are changed. Here where there was an ash, is an oak, and here where there had been an apple is a hazel. But you never see them actually in motion.

And there are the creatures, tall necked, sinuous creatures with long tails sliding along the deep rivers and into the deeper pools. They are very curious and poke their heads up comically if they see me, or another creature, and there are my favourite sea serpents who come up the rivers when the weather at sea is bad. They are very wise and humorous and tell tales of Lost Atlantis, or of outwitting the mages who seek their red eggs.

There are bears, of course, but you have to be careful. When they come from their hibernation, they are very grumpy and annoyed at having to wake up, or hungry and sleepy and annoyed that you are disturbing their sleep, or jealous and suspicious if they have cubs, and angry if you are in their territory. There is always something with them, so it is better to be polite and leave them alone.

There are the big cats too, one sort spotted beautifully, another sort black as midnight, beautifully glossy. I love the big cats. Like all cats they have a great curiosity, and an eccentric sense of humour. There was one I knew well who liked to lay along the branches of a tree and let his tail fall down on my head when I was passing, enjoying my screech of surprise. Then he would extend a long paw, laughing at me and haul me up into his tree. He always worried that I haven't enough fur to keep me warm and tucks me close up, into his belly, which is like being smothered in a feather bed.

Apart from the animals and birds there are other, stranger creatures. Not just the fairies and the dryads, the woodwoses, and very little people like moss who peer from the cracks in the tree trunks, and the elven people, and the small dark people who lived in these islands first, before the Great Ice came, they told me, and who live in long burrows deep underground They know the old magic and move so silently and invisibly that you can never know they are there unless they want you to know. They are my particular friends and teach me their magic and healing, which is different from Atlantis, based on the magnetic energies of the earth.

There are some scary places where I do not go, strange pathways where the dead pass, and I will not walk there, and odd spaces often between two great stones like a portal, where at dawn or dusk, a glow appears or a brilliant mist and out of the mist will come a creature so strange that you know at once that it is from another world, or another time perhaps. It might have a brilliant-coloured hide of scarlet with gold markings, or bright green loose veils undulating around it so that you aren't sure if it is a plant or an animal, or a giant fish. And there is another, with long brilliant coloured purple fur and a tufted tail, who is not as friendly as I hoped and chased me up a tree, until my big cat came padding along to see what all the roaring was about. It was a pity that the tail was so temptingly tufted, because my friend could not resist it and the poor creature shot back between the stones with much of it missing, and my friend pranced about tossing it high like a tassel in the air with pleasure and amusement.

I had many such encounters, learning all the time. In the forest I am never frightened and never feel in danger. I do not act foolishly or insensitively. I am polite. I feel am a guest, and I do not damage the trees and plants. Something looks after me as well as my ravens, who will never say who has sent them or why. They are there, they say, just because they want to be.

Once I saw a unicorn in the distance under low branches staring at me intently, but when I went towards it, it ran away. Already they are becoming rare, and I never managed to have a conversation with one. But there are fauns, who are there in abundance, and are a nuisance sometimes, giggling and wanting to dance rather than talk. And I met a centaur hunting party once, and ate with them, a guest in their camp. They were very handsome and serious. Very grand and formal, so that you felt you had to curtsey and be on your best behaviour.

In contrast there are the very lively little furry creatures who swing from branch to branch, following you , chittering and shouting jokes and plunging into the deep pools beneath. The pools in the forest, are strange – dark green and purple, where golden fishes raise their heads and frogs sit on the floating lily pads, croaking at me, crossly, for disturbing them. Sometimes the green thins out and the water becomes clear and sparkling, and the fish come up to say hello and nibble your fingers.

But I think of all the creatures in the forest, the finest craftspeople are the wonderful spiders who spin huge, many coloured shining webs between the trees, so fine and intricate I could sit looking at them for hours, wishing I could weave structures as fine as that. But it is difficult to talk with the spiders, as with the other insects. Their voices are so high, nearly beyond our hearing range, I think. I don't remember when I first learned that I could speak with the animals and birds. I think it must have been about the time I learned to speak my own human language, and, of course, I thought at first that everybody could do it, and it was sad and painful when I learned that it was a rare ability and nobody believed me. The children in the village called me Little Liar. For a time, I was very lonely, and spent more and more hours in the Forest, away from the village and learned many things, developing powers I did not know I had, but I kept them secret and did not share them with anyone, not even Aella.

One day, my ravens came, excited, dancing on the stones of the porch. 'Come,' they cried. 'Come, come.'

'Where? What?'

'Come, come, come. It is time.'

So, I followed them into the Forest depths, in a new direction. When I stopped, tired and doubtful, they shouted at me, urging me on, until we came to a clearing. A perfectly round space, surrounded with the remains of a wall, built of enormous stones. There was a deep, profound silence. It was not that there were no birds or animals. Blackbirds, thrushes, song birds of all sizes and colours were sitting solemnly on the branches of the trees. There were hares and hinds motionless among the trees, all watching intently.

I took a deep breath and stepped cautious through the portal carved in a single great stone, into an even greater silence.

Within the circle lay a deep pool of crystal water reflecting the trees that stooped over it. I looked around, expectantly, but there was nothing there, just the reflecting pool, utterly still, like a mirror, and the deep peace and silence. It was clearly a sacred place.

'How beautiful, I said, quietly and moved forward, kneeling on the soft moss that surrounded the water, and peered in, expecting to see my own reflection, and hoping to see fish moving in the depths, but the face that looked back at me, was older and smiling, very beautiful.

I was so surprised that my hands slipped, and I nearly plunged in.

'Careful,' said the face, laughing, 'Rhianna, welcome.'

'Lady,' I said, trying to recover myself, 'You sent for me?'

'Indeed. It is time. We have work to do.'

'What may I call you, Lady?'

'My name is like yours. You may call me Rhiannon.'

Rhiannon. I knew that name from my Avalon studies with Aella. The Goddess Rhiannon. The Ancient Goddess of the birds and animals and all nature and I was overwhelmed and fearful.

'L-lady,' I said again and bent my head.

'Come, there's no need to be fearful. I will not harm you. You are of my own line, many times descended. We have known each other in many lifetimes, Rhianna, my daughter. In this lifetime you have a high destiny, and must prepare yourself. You are gifted with many powers and we will work together to develop them. You will come here to me?'

'Yes, Lady.'

'Today, we begin. Do you know that you are a shape shifter, like your mother?'

'You know my mother?'

She smiled broadly. 'Indeed, I know your mother. A remarkable woman, with many gifts, but you are gifted beyond her. What animal would you like to be?'

'A r- raven?'

'Very well. Fix your mind on the bird. It's proud bearing. It's glossy coat. Imagine the strength in your arms becoming wings. Feel the claws on your feet...

Her voice went on, becoming muffled because now I could feel the change, the muscles changing, my head shrinking, the balance of my body moving forward, holding the tail feathers folded behind, I took a step forward and another and lifted into the air, effortlessly, I was flying.

I was so shaken and amazed that I plunged back to earth into my human body, and heard my ravens cackling with derisive laughter. The Lady was laughing too. 'Well, that wasn't bad for a first attempt. You will get better. So this is your first task. You must practice changing your shape and becoming other creatures until it is easy and natural. We will meet again soon.' And the pool was clear, reflecting only my own shocked and incredulous face. And my ravens were pacing about on the stone wall shouting with amusement.

For the next weeks I secretly practiced changing into a raven, and became very adept at it, and then curiously, wondered how it would be to move as fast as a hare, and within seconds I was bounding along the edge of the barley field. For a while I forgot all else, changing myself into a variety of creatures, wild with excitement.

When the Goddess called me next though, it was to show me how to change the weather, how to make sunlight spread, how to make rain fall, how to call the thunder, how to drive water along the river channels, how to form ice over water, how to raise the wind...

And so it went on, week by week, and I learned the secret powers and how to use them for the benefit of all. The most difficult was how to work on fellow human beings and change them, even against their will. But in this the Goddess said I excelled, and must be careful to use the skill always to help and never to injure – or there would be dire consequences.

So my initiation continued secretly. I don't know why I didn't tell Aella, except that it seemed to me that the Lady would not approve, and it would trouble Aella. This was just between the Lady and I, and not for babbling about lightly. The powers were sacred and private and I knew too, that they might be dangerous.

But of all the powers, the one that pleased me most, was the opening of my full healing power. Of course, I had always helped Aella with her practice, gathering the herbs and learning how to prepare them, and helping her with her midwifery and physical treatments, but this power was truly sacred and I spent much time finding injured animals and other creatures that I could hold gently and feel the power flowing through me into their bodies and feeling their hurts disappearing as the broken body healed miraculously. I knew that this power was coming from the Goddess herself, but it felt very familiar, as though I had done it before.

Of course, Aella soon noticed this, and made the sign of the Lady, but she said nothing, for truly there was nothing to say, except to give thanks.

Of course, I did eventually tell Aella that I could speak with the animals and birds, and some of the insects. All the animals had voices, sometimes very high almost beyond my hearing like the insects and birds, but the animals spoke very clearly according to their species and were wise with the learning of their generations.

Aella was very quiet for a time, as she had been when I showed her the tiny flame that I could make dance on my hand, and then asked me many questions, about what the animals said, and how much I understood, and somehow I did not think she was very surprised.

'Rhianna,' she said, at last. 'It is a very great gift, and I don't know what to say, except it is very dangerous. It is a very rare ability. Few people have such a gift, and I think it would be wise if you did not tell other people.'

It was what I expected her to say. Aella had long had this fear of exposing our secrets to others, and to be honest I did not take much notice of her warnings. I could not understand why she was so fearful. 'But wouldn't they be interested?'

'Oh yes, but they might think you are boasting, or they might think, because it is so very rare, that it is unnatural and you are strange or even evil.' I laughed at her, but soon she was proved correct, and I stopped laughing when the dreadful business of old Warrior happened.

Warrior was one of my favourites. He was an old dog who lived with my friend Aine. He usually lay outside, on their doorstep, his nose on his paws and I felt very sorry for him. He was very sad because he missed his master, who did not come home often, and Aine's mother and her grandmother did not like dogs. Gitta, and Aine, he said, were frightened of him and thought he would bite them, and Senomamma hated dogs because she thought they were insanitary and dirty and ate too much. She was a mean woman and did not feed him properly, he said. He had been left behind to take care of the women, but he couldn't do that because they chased him out of the house, and he had to live on their doorstep even when it was cold. He had the bone pain in his back legs now. He was so sad and lonely that I made a point of stopping by him for a few words and giving his ears a rub, and when there was nobody looking, I gave his legs a few minutes deep healing, which he thanked me for profusely. So we were friends and I encouraged Aine to look after him better. But she was annoyed that I took an interest in him, and said that he was their dog and she could do what she wanted. That should have warned me, but one day when I saw he was really ill, and he told me he had a strange big pain in his stomach, I had to tell her. And a couple of days later, when he put his head on his paws for the last time and died, she told her mother what I had said – that Warrior had told me about his pain. The resulting row was awful and upset me very much.

Gitta was one of the first converts to the White Christos a few years before, when a malevolent travelling preacher had come to the village and made much trouble telling people that the Goddess was evil, and they were all wicked sinners, until Rhoswen had ordered him to leave. Now Gitta was hysterical, shouting that, just as she had been told, Aella and I were wicked witches, and I had cursed her dog.

I was very angry about this because I loved Warrior. I said that on the contrary, she had been needlessly cruel to him, throwing him outdoors when all he wanted was to crawl into his corner to sleep, and that she did not give him enough food.

Of course, this fanned the flames of her fury, and other woman joined in, crowding round, shouting for and against me, until it turned violent. One woman hit another on the nose, until the blood started to flow and I was very frightened that they would beat me too. To my great relief, Aella arrived and calmly pointed out that as they all knew, she was teaching me to understand the symptoms of illnesses and I had merely guessed that the dog was ill. I had just explained it in a childish way, and, of course, the dog had not actually spoken to me. I kept quiet, horrified at causing so much bother and because of the trust they had in my grandmother, it was all smoothed over. But I could not forget or forgive Aine's betrayal and could not speak to her again. Aine was forbidden to play with me, and to my guilt and horror she grew thinner and thinner.

Aella was very angry with me. Her anger, slow to arouse was formidable, and she made me understand how dangerous the accusation of witchcraft was, and what they did to people with unusual powers.

I did not lose all my friends in the Village, although most of the children thought I was strange and a liar, but Gwyri came and said he did not care if I was a witch, if I could go on kicking the ball so accurately in our games with the West Stillwell children. I did not tell him that it was a spell I had devised to make the ball go where we needed it to be, and nothing to do with my superior kicking.

So the whole thing taught me a much needed lesson about superstition, and how unnecessarily fearful people were. I saw that Aella had been right all the time and I became very careful of revealing my gifts openly. For a time, I was very lonely and spent more and more time in the Forest, away from the village.

Rhianna 6

For as long as I can remember I have been interested in healing, at first just trying to save the injured animals and birds that I found. Later I trotted after Aella, first learning where to find the herbs she used, identifying them and what they were for, and then under her supervision preparing them and carefully making up the ointments and medicines with the correct amount of each herb and, perhaps, combining them. Some herbs are poisonous but can be sovereign in small doses.

But there is much more to being a healer than the medicines. You have to know about the way the body works, how to cut and bind, the great and holy mysteries of childbirth, how to treat wounds and injuries – oh, hundreds of things. As I grew older, Aella allowed me to help her, at first just watching, and then holding the bowls, bandaging, sewing up cuts, setting broken limbs. I decided that I wanted to be a healer, a surgeon, a proper healer. I discovered that there is a completely secret branch of healing, not written, involving chants and spells and using the mind in particular ways. Some of the Priestesses and Druids learned this secret lore, which had been handed down from Atlantis and ancient Egypt and I begged Aella to take me as an apprentice, but she said I was too young to make such a serious choice. But I went on learning all I could and hoped that one day she would change her mind.

And now I think there is a chance that she has, but I have to take an Oath, and I am not sure that I can do that.

Yesterday morning they sent for Aella urgently to come to Gladius, injured in an accident. Of course, I went with her. It was serious. He had been trying to fell an elm tree, on the edge of the communal fields, and unexpectedly it had fallen in the wrong direction. His legs were crushed and a long spike had driven into his stomach. They cut and lifted away the tree and fetched Aella to him.

I was very upset. Gladius was our special friend, an old soldier, who had fought with the Roman Legions against the barbarians in so many far-away places. We listened to his wonderful stories whenever we could persuade him to spare the time. He had returned to his homeland hoping to spend a peaceful old age, only to find he was called to defend it against the invading Saxons. And this was the first year he had not gone with the muster. He was much respected and everybody liked him.

Of course, his bone pain and wound made it difficult for him to run or move quickly. I looked anxiously at Aella. His legs were totally crushed from the knee down. How could we put all those pieces of bone together again? He would, surely, never walk again. Aella was on her knees, examining his stomach wound, where the blood was pulsing free while I tried to staunch it. I saw her face settle into a pale gravity I had never seen before and felt cold move down my spine. She shook her head, and the people standing around groaned.

Gladius opened his eyes, conscious again. 'Can't feel my legs,' He squinted, trying to see her. 'Can't feel my legs, lady.' He was speaking in Latin.

Aella put her hand on his forehead, to reduce the pain. 'Gladius.' And he relaxed a little.

'Can't feel...Stomach?' He took a long shuddering breath, as the pain hit him.

'Stomach,' Aella confirmed. 'A spike of wood.' She took his hand and held it tightly.

Gladius groaned. He was an old warrior, he knew what that meant. 'Death wound. Long time to die... Death wound, lady?'

'Yes, Gladius.'

He was silent a while, clutching her hand, 'Finished. Terrible pain...Please, my Lady, please...'

She was very pale, holding his hand tightly between both of hers. 'Gladius, what are you asking?'

'Please, lady.'

'Are you sure?'

He tried to smile. 'Very sure. Now, quickly, please.'

Then, to my horror, I saw Aella pull out the thin, beautiful, sharp little knife that ever hung on her girdle.

She lifted his hand again. 'You will not stay?'

He shook his head, gasping, 'No, *now*,'

Aella closed her eyes for a second, and spoke, high and clear: 'Mithras, Great Lord, receive your good son. A brave life, lived bravely and well,' and with a quick, practiced move, she slit his throat.

Unbelievably there was the beginning of a smile on Gladius face.

Aella bent her head, but I could see the tears running down her cheeks, and her hands trembling. After a few moments she rose, wiped the blood from her knife on her robe and walked away, her skirt dragging in Gladius' blood, pooled on the grass. The crowd parted for her respectfully, murmuring voices thanking her, and I followed her.

Later in the evening, Aella called me to her. I had spent the time in the Forest, crying, trying to understand why she had killed Gladius. He would have died anyway, so why had she taken even the last few hours of his life?

'Why?' I said. 'Why did you do it? You have always said that all life is sacred, and yet...'

'Rhianna, since you were a little child, you have ever trotted at my heels, helping me heal. When we were at Lot's Castle...' she stopped, suddenly. 'I mean, when you were very small you were always trying to heal the little injured animals you found, do you remember?'

I nodded, doubtfully. 'When we were at Lot's Castle?' What was this? 'I think I remember a little mouse, and what was it, a rabbit?'

She nodded. 'And most times they recovered... I think you have a gift for healing. You have learned much and are a great help to me with the herbs and medicines. And the garden.'

'You know I want to be a healer, a great healer, like you. I've asked you again and again if you would take me as your apprentice and teach me. I would know the words, too. The spells, the secrets, all of it.'

She pulled me to her, and stroked the hair away from my cheeks, and saw the tear stains. 'You were very upset this morning?'

'So were you. Why did you...'

'To be a healer, you must take a most sacred, binding, Oath, sworn to the Goddess.

From time beyond time there have always been those who healed, and always there has been an Oath taken, not to harm, always to do good to people, to remove pain.

'But you harmed Gladius. You killed him.'

'Aye. But you see, Priestesses of Avalon swear a Sacred Oath too. Gladius was in agonising pain. You saw his legs. He would never walk again, and he had the stomach wound that soldiers everywhere dread. We have no way of repairing the internal organs, and they die very slowly and painfully, their own bodies poisoning them.'

I nodded. 'I know that.'

'Gladius would have died by now. He was in agony. But he begged for help. He knew we are sworn to help people into life – and out of it, if they ask.'

'He said, 'Death wound.' He knew.'

'He did, and he passed quickly.'

'How did you know his God was Mithras?'

'Mithras is the secret God of many soldiers. But Rhianna, the important thing is, if you wish to be an apprentice healer, you must take the Oath – and it will include the need to be willing to take a life, if you are asked by a dying person, as well as heal it. Are you willing to accept that? Are you strong enough? Will you kill if you are asked?

'I don't know.'

'Then you must think very hard about it. Let me know when you decide. There's no hurry. You must be absolutely sure.'

Well I have thought long and hard. I went to the Lady's Pool this afternoon, and discussed it with her.

She was surprised. 'Of course, Aella is right. You must never leave any creature who has its death wound or disease. You must release its soul for rebirth when it is ready to go.'

'But, suppose I am wrong, and they are able to recover? I have known people recover from very bad illness when it seemed certain they would die.'

'People know when they are ready to leave. Do you think you have only one life?'

I stared. I did think that. But if we have many lives, it changes everything. I must think much more about this. It is a revelation to me.

I said, 'But suppose it is something silly like Babitha saying she wanted to die because Tori had walked out with Eda?'

The Lady laughed. 'I'm sure you will know the difference.'

I pondered all these matters as I walked home. I knew that if I was injured like Gladius I would not want to live in such pain and disability. I would rather go to my next life quickly, and I would be grateful to the Priestess who helped me to it.

When I got home, I told Aella that I was ready to take the healers' Oath of life and death. At the next full moon, we will go to the sacred Spring and I will swear to the Goddess, and become Aella's Apprentice Healer at last.

Rhianna 7

It is done! I have sworn the Oath of life and death to the Goddess, and I am now Aella's full apprentice healer. At Lughnasadh we went privately to the famous Sacred Springs in the valley along the Sabrina at the full moon, prayed to the Goddess, made offerings of fruit and flowers. To my surprise there were a number of other dark cloaked and cowled figures there making oath.

I held out my hands, and the Priestess poured spring water over my head and hands. It was icy and smelled of rosemary. I recited the Sacred Oath that Aella bade me speak, and she poured more spring water, that glinted silver in the moonlight. Then we waited, silent and shivering. An owl hooted three times in the distance, and suddenly my hands began to glow with an inner light. I could not feel anything, but the glow increased, to a brilliant white, which turned gold, and then after a while began to fade into away into blue violet and then it was gone. I was almost afraid to move my hands; they did not seem to belong to me.

Aella drew in a deep, relieved breath, wiped tears away from her cheeks. 'It is done,' she said. 'The Goddess has accepted you. You are my apprentice healer.' And she put into my palm a most beautiful small knife, chased with spirals and glowing rubies – beautiful and deadly, which sent a shudder down my back. It was a reminder of the full responsibility of what I was undertaking.

I put my hands now again in a bowl of spring water and swear the Oath to myself. I will serve and do good.

Part Six

Rhianna 8

Gena says Rhoswen says that there is a new Holy Hermit come to the old bear cave along the river. This is good news. Everyone knows that hermits bring good fortune and with their prayers, make the village safer. We were all missing Father Drusus, and his gentle advice. There was no one to talk over problems with, or get a second opinion.

Dewi, the shepherd was sent to welcome the new hermit, with a pack of fresh bread, cheese and milk, and to ask if there was anything he needed.

Dewi is as ancient and wrinkled as any hermit, like a piece of bog oak, but he is very dignified and has this deep musical voice. He sometimes deputises for Maglos, our Head man, when he is away fighting.

Dewi came back. giggling, with the new hermit's thanks and good wishes to the village, and offer of help or advice, should anybody require it. Dewi said he thinks the new hermit can very well take care of himself. He would not say why he was giggling, but I heard that offer of help very clearly! I wondered if the new hermit was a scholar, and knew Greek?

* * *

I always enjoy going up to the Hermit's Cave, it is such a lovely peaceful place. The first hermit, whoever he was, had chosen well.

The path runs alongside the big river for a while, and then lifts into a rocky cliff, climbing more steeply until it emerges much higher, onto a hill overlooking the river. The higher I got the more I heard, through the morning mist, the sound of someone singing. It was an astonishing voice, bell-like and joyous.

The path wound around, still climbing, until it passed two standing stones, half-buried in deep grass and flowering shrubs. Stepping between the stones you are in a round, hidden space, surrounded by higher rocky outcrops and apple trees, very sheltered, with a cave opening to the side, turning away from the prevailing wind. A tiny convenient spring feeds into a rocky basin beside the cave, and across the grassy space between two high rocks there is a waterfall, which tips over the edge in haste to get to the sea. The clearing seems to collect light like a pool, light and warmth reflected off the rocks, and on sunny days there is always the murmuring sound of water and bees among the blossoms and birdsong. It is a truly magical place.

I saw at once that the new hermit had been busy. He had already planted a lot of vegetables and herbs, all the ones we used ourselves, and had plaited two skeps for the bees. Father Drusus had been too old and infirm to look after a garden and everyone in the village had worried about him. I had climbed up here twice a week since I was seven, to bring him food and medicines, and he had talked to me about good and evil, and the great prophets and philosophers. And he had taught me the harp and to sing the old songs. This last winter which had been a hard one, he had taken ill with the deadly lung sickness. They had brought him down to Aella, but it was too late. He had neglected himself, and stopped eating and even she could not save him. He was such a saintly, lovely old man, we were still grieving for him. We were uneasy without a Hermit, and there was great relief that a new one had come.

There was a man standing under the waterfall where it fell away to the trees below. He was stark naked, scrubbing himself vigorously and singing at the top of his voice, I withdrew a little behind a large bush, not wanting to disturb his enjoyment.

He was so far from my idea of a holy Hermit, who would be wrinkled and bent, that I did not at first think he could be the one I sought. He was very tall, with broad muscled shoulders, his hair silver, thick and curled, shorn close to his head.

'I know you are there,' he said, 'Come forth. Don't be shy.'

I moved forward. 'Good morning. I didn't want to interrupt you. I'm not shy. I have seen many bodies. All of them wondrous.' His member was small, curled close from the icy water.

He seized a drying cloth hanging from a knob of rock, and began to dry himself. 'Cleanliness before godliness.'

I was surprised – that was one of Aella's constant chants. 'Heresy, the Christian priests would say.'

'Cleanliness for good health then.'

'And lavender, woundwort, marigold...'

He nodded. 'All useful against infection.' And flung the cloth over his dripping head.

'You have many scars,' I said clinically, looking at his back. 'Knife cuts. Sword. Lance? No, spear, I think.' I paused, again surprised, 'Whip?' He did not seem to be the sort of man who would allow himself to be flogged. Had he been a slave? 'And...' I hesitated, worried, there was big deep wound near his shoulder blade, recent, and not healing well. An axe?

'That's right,' he said, 'An axe.' He had read my mind.

'You nearly lost an arm there. You are lucky to be alive.'

'Aye, I'm a bit battered, right enough.' He laughed, and pulled a thick, clean robe over his head. It was well worn, plain, but excellently woven. Not hermit poor.

'Are you a soldier?'

'If need be.' What did that mean?

'So, you are a healer?' he said, buckling an astonishing belt round his waist.

'An apprentice only,' I said, staring at the belt.

'To?'

'To? Oh, to my grandmother, Aella. She is the Healer in the village down there, Stillwell. That is a marvellous belt. I have never seen anything like it.'

'Nor will. It was made for me by a leather worker in Constantinople. A great artist.'

He took it off and threw it to me, so I could examine it closer. It was heavy, strong, supple, black. I exclaimed. 'Not black! Purple! How did they ever find such a dye? We can't...'

'Tyrian purple from Carthage. They get it from sea snails, rock snails of the family Muricidea, originally known by the name Murex. You need many hundreds of snails.'

Into the leather was impressed a constellation of stars – the Bear? – a real gold sun, and a glowing moon, a shining white gemstone. And then I realised that all the glittering stars had jewels glowing in their centres. 'Why the Bear?'

He turned. He had been heating a can of water on a small fire he had on the stone hearth he had made near the cave mouth. 'You are well educated.'

'Do you think so? Aella would be glad to hear you say so.' I grinned.

Along the base of the belt ran a procession of gold animals, so real they seemed to be alive. They were all running towards the buckle. This was another wonder, in woven gold, with tiny leaves. flowers, fruits, birds, even a little squirrel, a crafty link, in the middle, and suddenly it was whole. A tree.

I took a deep breath. 'It is a Tree of Life! With all the animals, the Sun and Moon, the Bear and the Pleiades. It is magnificent! Oh, I wish...'

'You may have it.'

My jaw dropped and I stared at him. Was he mad? Dangerous? And then I realised. I laughed. I got up and gave it back to him. 'No, no. I was going to say I wish I could make something like this with my hands. So beautiful. And travel to Constantinople to see more such things.'

He stared at me for a moment, then turned to put a cup into my hands. I sipped the tea. Rose hip with honey. Delicious. 'Thank you, my favourite.'

'Mine too.'

He was a very special hermit I thought. If indeed, he was a hermit.

'Your Grandmother? Aella, you say?' He sounded puzzled. 'I would like to meet your "grandmother".'

'I will tell her. She will come.'

He looked at me. Amber, penetrating eyes, like the sun reflecting in the darkest water.

Old eyes, full of knowledge and wisdom, somehow entering into my mind. I sank down and down, and found only immense tenderness, love and understanding. I was not afraid. I knew he was a friend. I had known him for aeons. We had been friends over many lifetimes. He put out his hands and took one of mine. His very long fingers closed around my small brown hand, protection and a promise. 'Greetings, Rhiannon. Never fear me.'

'No,' I said. 'I am so glad to meet you again.' It was simple as that. It felt as if a broken chain had been mended.

'You came to talk to me?' he said.

I came back to myself and remembered my errand. 'Yes. I came to ask if you were a scholar, as well as a hol..., well a hermit?'

He laughed. 'A hermit. But not holy?'

I coloured. 'I hoped you would be able to teach me Greek, or maybe, Aramaic.' I held my breath.

'Greek?' he said, surprised. 'What about Latin?'

'I have the Latin. I can speak it well, Aella says.' I went on in that language so he could judge, 'But we have this book you see. A book on healing, in Greek. It has some drawings, and diagrams and it looks as though it might be very useful to me. I would dearly love to read it. But there is nobody in the village who can help.'

'I will teach you Greek. And Aramaic, you say. Why?"

'Well, I have heard that in Spain they have some wonderful healers who are translating from ancient scrolls by a man called Galen...'

'Aye. Jewish philosophers. You are determined on the healing then?'

'Well, it will be my living.' I dug my toes into the soft earth under a stone, not seeing it . 'I love to heal, but sometimes... like now, my hands want to move and make, and I don't know how to. It's like a gnat biting and it won't go away, and I can't find a way to scratch it.' I was astonished that I was confiding something so personal, so secret. 'There is something else I should be doing.'

'Ah, I understand. You don't have to choose one thing. Choose all. Let all come that you would do and learn. At your age that is very important. Later you will find that some things will become more entrancing, more demanding, and you will find yourself pursuing them...spending more time on them... But for now, try all. There is so much in the world.'

I relaxed, smiling. 'I would like to know more of our beginnings, about the other peoples, and how they think, about the wind and rain and lightning, and about the universe and planets. I love to find new plants and help them thrive, and make the herbal draughts and powders...'

He broke in, 'I can help you with some of that...You find new medicines?'

'In the deep forest. I bring them home to our garden and plant them. I have made a collection of them. We try to find out what they can do and...'

'How do you know they are healing plants?'

It was the first time anyone had shown interest in my collection. I ran on excitedly, 'Well, they have a kind of bluish haze around them, and when I ask the little people or the animals, they can sometimes tell me...' I ground to a halt biting my tongue. His strange eyes had dilated to darkness, and I realised I had given away too much. I had talked about something that must be kept secret.

'You are able to talk to the animals?'

I tried to laugh. 'Well everyone talks to the animals, don't they? You say, 'Come in Warrior, it's raining...' I could see that he was not being deflected.

'The animals speak to you? You understand what they are saying?'

Under his penetrating eyes I tried to lie. 'Well not exactly...'

'Liar,' said Glossy, one of the ravens, sitting, almost hidden, in the birch tree next the cave. 'Liar, liar,' said Dark Claw, above me, and they both laughed.

The hermit raised his eyes and found them in the surrounding trees, counting them. There were only five today. He looked back at me, his eyes glowing with triumph and laughter.

'Liar, they say. I understand.'

I shrugged, but I knew that he did. Not just understand what the ravens had said, but that I had developed special powers which I must keep secret. But he said no more about them.

We arranged for me to come regularly twice a week to begin learning Greek.

As I left, I said, turning back. 'My name is Rhianna. What should I call you, sir?'

He stood, very tall and broad-shouldered, 'You may call me, Emlyn.'

Of the Cymry then, I thought. 'Goodbye, Master Emlyn, and thank you.'

He watched me leave with the ravens flying after me, until the path turned.

Rhianna 9

I couldn't wait to tell Aella about Master Emlyn and his promise to teach me Greek, but she was much less pleased than I thought she would be.

'He might have been dangerous – a mad old man. Many hermits have lost their minds, in their solitude, and pursuing their religion too intensely.'

'He could be dangerous, I think,' I said. 'But not to me. The Ravens liked him.'

She snorted. 'I will see this hermit for myself. What is his name?'

'Master Emlyn.'

She paused, a strange look on her face. 'Emlyn? Of the Cymry?'

'Do you know him then?'

She shook her head. 'I'm stupid. It can't possibly be.'

When she came back from her visit, there was an even stranger look in her eyes. A mixture of worry, relief and even amusement. She refused to tell me what had happened, other than that they had come to an agreement that I was to go to him twice a week for Greek and Sanskrit, and to take fresh bread and milk in payment.

I opened my eyes wide. 'Sanskrit?'

'An ancient language. He says, for the philosophy and Ayurvedic medicine.'

Aella tried to make it sound commonplace, but I was wildly excited. I never dreamed that I would have the opportunity of learning Sanskrit as well as Greek. 'What kind of medicine is that?'

'Very, very ancient from the Land of Spices,' Aella said, 'Herb and mineral based, I think, but much more than that, different foods, healing movement and as Mer...I mean, Master Emlyn says, philosophy – ideas new to us.'

It got better and better. I had often thought that the way we moved could help in the healing process, for bone pain for instance. I had heard that the Romans had traded in the Land of Spices for powerful healing herbs and spices which did not grow in Europe. I would love to find out more about them. Turmeric had been mentioned in one of the Latin books. Ginger, that was another, and Boswellia...I wondered if they were available here, and maybe I could try to grow them...

'And – are you listening, Rhianna? He will oversee your written Latin too. So you must take your Chronicle to show him.'

Not so good. I groaned, and Aella smiled. But I did not mind really. It was nothing compared to the joy of finding such a teacher. I said, 'I have to take a pot of our healing salve too. He has an axe wound that is festering.'

Aella 24

'Emlyn', Rhianna had said. I knew only one Emlyn, but surely it could not be. What on earth would he be doing here, pretending to be a hermit?

I went to see Rhianna's hermit, half prepared, suspicious, but it was still a surprise to find Merlin himself, sitting comfortably outside the cave, mending a sandal, as though he had lived there for years.

He looked up, setting aside his work, grinning. 'Aella!'

'My Lord Merlin,' I said, formally, and bowed.

'Aella, my dear!' he came forward, flinging his arms wide, hugging me. 'So many years! Come, sit down. That boulder is comfortable.'

I sat, arranging my skirts, and watched him. I had always liked Merlin, but he was tricky, and did not always understand the consequences of his actions, or care, if the truth be told. And why should he? The Lord High Merlin of Logres, did not concern himself with trivial matters. 'Why are you here?' I asked bluntly, and remembered then that he had caused all Morgan's trouble. Well, he and Vivienne together. I was worried too. If he knew where we were living, others would know too.

He grinned again. 'I thought you'd be surprised.'

'That's no answer.'

'Morgan told me.'

The tension went out of me. I was excited. 'How is she?'

'In health. Well, overwhelmed with work. The King's right hand. They are re-building Logres. New Councils. New Courts of Law. New just laws. New land laws. Throwing out the old. Total reform of the old ways.' He paused, and stopped grinning. 'Order, justice, security, well-being throughout the land. She hears the voice of the people.'

'She always did,' I said, fondly.

'Aella, you would not believe the wonderful changes they have already made together.' He stared beyond me.

'In spirit?' I said.

'Aah!' He stood, suddenly, hesitated, needing to move. 'Leashed.'

'Leashed?'

'Like a hound. Straining. She wants her own lands. Anything. Away from him.'

'Oh.' I said, understanding, my heart dropping.

'Oh indeed!' he said, viciously, and kicked his sandal into the cave behind him. 'She grows thin. She transforms too often. She takes risks. She will kill herself, one day. You know that she is my daughter?'

'I knew Ygraine was pregnant when she married Gorlois. I thought... Beltane...' I stood up, wringing my hands in distress. 'Why doesn't he let her go?'

'You know why. She is his soul. His reason for living. His.'

I took a breath. The damage was too deep. It could only be

borne, mitigated, perhaps, not cured. 'The Queen?'

'The first one? Nice little nitwit. Did her duty, produced a son. Scared of Arthur. Scared of everyone. Died in childbirth with the second child. The current one... another Gwenivere, King Leodegrance's daughter. Very rich. Very beautiful. Very confident. Bringing two hundred trained knights and warriors with her. I advised against it.'

'You don't like her?'

'Aella, she is a Queen Bee. Everyone must do her bidding, must surrender their souls. She is very charming. Well trained. Efficient. The Court is very civilised. Good food. Clean beds. Wine. *Lutes.*'

Oh dear, Merlin really hated her.

'The Ambassadors are full of praise. The King does his duty, sometimes, but she does not conceive. Isn't that strange? His bed partners have aborted twice.'

I looked at him coldly. He bared his teeth, a mock smile. 'Don't worry, the King is well serviced. Only Morgan suffers.'

'It was the nuns,' I said, remembering.

'Lancelot is deep in Gwenivere's toils, poor fellow. Riven. She is working with the Archbishop and the Christians against Arthur, and she knows about Morgan and does everything to try to destroy her. A great enemy, Aella. I think she will get her revenge in the end.'

'There is nothing you can do?'

'I do what I can.'

A bad situation that could only get worse. I picked up my shawl. The afternoon breeze suddenly felt chilly.

'I am sorry I bring bad news of our favourite.' He sounded contrite; his anger gone.

'But why did you come?'

He flung out his hands impatiently. 'I was bored, Aella. Bored. When we were fighting, I was needed. Good comradeship. Healing. Exciting times. A clear aim. Victory! Now is the time for rebuilding. Making a new future. I am King's Counsellor, of course, but Arthur has grown into his Kingship. I do not like Gwenivere's intrigues. I do not like how the religious are changing our land, getting a great hold.' We were silent, thinking.

I took a deep breath, 'What of Vivienne? The Lady of the Lake?'

'She does nothing.'

It silenced me. Could he be right? What was happening in Avalon?

'And then there is the future,' he said, in different tone. 'Lachau is a warrior, like his father, his life is uncertain. I thought I must look for 'Sisters' child' to make sure of the succession. Of her education. Of her abilities.'

I tried to smile. 'I came to talk of Rhianna, arrange her Greek lessons.'

'Yes, she must come to me for her Greek and Sanskrit, but she is already beyond us, Aella. A major soul. You have done very well. You have shaped a miracle. She is the most remarkable of our line. A green Mage.'

I brushed away tears. 'She is the child of my heart. She has a spirit and intelligence full of clarity and light. She has given me a fulfilled life. I have been able to serve the Goddess, even outside Avalon. It is ending? We have been happy here.'

He was silent, but put his hands on my shoulders – a blessing.

I stood up. 'Thank you, Lord Merlin.' I took his hand and kissed it. 'I will send milk and bread with Rhianna when she comes.' I walked away down the track, my eyes blurred with tears.

To my surprise, he came with me. 'There's something else, Aella,' he said, hesitating.

'I came to warn you. There is something... I can't see what it is. But there is real danger coming to you both. Be careful. It isn't clear to me yet.'

My heart turned over. 'Mawgawse, has she found us, do you think?'

'Not Mawgawse. Something else. My mind is drumming with it. Something comes, but not quite yet. I can only say, take care.'

Merlin's second sight was famous. 'Thank you,' I said. 'I will renew my wards and make preparation.' What would happen, would happen. But it would not catch me unaware.

Rhianna 10

Master Emlyn is a magnificent teacher.

On my first morning, bearing the fresh bannocks, a jug of milk, and the healing salve, I climbed up the muddy track to his cave. It was raining heavily and my cloak was soaked through but to my surprise, the cave was warm and dry, with a glowing fire in the hearth stones, and I realised that he had warded it from the clinging damp. He took my cloak and draped it over the end of a bench which he dragged near to the fire.

'Good morning!' he said. 'Sit. Dry out,'

'Master Emlyn,' I said, straightly, 'I don't know what to call you. I don't believe that Emlyn is your real name. Aella has given the game away. She started to call you something else. You know each other. It's another of her mysteries. But I would know the truth, if you please.'

He grinned. 'She knows me as Merlin. You can call me that if you like.'

The name rang a bell, but I could not remember where I had heard it. 'Merlin.'

'It is a Druid title. A high priest.'

'Does that mean you are a Druid? I thought hermits were all Christians.'

'I have been both, but no longer.'

I did not know what to say to that. I had never known anyone who had changed their religion twice. 'Why did you tell me, Emlyn?'

'It is my birthname.' He grinned again.

I was relieved. 'Ah, that is why it did not seem respectful to call you that somehow. I will call you as Aella does, Merlin.' But I still wondered why they had both tried to keep the name secret.

Merlin's teaching is like none other. No boring exercises to be done over and over again. We started with the Greek, and Merlin spent most of the time telling me all about the Greek people, where and how they lived. He knows how much I long to travel to see other places.

'Look there', he said, pointing. There was a glowing patch on a smooth wall of the cave, almost like a window with brilliant sunlight coming through. As I stood watching the edges seemed to expand, and then disappeared altogether, and I was standing in sunshine in this other place. I was really there, alive, and there were people passing me, wearing robes and cloaks, walking up the hill to a high place. I looked up, and gasped. There was a huge building there of white stone, bigger than I had ever seen. I didn't know that human beings could make buildings that tall. It was many times the height of a man, taller than the tallest trees in the Forest. And indeed, it reminded me of the trees because there were tree-like pillars along the front, and sides, holding up the roof and a great sculpture of giant-sized people, like Gods, painted in rich colours, above the entrance.

'The Parthenon,' said Merlin. 'A temple dedicated to the Goddess Athena, in the city of Athens, one of the City States I told you about.'

'They have the Goddess too?'

'And Gods. A lot of them.'

I stared and stared, hardly believing that it would not fall down, it was so large. Merlin chuckled and the sunshine darkened and we were back in the cave. Outside the rain continued to batter at the rocks

I looked at Merlin, and he looked back smiling. 'I thought so.' I said. 'You are a magician. A very great Mage.'

'Thank you,' he said. 'We are a pair.'

I burst out laughing, it was so silly to compare us. But Merlin was not laughing. 'You will see,' he said.

He gave me a piece of vellum with the Greek letters beautifully written and told me to practise writing them until I knew them thoroughly by the next lesson, and then it was time to go home. But I really didn't want to leave.

The next lesson the sun was shining, and we marched around the space outside the cave, pretending to be Greek soldiers – hoplites, Merlin said – shouting out the words of a marching song, a rude one. He explained about their weapons – a spear and big round shield and how they fought in a rectangle form called a Phalanx, with their shields linked, so the arrows of the Persians, their enemies, could not penetrate. Then Merlin showed me how to hold and move a spear, and we fought a mock battle with two shafts of wood, with Merlin calling insults at me – in Greek, I realised after a while, shouting them back at him – 'flat foot piglet', 'cross-eyed tortoise', 'ham-fisted fat bum'.

I'm not sure how I knew what the words meant, but I ended up rolling on the grass, helpless with laughter, while the ravens flew around, excited, laughing raucously and making up their own insults.

And now I realise that I have learned the sound of the letters I have learned to write. Crafty Merlin.

Merlin said that this week we were to travel again, but back to the past. The glowing patch of wall appeared, showing a garden, and we were there, sitting listening to a man called Homer. He was an old man with a long craggy face, a very big nose and a short curly beard. He was wearing a flat cap on his head, and a loose white robe. He was reclining in a low-slung leather chair, reciting what sounded like a poem, waving his arms around to emphasize the rhythm of the poem, and a young man, sitting opposite, was writing it down, both of them were laughing and enjoying it. I could see over the young man's shoulder and was able to see the words, dark on the surface, moving along, jumping about like naughty children, finally settling into sedate lines as Homer spoke them. I thought, why, he is making up the poem as he goes along! Then I saw that his eyes had a white film covering the iris, and realised he was blind.

I loved the sound of the words, and Homer's voice, and it seemed I could understand more and more. I listened eagerly. It was a story of a war, with great heroes, doing terrible things, and then the vision faded. I was so disappointed I wanted to go on listening.

Merlin was there, grinning with satisfaction, holding a scroll. 'Here it is, The Iliad.

'You can borrow it and begin your own translation.'

I stared at him, dazed. 'You mean it is a real poem, written down?'

'You saw! Some say about real events.' He pointed at the wall, and the light expanded again, showing a group of people, men and women, standing on a very high wall. They were rich with fine clothes and gold jewellery, one with a crown on his head.

'King Priam,' said Merlin.

Below them, the land dropped away to a flat plain stretching into the distance, where the sea shimmered on the horizon. There was an army camped there, with tents, but the warriors were lined up watching, strangely silent, and in front of them, on the plain was a wooden platform with a bound body awaiting cremation.

'Patroclus, Achilles friend and lover.'

Then from behind the pyre, came a light war chariot, with two horses, driven at speed, by a tall warrior with brilliant armour and a helmet with a great black plume and tail like a horse. 'Achilles.'

Horribly, tied to the back of the chariot, raising a cloud of dust, as the horses raced forward, was a body, another warrior, battered, half his armour gone, his body falling apart.

'Hector,' said Merlin. 'King Priam's son. The Hero of his people. Hector killed Patroclus. Achilles is taking his revenge. He has been dishonouring the body for nine days in front of his parents.'

The King on the wall was crying, his tears sliding down his face, unstoppable, but his mother, was dry-eyed, not moving, like a piece of white marble, but I could see clearly a green glow of hate and rage surrounding her, and I wondered if she was an enchantress. If she was, Achilles would not be enjoying his revenge for very long.

'Achilles is dishonouring himself,' I said. 'That's why his warriors are silent. The man is already dead. He has paid already for Patroclus death.'

I was suddenly angry. 'Men are stupid. They waste lives and think they are heroes.'

'What happened then?'

Merlin's eyes glinted. 'That's for you to find out. It's all there in the scroll.'

Rhianna 11

I have been to the Land of Spices! We started Sanskrit today and Merlin showed me some of the lands of the East, with wonders beyond description. There were great temples, with intricate carvings all over them, but it is the fabrics I remember most. Silk! A smooth, glistening fabric, brilliant with colour, fluttering like butterfly's wings. Velvet, thicker, deep rich colours glowing, and soft! So very soft, like the fur of moles. And wondrous silks woven with real gold into patterns of flowers and birds, shot with silver. I looked at these for a long time, wondering how they made them, and wishing I could make them myself.

The spices were there too, dozens of them, heaped carelessly into big sacks and stacked against the walls of little shops. Oh, and the carpets! How could I forget the carpets – most wondrous of all? Hanging on the walls, as well as on the floors. Fine wool woven into pictures, like gardens, and patterns of symbols. I had never seen such colours. Where did they get their dyes?

We went into a temple, with many chambers carved out of the solid rock, and huge breath-taking decorations and sacred sculptures and the walls painted with huge serene gods and goddesses in colours like a dream of gold and pink and green... And there were people too, alive, sitting cross-legged and chanting. I saw scribes copying scrolls in Sanskrit and illuminating them with wonderful paintings and patterns, done with such skill and care that it seemed as though they had been done magically, but I saw the artists actually drawing and painting them with fine thin brushes, their colours liquid in little dishes.

I have another new script to learn. This one is very beautiful on the page, with curly letters under a straight black line. They make patterns that could be embroidered on a braid. If one could make one word, say 'peace' for the edge of a cloak, I wonder if it would make the person who wears the cloak feel peaceful or happy – like the yellow monks who were chanting a song?

I am so excited at this idea, that I must discuss it with Merlin. I went up to the cave especially, but Merlin was not there. There were ashes in the hearth, and the bannocks I brought last week are stale. Where has he gone?

Rhianna 12

Master Merlin was back, to my relief. A turf fire glowed among the big stones of the hearth, but he was absent. I found him at last, down by the stream, fishing, placidly, as though he had been there all the time.

'Ah, there you are,' I said, 'Where have you been? Aella has sent food three times, but you weren't here.'

'My thanks to her and to you for bringing it. I found the pot of soup and pie in the box of ice. They were still edible.'

I would not let him turn away my enquiry. 'I have finished translating the Homer that you set for me. And have had nothing to do.'

'Good. There's plenty more.'

'But where have you been?' I scolded, exasperated. 'We have been so worried.'

He said, at last, 'There has been another battle. I went to help.'

I sat down next to him. 'The Bear?'

'Aye,' he said dryly, 'Another glorious victory they will remember in the Annals, Badon.'

'So why are you so upset and gloomy? Are you wounded?'

'Fine young men, scattered and dead? A field of blood. No. A few scratches only, thanks be. Your healing salve worked wonderfully.'

'Why do men do it?' I burst out. 'Aella and I bring many children into the world. It is hard, birthing. Hard, bloody and dangerous. Then they have to be looked after carefully for many years, only for them to end up dead, fighting each other. It is waste. Destructive waste. Why do they waste their lives like that? It is pointless.'

'You'd rather be a slave?'

'Better than dead. Are they so very bad, these Saxons?'

'Like all men and women, some good, some bad.'

'There is a Saxon family in West Stillwell. They say they came through the Perilous Forest, twenty years ago, lost and fleeing. The Head Woman said they could stay. They are good people. Algar is a good farmer. He has made an assart in the Forest, raises pig and goats. His children are mannerly and help with the Village harvest. They all speak our language. They are peaceful people, and neighbourly.'

'Very likely. The tribes are farmers, generally.'

'But, Merlin, why do they come here. Why don't they stay in their own countries?'

Master Merlin sighed. He pulled a stick from the thicket, next to us, and began to draw in the sand by the river bank. 'See here. This is Britannia, as the Romans called us. This is the whole island.' He drew a curving, slashing line through the middle. 'All this land to the east is Saxon, Angle-land. Jute-land. right along these eastern shores, as far as the land of the Picts, here in the north... Here to the west we have the mountains of the Cymry, the Summer lands, Cornwell, Lyoness, the Valley of the big river Thamesis, the Middle lands. Arthur seeks to secure a border here, to hold these lands for the Britons. But the Saxon Princes are greedy for more and more land for their people, greedy for power, greedy for riches. They push forward. Arthur and the British kings seek to drive them back.'

'Into the sea,' I nodded. 'That's what the village men are always saying.'

'They delude themselves,' said Master Merlin. 'More and more come and will come yet.'

'But why? I don't understand.'

He began to draw again, a much bigger area. 'Here is Brittany, where many of our people went to live. Here is Northern Gaul. Here are the lowlands of the continent, and to the north, more land. This is where the Saxons come from.

The drawing got bigger and bigger, spreading along the strand. 'Here the Angles, here the Jutes. Here the Franks, fighting into Gaul. Here the barbarian tribes spreading down into the Roman lands...'

'But Master Merlin, you must be wrong. You have made it too big. It is bigger than the whole of Britannia.'

'Aye, and so it is. Many times bigger.' His eyes crinkled with amusement. 'Did you think this small island was the biggest land in the world?

'Yes,' I said soberly. 'I did not guess that the world was so big.' My stomach felt hollow.

'Even this is only a small part. There is Africa here... and China here ...'

'Where is Constantinople?'

'Down here.'

'And Rome?'

'Not so far, here.'

I stared at the map.

'But if it is all so big, why do they come here to our lands?'

'Rhianna, this is a time of great movements of peoples. Here, out of the east have come nomadic peoples, bloodthirsty, swift on horses, great warriors bearing down on the peoples of Europe, driving them westward. They, in turn, drive the people already living there further west, and further. These low-lying lands, are marshland, wet and boggy. The soil is poor, difficult to farm. So, they have looked westward and seen that this land has rich soil, good farming land, left derelict from the migration of our people to Brittany after the Romans left, and they have come. Many keels full of men, ready to fight fiercely for new land. At first, they made treaties, and were welcomed, but more come from many tribes and they try to take what they are not given. Their princes are strong and greedy, wanting lands and riches and above all power, like all princes.'

'And Arthur?'

'Arthur seeks to defend what is left, and unite all the British Kings against the invaders.'

I said, 'I do not think most of us care who struts about with a crown on his head and a gold torc round his throat in Winchester, or Carnarvon or the City of the Legions, if all we get is war, starvation and destruction, and our men lie dead in some field far from home. We women want to live in peace, feed our families well. Bring up our children so they live long and healthy lives.' Master Merlin stared at me. 'And you know, Master, I do not believe that men go off to war reluctantly, just to save the Cymry. I have seen them go, excited and singing, anxious to get away from the village. They like fighting and killing. They enjoy it.'

He smiled, reluctantly. 'I am afraid there is much truth in that. We are a warrior people, quarrelsome. The way to gain respect, fame, a fine wife and house, is to become a great fighter, a hero who will feast with the Gods when he dies.'

'And nobody cares about the people who grow the food, or weave the beautiful cloth, or make comfortable houses and wonderful gardens...'

'You need to hold the land first, to do any of those things, Rhianna.'

I did not answer, but collected up my cloak, and prepared to stalk off.

'Don't you want the second book of Homer to work on?'

I turned quickly, eagerly, 'You truly have it?'

'Where is your translation of the first book?'

'I left it on your bench.'

'I will look at it and we will discuss it next time you come.' He swung his stick along the strand, obliterating his drawings from the sand, but not from my mind. He put his hand on my shoulder. 'By the way, I have found a new Galen treatise about the action of the heart, which you will find very interesting.' And we went up the path together to fetch it.

Rhianna 13

I am very busy. There are not enough days to do all I want to do.

With Master Merlin's help, my written Latin has improved. It has become fluent and it looks more accomplished. Even Aella has ceased to complain.

I continue with the Greek and Sanskrit studies, learning the new words, translating texts of marvellous poems and stories, finding new healing knowledge in the Master's collection of scrolls. We go to wonderful places where I can hear the languages spoken and see temples and palaces, sculptures and paintings and once, a huge tapestry, covering the whole wall with brilliant people and animals in a garden sewn with real gold threads.

I am very busy in the garden, always increasing our stock of plants and vegetables. I love finding new plants in the Forest, and bringing them home. They grow well and Aella says it looks like a Paradise garden. Perhaps it would make a good tapestry, if only I could weave. I have tried to paint murals similar to those I saw in the temple caves, on the inside walls of our house, but I cannot find the colours I would like. How can I make that glorious sky blue? Or sunset red? I asked Ethne who makes dyes for the Weaving Hall. She said that blue is impossible, but I might get a good red from the madder plant. I have tried, but it is the wrong red. I want a bright orangey colour. I will have to experiment mixing several colours and I will start to look for plants that will make dyes.

The apple tree I planted last year has grown to six feet and has blossoms, so we may have apples this year!

What else do I do? Oh yes, I make all our medicines and ointments, and even the little clay pots we put them in.

I go to the Forest, see all my friends and the Lady in the pool.

And, of course, I accompany Aella to her patients, learning all the time.

And then there are my magical studies, which are the most absorbing, exciting and wondrous, of all the things I do but I must be very careful what I write down about them. They are secret, and with good reason. In the wrong hands there is potential for immense destruction.

From my earliest years Aella taught me simple Avalonian spells of repair, renewal and protection, useful things like making fire and light, but, of course, Avalon inherited its magic from the survivors of Atlantis, via Ancient Egypt, which is an extensive labyrinth of scientific ideas, based on the particle theory of matter, involving gases and liquids, as well as the manipulation of particles as well as matter. And I have been doing advanced research for a long time, exhausting Aella's own knowledge, she says, so I was very happy to find that Master Merlin could take me further. His own magic has evolved to include other systems he learned in Persia and the East, which has greatly added to my range. I know now how to travel to the past, and other places in the present, but the future is only allowed briefly and unpredictably, according to the Goddess' will. Master Merlin has concentrated on showing me ways of developing and controlling my mind, like the meditation practice which we saw in a Temple, and I think that this might be the most valuable of all in the long term. It is certainly the most difficult. And I have learned to move swift and invisible, which he says is an advanced practice from monasteries high up the great Himalayan mountains, which are spectacular.

There are so many kinds of magic. The other one I know best, is that used by the little dark people. I made friends long ago, and they taught me their magic and healing, which uses the energies of the earth. I find this magic very sympathetic and use it frequently.

And then there is the magic of the Word, for spells, and spellbinding but I am not always happy using the latter. It has its place, but I do not like to make people do things against their will. It smacks too much of the dark side.

Anyway, what I want to say is that I have a very satisfying life that I love. It is busy, wonderfully interesting with an incredible teacher. I am so very lucky, I know that. But... But there is something missing. Sometimes my hands ache to do something else, but I don't know what it is. There is a gap. A space which I need to fill. Something very, very important. I have asked the Lady. She says, 'Have patience. It will come.' I have consulted Master Merlin, and he too says 'Wait.' But time is going past and somehow, I feel that there is an urgency to the problem.

Rhianna 14

One day, when I got back from the Forest, I was astonished to find Ailidh in the healing space with Aella.

She was holding both arms out, exasperated. 'What am I to do with these? Every year the same thing, and I am as helpless as a six day babe, just when we need all hands at the weaving.' Both arms were red and swollen to the elbow with a weeping rash.

Aella examined her skin carefully. 'I have seen this before.'

As had I. I pushed away my spinning, and was already at the narrow board grinding the mix of centaury and camomile into the ointment she would need to take the heat from the skin, and assist the healing. I added a little hypericum for the sharp pain, and chanted under my breath the healing spells to seal them.

I knew that as she held Ailidh's hands, Aella was using her healer's touch. 'It is the lambs,' she said. 'Or rather, the oils in the fleeces. You have been handling the raw fleece. Your skin does not like the oils, You must let others handle the raw fleeces until they are washed, and then perhaps, bind up your hands before you work.'

Ailidh stared. 'Yes, it's true. Every year when I work on the fleeces, my hands break out into these pustules. You would think that after all these years they would be hardened. You are sure it is the fleeces?'

Aella fetched a bowl of pure spring water, and sprinkled some ground herbs into it.

'The oils in the fleece. Many people have the same trouble.'

'Can you give me something to help the healing?'

'This will reduce the smarting and cleanse the open places. Rinse your hands and arms and dry them.'

Ailidh plunged her hands into the water, heaping it over her forearms and shook them both dry, smiling.

'You are a miracle worker, Mother Aella, and we are lucky to have you in the village. It was a great day when you came here. Already the smarting has gone.'

'Rhia is making you an ointment. Use it three times a day. Will you sit? She will take only a few minutes.'

Ailidh sat down and spread her skirts. 'I'm glad to take a few minutes in a busy day. It is comfortable here. Peaceful.' Idly she picked up my spinning and examined the thread professionally, 'You know this is remarkably fine. Very delicate and even. No knots or fraying. I've noticed it before, Rhia, you are a champion spinner, do you know that?'

I went red. 'Thank you, ma'am. I like spinning and making the dye bath from the herbs.' While they watched, I scooped the ointment deftly from the bowl into one of the small baked pots we made for the purpose, smoothed the top, and secured the shallow lid with a spot of warm wax, and presented it to Ailidh with a little curtsey. She smiled her thanks.

Aella said, 'Of course, weaving is what she wants to do. But I have no skill there. In the place where I was born it wasn't necessary. We had master weavers who did all the household weaving.'

'I have heard of this.' Angeal sighed. 'I wish it were so here, but we have to keep at it or we would all go bare arsed! Too many bodies. Too little time.' She got to her feet still staring at the spun yarn. 'She is young yet,' she said frowning with thought. 'But very neat handed.' Then she made up her mind. 'Yes, well why not? Listen, Rhia can come to me. Yes, that's it, Mother Aella. If you would agree, Rhia can come to me and I will teach her. We need good weavers, and I can do little at the moment. It is a useful skill, and will be serviceable in her future.'

Aella looked at me. I was scarlet with excitement, unable to speak for a moment, then I stuttered out, 'Please, grandmother!' And she smiled. 'Very well. Thank you, Ailidh, if you are willing.'

All I could do was to give a little dance of excitement. 'Oh Ma'am, thank you, thank you. May I come tomorrow?'

Ailidh laughed. 'My, you are enthusiastic! May it continue! Tomorrow then.' She put two coins on the table. But Aella pushed them back to her. 'The teaching of such a skill is more payment than is owed for a pot of ointment.'

Rhianna 15

I can't think of anything but weaving. The ideas are bursting out. It is as though they have been penned up and have now escaped. Ailidh is an exceptional weaver, known through all the near villages and beyond, for her skill, and I find she is a wonderful teacher too.

She started me on the narrow tablet loom, which made girdles or baldrics for swords and bags, or borders for cloaks and tunics and skirts, or could be sewn together to make wider fabric. It was easy and quick to change the patterns and the fabric grows quickly.

And then she showed me how to weave without a loom, using stones tied to the warp thread, as our people had done before the Romans came, or even across a table or board. And then she showed me how to set up the big, complicated loom in the Weaving Hall, with the rows of the lark's head knots. But most of all she taught me the patterns of the weave – the plaids and stripes our people like so much, and their subtle changes of colour, so that dull brown became bright russet with red threads added and could be made to glow beautifully when a blue-green was placed alongside.

And I soak it all up, learning quickly, as though I have known it before. I am happier than I have ever been. I am wild to experiment, invent my own patterns, and I know, at last, that the gap has been filled and I have found my life's work. I remembered the woman weaving in the room that the Lady of the Pool had shown me, and realised it was myself in the future.

The village trades its woollen cloth for the goods and materials it cannot make for itself, and within a short time my cloth was being sold. I love weaving so much and want to do it all the time. Very soon I began to add touches to the designs, a different kind of stripe, knots that altered the texture.

I experimented with the border designs and found that I could do so much more than the traditional geometric designs. I could even make the twining, trailing patterns with the birds and animals that peer between the leaves and then became something else, like the illustrations some monks are using in their holy books.

My work is becoming known, Ailidh said my designs were the first to be chosen at the Fairs, and she is very proud of me and my contribution to the well-being of the village. One good at least has come of it. The bullying and name-calling have stopped and I feel safe.

I am always busy. The Lady of the Pool said, 'Don't forget your healing. That is important too. Find new ways to heal. Join up your thinking!' I am not sure what she means, but I went back to the garden, which I had recently neglected a little, and began a collection of plants which might make rich colour when I dye the spun yarn.

Aella 25

I began to hear more frequently from Morgan, which reassured me that we were not forgotten. She, too, was exceptionally busy, involved with Merlin in law-making, setting up local councils, and developing trade, receiving trade delegations, involved in taxation and raising monies for the High King, always complaining that most of the work was left to her, and that Merlin was often absent for long periods, nobody knowing where he was.

Well, I could have enlightened her on that!

It seemed, according to Morgan, that great strides were being made, and that the land was becoming more secure and settled. Arthur, since the great victory at Badon, had begun to build a huge new castle near Cadbury in the Summer Country, called Camelot, which he intended to make his capital, and once this was built, she had great hopes she would be granted her lands in the west, where we could all live together again...

On this point I held no great hopes. I could not see why Arthur delayed. He clearly needed her for the rebuilding of the civil structures in the broken land, but nothing prevented the assignment of her inheritance. He was using it as a tether to keep her at his Court. I wondered what would happen when her patience ran out and she realised she was trapped. Morgan needed her freedom like she needed air. She was a wild creature who could not live in captivity. She became mad and destructive when confined. I remembered that wild-eyed mad child with tangled hair, spitting and screaming, as I had first known her, ready to kill herself rather than submit, and I was, once again, filled with anxiety and pity for her.

Meanwhile Rhianna and I thrived. We had our work and the respect of the community. Rhianna made great advances in her studies, and Merlin opened the whole world to her. Books of all kinds flowed to her, on healing and herbs, and very soon she was surpassing me in surgical techniques and knowledge of the mental healing of people and animals.

She still disappeared to visit her friends in the Forest, and our garden expanded with all manner of plants for many illnesses. Our reputation spread in the villages around and always there were people waiting for our help.

One thing I could not understand and worried about, was Rhianna's growing obsession with weaving. This most basic of domestic activities was not fitting for a mage of her lineage. Most women of her kind had others to weave for them. It was a servant's job, but Rhianna would not give it up, however busy she was, and slipped away to the Weaving Hall whenever she could. Ailidh, the Head Weaver, reported with misplaced glee and some awe, I thought, that her work was of the very highest quality, innovative in techniques and colours, and was selling well for the village in Glevum market.

I knew about the colours, of course. Rhianna had set up

her pottery bowls of colour in a lean-to shed she had persuaded Julius and Titus to make for her, in return for a big pot of her most successful salve for the bone pain. She was using many plants and grasses to make the new colours, and I suppose it was a natural extension of her interest in herbs and medicines. She did not stop at plain weave cloth either, but began using patterns and shape together, and I realised at last that she was weaving hangings such as my father had on his walls, and which came from Gaul at great cost.

But why did Rhianna want to make them when her business was healing? She could not seem to explain, and eventually I just accepted it as a strange quirk of personality, as we do with all those we love deeply. I could not complain because she did not neglect her healing, which grew deeper and stronger.

At first, I was worried that her extraordinary abilities and the attention they brought her might make her conceited and spoilt. But it did not occur to her that she was in any way unusual. She went about her daily activities with great interest, always busy, always trying to discover better ways of doing something, and always with love and joy.

I could not conceive of a better, more dutiful granddaughter. I relied on her more and more, and she repaid my trust a thousand -fold.

We continued our magical studies, of course, Atlantean as it was in Avalon and scientifically based, but I knew that she had learned a different, earth-based magic using the magnetic flow of the earth, from the little dark people, and Merlin began to teach her his own esoteric magic, learned from many sources and his travels in distant countries. He passed this on to her judiciously, very carefully, as he had done with Arthur, and it became obvious that he was here for exactly the same purpose – to protect her, but also to educate and prepare a possible heir to the High Kingship should Arthur and Lachau die untimely.

This brought Medraut to my mind. What had happened to him? He was the younger child and I pondered what Mawgawse might have taught him. He was 'Sister's son' and so was her own son Gawain. A cold feeling moved down my spine as I wondered if either of them had inherited the family's magical abilities.

We kept all the magical studies secret, and Rhianna never spoke of them. Her early betrayal had taught her well the dangers of it becoming known, and she used magic with extreme discretion, so that even I did not always know when she had exercised it – except when she played jokes on me – causing my bed fur to leap on me like a wild animal, and set me screeching was a favourite, or making my bowl of porridge jump around the table like a frog, or turning our hens invisible so that I searched for them for half an hour to shut them safely in the hen house, only to find that they were already assembled there and looking at me as though I was totally mad.

I flattered myself that my girl was as highly educated as any of the noble maidens at the Avalon school. I did not think that Morgan would be disappointed when she met her daughter again. It had been a daunting task to take on the raising of such a special child, but I thought that I had done as well as I could and had succeeded, for which I heartily thanked the Goddess.

Rhianna 16

Since she came back from meeting Master Merlin weeks ago, Aella had been even more mysterious than usual. Regularly, at least once a week, she leaves the house, at dead of night, returning noiselessly an hour or so later. After a while I could not stand the mystery any longer, and I followed her.

She circles as many of the village houses as she can without waking the dogs, whispering spells. I listened carefully, caught several words, and realised, with astonishment, that Aella was casting warding spells, weaving a net of protection over the village. I knew that our house was triple warded, but now she has renewed all the wardings and extended them down and around our nearest neighbours.

I knew that Aella had an obsession about safety. From as far back as I remember she has issued warnings to me. She explained to me that we were hiding from powerful enemies, and must remember to hide ourselves as much as possible, and not draw attention to ourselves. It was a relief to her, I think, that we lived in the very last house of the village, not overlooked by other houses and she suggested to me that we grow plants over it. I was delighted with this suggestion and I brought back from the Forest some lovely flowering and climbing plants like honeysuckle and wisteria, that quickly formed a sweet-smelling screen all over the thatch. But Aella was not interested in the decoration, she was hiding it from view, and if you came up the track you could easily overlook it as just another part of the Forest.

I didn't understand her anxiety for a long time, and thought it one of her mild eccentricities, a paranoia caused, perhaps, by some incident in her early life. I mean, why would we have enemies, living so quietly, when we had never harmed anybody? Who were these enemies? But Aella said that they were my mother's enemies, who would like to harm us to punish my mother. And, in any case, if you had unusual abilities, you did not need to do anything, for some people to dislike or even hate you. There was fear and jealousy, for instance, and differences of religion.

I knew that her fears were not entirely imagination. There was the woman, a wholly malevolent force, who tried to scry us from a distance from time to time, and tried to come into my mind. I was not afraid of her. My powers were already so much greater than hers, that it amused me, and I would step into her mind instead, and make her do stupid things, until Aella said that it was a black art and I must not do it. As I grew, her attacks virtually stopped, and I almost forgot about them. But Aella did not.

'She's gone!' I said, 'Nothing to worry about.'

Aella smiled grimly. 'For people like us, people with rare abilities, there are always enemies, Rhianna. Be alert. Be aware. Keep secret. Keep hidden. Do not tell even your friends.'

'Yes, yes. I understand. You must not worry so much.' I would say to sooth her, and then forget all about it. Until the trouble over Warrior, and the lesson I learned then, I have never forgotten and never will.

In the autumn, Rhoswen, Ailidh, and Brigitta, packed up all our weavings and, with the help of a couple of the older men to carry the heaviest packs took them all off to the Autumn Fair, at Glevum. They came back triumphant, calling and laughing, having sold everything at very good prices. They brought with them much needed goods – thin needles and cotton thread, combs, iron cauldrons, well-made leather boots, furs for the winter, and. as a special treat, ten large jars of wine from Gaul for the end of year feast.

I had made a few wall hangings, as well as cloth for clothes, and I was delighted to find that they had sold very quickly, Ailidh said that perhaps I should concentrate on more of them, but for the moment I was planning a new project.

As the last few leaves fluttered on the trees, to my annoyance Aella had once again brought forth her tattered and torn old cloak, with its frayed edge. I had no idea how old this cloak was, but enough was enough and I was determined to make a new cloak for her. I spun the yarn smoothly and began to think about the colour. A deep violet blue colour was her favourite, a Priestess colour, but I wanted to make it paler at the top, darkening as it went down to a darker smoke, so that a person could disappear into the mist or moonlight, and fade into the shadows at dawn. Aella would like that. She liked soft, quiet colours. I collected a basket of blackberries, which would form the base of my violet dye bath, and it occurred to me that it might be a good idea to include a spell to overcome her chronic anxiety, which seemed to be getting worse. The only trouble about that was that the spell would need to be renewed regularly, as it faded.

And then I had my idea, an idea that afterwards gave me my small fame, or infamy, the Christians would say. I made a invocation to the Great Goddess and began to chant spells and prayers deeply into the cloth as I wove it, so that they would be there for all time.

I tried to work quickly, because I had begun to feel somehow that the time was running out, but I found that it took longer than the old way of weaving, and I was afraid the danger would be upon Aella before I could finish it. I rose earlier each day and worked into the night, snatching every moment during the day to add a few inches. I worked on Ailidh's loom, and we kept it as a surprise for Aella.

As I got used to the new way of working it grew more quickly It was good to look at: Soft, rich cloth, graduating in colour from palest blue-violet to deepest violet. I needed many lengths of cloth because the loom was narrow and the cloak must be shaped to hang full and comfortably.

I used up every spare moment. Aella still had no idea it was intended for her, but she came sometimes to see its progress. Ailidh was full of admiration, saying the cloak was fit for a queen.

But I was not entirely satisfied. There was something missing.

I worked all winter, and when there was a smell of growth and damp in the air and tiny buds appeared on the dark fretwork of the tree branches, I became increasingly restless, unable to settle to anything. It seemed that something was about to happen. I went to see the Lady of the Pool to see if she knew what I should expect.

She appeared very quickly and seemed a little agitated. 'Change and danger,' she said.

You must beware. Something comes. Use your knowledge. Practice the spells for protection. Look to the herbs. Use your gifts.'

I was shaken. The pool was shivering as though a wind was moving the surface. But there was no wind. It was the Lady's agitation.

'What gifts, Lady?'

'Power. Fire. Transformation. Tell Aella. Lose no time.'

But when I got home, I found Aella was already packing our few treasures into the plain wooden box, which she later buried deep under the hearth stone that bore our fire. Over the next weeks, the house became stripped of anything anybody would want to steal. The hangings I had made came down and were rolled into a skin and were hidden under the thatch.

Aella began to go through our stocks of herbs and medicines, carefully setting some aside which she packed into little cloth pouches, which she folded into the deep pockets of her robe and tunic. I looked to see what had disappeared from the shelf and was shocked. Aconite. Hemlock. Digitalis. Arsenicum. And the dark berries of Nightshade – all of them deadly poisons, unless you knew the exact dosage for their healing uses. All of them were sovereign for certain illnesses. The rest of the herbs she packed into wooden boxes which were hidden in an old hut in the fringes of the forest.

I was bewildered. 'Are we going somewhere, Aella?'

For the first time in several days, she stopped her whirlwind activity and stood staring at me.

'I don't know Rhianna. I feel strongly that there is danger.'

'A foretelling?'

'It is not my skill, but this time I believe that something is coming. Perhaps the Mother has whispered to me. She tried to smile but only succeeded in looking uneasy.

'I have that feeling too. The Lady of the Pool says we must look to protection.'

She looked relieved. 'Aah, I was right then. I am not just a scared old woman.' She got up, staring into the roof. 'And now we must make a hiding place, and another way out, perhaps,'

I looked around at the small space and could not help laughing. It was so bare now and everything could be seen at a glance.

'In the thatch,' she said. 'A space for you and a hole in the roof that you can get out of and slide down the thatch to the ground, and hide in the Forest.'

After some thought she went along to Rhoswen, our Head Woman and borrowed her wooden ladder, explaining that we needed to attend to the thatch after the winter rains. High up in the most shadowy area we had a shelf for the drying of herbs. We added another plank across the two house posts and packed thatch around the planks, so they could not be seen. Aella cut a hole in the roof with a knife. It was big enough to put your head and arms through, and draw yourself up and out. Then she covered the hole with a loose layer of rushes so that all that was needed was a quick push to allow an easy exit.

'There's room for only one person, Aella.'

'For you. They won't bother with me.'

'They? What are you expecting? You have always said we

are safe here.'

'So we have been for many years. But the Spring is coming. In a few weeks our men will be gone again. Morgan says there was raiding along the Cymru coast. Or there could be a a war band from some great lord, out of control and looking to line their pockets.'

I said, shocked, 'Surely not the Bear or his Companions. They wouldn't do that would they?'

She smiled bitterly. 'Perhaps not, but it hardly matters to poor people who comes. The country is still in turmoil with Lord fighting Lord, despite all of King Arthur's efforts. These wolves take what they want and leave death and ruin behind. This is a village of woman and children and a few old injured men. We are vulnerable, although fortunately we are further inland, hidden along our river, not visible from the estuary. But our cloth and weavings are well-known and desired. Rich pickings. Word gets around.'

I was beginning to be alarmed, understanding that we might be in real danger and from that moment on I worried about Aella. I thought about her as I climbed up to my studies with Master Merlin, and when I walked behind her on our healing rounds, and I thought about her, when I worked in the herb garden. And when the solution came to me, I laughed, because it was so simple.

'Aella, can you make yourself invisible?'

She said sourly, 'I'm a wise woman, not an enchantress.'

'So how are we to protect you?'

'Don't worry about me. You would be the one in greatest danger.'

But I already knew what to do. The cloak I was weaving

for her, I would make into a very special cloak. I would add to the spells for protection, against disease, and all the things I could think of, another spell that would make her invisible if she desired that. Invisibility was the answer to keeping her safe. Unfortunately, the invisibility spells did not work very well. They faded quickly and needed to be renewed constantly.

I worked very hard trying out new ideas, and eventually, as I began to look forward to my fifteenth birthday, the answer came. This time I spun thread so fine that it seemed that a spider might have made it, and I wove it into a series of narrow panels, light and airy, that lifted in the breeze, and these I attached to the cloak, like a shoulder cape, wing-like. This time, when the cloak moved the panels drifted gently before settling against the wool, and softened the outline of the cloak, so it became difficult to see. I had woven into them a thin silver thread which I found in the silk market of Athens, which held a strong glamour against recognition.

'Are you finished, child?' Aella said at my elbow, a strange note in her voice, of respect or awe, I thought. 'It is a great work. Beautiful. We have never seen anything like it before.

'A cloak!' I said gleefully. 'A cloak for you. I have finished it. Try it.' And I slipped it around her shoulders and turned her around so that the thin panels fluttered, rose and fell. It is a cloak of protection for you. A cloak of invisibility. See when the scarves move you are almost impossible to see.'

She turned, drawing it around her, feeling its softness and warmth. There is more than invisibility here. I can feel it. There is...healing...and protection against...disease, fire...'

'Oh, dozens of things. Everything I could think of. Do you like it? It is my first real weaving. I think.'

She drew a deep breath. 'Oh Rhiannon, it is so beautiful.' She let the cloth slid between her fingers. 'It's wondrous, out of this world. It's too good for me.'

'Nothing is too good for you! You have loved and looked after me and taught me all my days. It is a thank- you present.'

'As Ailidh says, it is a cloak for a queen.'

'You are a queen. It will keep you safe and invisible.'

She hugged me tightly, tears brimming in her eyes. 'The Goddess' blessing on you child, but when will I ever wear it?'

'When the raiders come.' I said grinning, because I was still half persuaded that this was a figment of our imaginations. After all I had heard similar stories all my life around the hearth fires, and I'd never seen any evidence of them. All was normal. Imbolc had come and gone and the Spring had come, the Branch had come and the men had marched off as usual with the Lord.

All the same, I was very glad that I had finished Aella's special cloak, and felt much less worried about the possible dangers.

Together we finished collecting and packing the herbs, and storing them in the Forest, and then Aella made the village women stand together in a dawn ring and chant the old spells of protection against fire and injury, but some, who followed the Christ, would not join in.

But for all our preparations, I was away from home deep in the Forest, consulting the Lady of the Pool before first light, when the raiders came, two weeks after I had finished my first cloak. Aella was right. They came from the sea in their curraghs, Irish raiders, along the Sabrina Sea and up our tributary river, sacking and burning the houses along its banks. A strong pungent smell spread over the trees.

'Burning!' we said together.

'Go quickly,' The Lady, cried. 'The killers are at your door. Go deeper in the Forest and hide until they are gone.'

I said, 'There's Aella. I must find Aella,' and heard the Lady calling, as I bounded back along the forest paths.

I was not stupid. When I reached the edge of the Forest, I climbed up a tall tree that I knew would give me a long view of the whole village path, as it sloped down to the river. It was a terrible sight.

Part Seven

Rhianna 17

The round houses on both sides of the path in the lower part of the village and by the landing stage were nearly all alight. Gangs of the tall, black bearded raiders were dragging their furnishings out on to the road and carrying them down to the river where I could see their boats, three of them, were drawn up. There seemed to be dozens of the men. And then I saw that they were dragging out the village people too. And I watched the slaughter and then the rape too, and knew what Aella had always feared.

Isarnos, our blacksmith, who had been severely injured at Badon, and Daft Jamie were already dead, motionless on the planks of the landing stage, where they had tried to stop the boats landing, and their bodies were kicked unceremoniously into the river to clear the planking for plunder. Our herd of cows were bellowing, being butchered, their bloody meat being loaded into the boats.

As I watched, a huge raider came out of Branwen's hut, where the thatch was well alight, laughing uproariously, head thrown back, with Branwen's little baby screaming on the end of his spear.

'Little pig, squealing!' he shouted, and tossed the baby back into the inferno behind him.

I stared and stared unbelieving, letting the horror penetrate my understanding and the red hate flooded my mind and through all my limbs, and I could feel the energies of it gathering.

The man went into the next round house, and dragged forth little lame Liath, an orphan, we had saved from pneumonia, and I wailed with despair, expecting him to spear her too and throw her into the fire, but he wanted some sport first. He ripped off her rags, leaving her thin, blue- white body naked, and then he was on her like a wild beast, thrusting his bloated, engorged member into her, and his men came along then, shouting about him, laughing and counting.

'Come on. Come on. Our turn, our turn.'

I felt the hate flooding. Poor little Liath, only eleven years old...

Then I saw my friend Ailidh come out of the Weaving Hall behind them. 'No,' I thought. 'NO!'

She was wild, like an Avenging Goddess, magnificent, cursing them and screaming, waving a big sword, a rusty old Roman sword, and she swooped at their backs, and one, two, three of the heads bounded away down the path, and another man fell as she chopped at his knees. But there were too many of them, and they were on her, trying to twist away the sword, but she had turned it and slashed at her own neck, and already her blood was fountaining over them.

'Ailidh!' I whispered, 'Ailidh!' And absurdly could only think that she would not need our ointment again.

The big man stood back laughing, and casually thrust his spear into little Liath as she tried to crawl away.

And then I could not hold it back. The red hate flooded, burned, and ran with a superhuman strength and energy through my veins, grew and grew. I stretched both my arms, reaching and pointing at the big man, and the power burst from my fingers, invisible but deadly. I had never done such a thing before, however angry I had been, and I had promised Aella more than once that I would never turn to the dark side of my powers. I did not know what it would do. He was too far away surely, but the power flowed out thick and strong with a beautiful, satisfying ease and release, snaked with incredible speed towards him and a second later he exploded into flames, and it was my turn to laugh, as he stood, his face transfixed with horror and agony before being engulfed. The flames died and the hideous shrunken thing only half his height now, toppled into the sewage ditch.

His men staggered back, horrified, staring, unbelieving.

'What happened?'

'Didn't see.'

'Must have been a spark from the hut.'

'He just burst into flame!' He turned away and vomited.

They looked over their shoulders uneasily. 'Sorcery.'

'He's done for, anyway. Let's go.'

'What of the huts up at the end there?' They turned and Isarnos's women came screaming down on them, the three girls, the sister-in-law, Lania and even the old grandmother, all wielding spears, a band of Furies, with Rhoswen, whirling a heavy axe around her head.

I was holding on to the branches, sick and giddy, the power

gone from me, so that I hung limp like a rag, unable to move. And how I wanted to move. I wanted to kill all the raiders, one at a time, but I could do nothing, the power was gone and oh, Goddess! Here came another party of them up from the houses near the river. Three of the men dragged Gitta and Aine down the hill.

'Poor pickings. Not enough to buy a goat.

'Put a brand to the rest of the houses and let's go.'

'Tried. Thatch won't burn. Must be wet.'

And I came alive again in horror. Aella, where was Aella?

Somehow, I found the strength to scramble down the tree, and ran the few yards to the back of the house and darted through the door.

Aella turned from the cauldron which she was, strangely, still tending, taking no notice of the shouting outside. She cried out in despair, 'Rhianna. Oh Goddess. What are you doing? Up, up. Up!' And thrust me upwards to the roof hidey hole.

We could hear the men nearby in Brigitta's house now, dragging out her kegs of ale, with triumphant shouts. Where was Brigitta? I hoped she had got away to the Forest.

'Where...?' I was peering down through the concealing thatch.

'Out and into the Forest with you. Now.'

'Where's the Cloak? You need it now.' I scrabbled around and found the cloak where we had carefully wrapped it, and threw it down to her. 'Here.'

'No. I'm alright, I tell you. I have scores to settle. Now be quiet. No sound.'

Aella suddenly was a different person. Her voice brooking no argument, was one of authority and power. And surely, she was looking different too, smaller, bent, incredibly ancient, crouching in rags (rags?) by the cauldron steaming on the hearth.

I pressed my hand to my mouth to stop the hysterical giggle when I realised she had wrapped herself in a spell that would deceive the eye. Not a moment too soon.

'What have we here then?' The man with the gold arm bands stood at the door peering in.

Aella whimpered and flung her rags over her head and crouched close to the floor.

'Food, by God! Food!' The cauldron gently simmered, with a wonderful smell of meat and garlic.

Armbands was looking round the bare hut. Nothing. A few pots. A bed place with blankets and a fur. He shoved his spear into the bed and scattered them over the floor. Nothing. No hidden gold pieces. He glanced up. Nothing. This village was poorer than his own at home. Just the cauldron gently simmering with a wonderful smell of meat and garlic.

'All clear,' said the second man, coming in. 'They're all dead bar ten slaves. But we've lost some, ten at the landing, and six in the lane. Some wounded bad.'

'Too many,' mumbled Armbands, still looking around. There was something here. Something wrong and dangerous. It was lifting the hairs on his forearms.

'We couldn't hold the woman. A berserker.'

'And Eoghain's gone. A hero. They won't like that.

'Eoghain! I don't believe it. Nobody could best him. What happened?'

The man's voice shook. 'It was horrible. He... just burst into flame. Like a burning log. Uncanny. It must have been a spark from the fires. He was careless.'

The other growled, 'He was my wife's brother.'

'You'll be the new Chief.' He coughed apologetically. 'Are we going to eat this?' He shoved his sword, still red with blood, into the cauldron and stirred it, releasing another burst of stew. I thought that my grandmother must have used up our entire stock of dried beef. But the smell was wonderful. I could feel my mouth watering. Garlic, Onions, Barley. Strong flavours.

Armbands looked around again. 'Nothing here. Let's go.'

'What about the food. I'm starving. Pity to leave it. All the boys have been searching. A few loaves. A bag of rotten apples. We're all starving. It'll be a long night on the seas.'

Aella came to life, crawling forward, and my heart jumped into my throat. What was she doing? They would kill her as they left.

'Oh no, please sir. Please don't take the broth, it's all we have to live on. Please sir. Everything's gone. We'll starve...'

I suddenly caught my breath. I remembered the little pouches of herbs in Aella's pocket. Surely Aella hadn't...' And then I was sure she had.

'Oh, very well. Drag the cauldron outside. No wait. Feed the hag a cup of the stew to see if it's safe.'

The other man had found a broken crock and dipped it into the broth. 'Drink Woman.' Aella took the cup with a palsied hand, muttering, whining. 'My stew...my stew...all I've got.'

I closed my eyes and held my breath, praying, reaching out to Aella. If she had already salted the stew with the deadly poisons she would be gone in the next few minutes.

'Don't worry, child.' It came into my mind clearly, amazingly, I had never guessed we could mind-speak. I opened my eyes and saw the two men watching Aella, who said resentfully. 'Good broth. My best broth,' and held up her hands pitifully. 'More?The second man laughed and kicked away the crock from her hands.

'Get the cauldron outside,' said Armbands. 'I don't like this place. Something unchancy about it. And get rid of her.'

Now that I knew Aella's plan, I wondered how I could distract the man for a few moments so that she could put it into action.

He put his hand to the cauldron handle, which he found was much hotter than he thought, and was now glowing with heat. He howled and stamped around the room blowing on his palm, and hiding it under his armpit. And Aella swifter than thought had hurled in her first pouch. But it might not be enough. She needed more time. I grinned suddenly, as he stamped around again, kicking the bed fur out of his path. I turned it into a large grey mountain cat, which jumped, screaming, past him out of the door. It was one of my oldest spells and never failed to delight me.

'What the hell...?'

He had ducked instinctively and followed the cat to the door, grabbing, only to trip over a log that he had not noticed before, because I'd only just moved it there.

Aella had finished her business. Five more pouches had followed the first, and she had crawled away into the shadows, under the invisibility cloak.

Swearing the man picked himself up and looked for his spear to kill the old woman, but that too had disappeared into the shadows, under the invisibility cloak.

He swore again. 'Here, what's going on? Where's she gone?'

'Where's this food then?' Another voice shouted, and two more men came lurching into the space and began to carry the heavy cauldron outside into the sun. 'Here, you, leave that alone. It's my broth...' He tore after them.

There was silence in the shadowy round house as we concentrated on strengthening the invisibility spells. He might still come back looking for the old woman. We lay silent, listening to the feasting of Armbands and his men.

The stew was potent.

In less time than it took to launch one of their boats, twenty men lay dead outside our house.

And next door twenty- five drinkers lay, dead drunk, I thought, but Aella, said gravely that they too were poisoned. Brigitta had salted the kegs with Aella's herbs before slipping away into the Forest, along with some of the village woman and children.

Rhianna 18

When we were sure they were all dead, we crawled from our hiding places and Aella sat on the hearth stool, rocking to and fro, helpless with laughter.

'That log,' she choked, 'And the cat...' She had been startled by the cat trick often when I was younger. I was laughing too, rather hysterically, but laughing.

It was the last laugh we had for a long time. We went through the village looking for the injured and the dead. There was no movement. Only a few village bodies lay along the path, and the smell of burning hung heavily. We met Branwen coming up, covered in blood, her eyes wide and mad, carrying a long dripping butcher's knife. 'Got them! Trying to crawl away. I chopped them. Injured at the boats. Chopped their legs. Chopped their necks.'

'Branwen, my love, will you come with us? Aella said.

'Not now. I'm hunting. Cutting their throats. They took my baby – they've hidden him somewhere.' Blindly she pushed past. 'Where are they all?' and disappeared down the path to West Stillwell.

I said to Aella, feeling sick, 'The man I killed had him on his spear. He threw him back into the burning house. Should I tell her?'

'She knows,' Aella said, heavily. 'Let us hope that some of the women and children got away to the Forest. There is no one alive here.'

We found little Liath, lying at the side of the path, her thin legs blood smeared, a blue bruise on her forehead and a spear thrust in her back, but as we turned her over, amazingly she was still breathing. We carried her to our hut and quickly worked on her while she was still unconscious.

Soon the second-best cauldron was steaming with spring water and cleansing herbs and Aella washed her body with infinite gentleness that made me want to cry. We found that in one respect at any rate she had been lucky, the spear thrust had hit her shoulder blade and slid off into her rib bones. None of her vital organs or her lungs seemed to have been injured. Aella soaked the deep cuts and ripped flesh and poured healing herbs into the wounds and I sewed the slashes together carefully using the thinnest thread with tiny even stitches, so that the scars might disappear eventually if she lived.

'The knock on the head is what I fear most,' said Aella. 'The skull is not broken, I think. I cannot feel anything amiss.' Her tender hands were feeling through Liath's sparse fair hair. She was a delicate child, a fosterling who always looked half starved.

'What of Beti, her foster mother?'

'Dead, I think, if she was in the house. He fired the hut then brought Liath out. I didn't see Beti leave.'

'Liath has that snorting breathing. Concussion, I think. All we can do now is to let her lie quietly until the Goddess returns her to us.'

'And the rape?'

'She's torn, but I have used the numbing ointment.' She looked at the inert white body and covered it carefully. 'We can heal the body but the mind is a deep mystery and hard to heal.'

There were very few others who required our help. Further down the path near the river, they were all dead. Flung higgledy piggledy and butchered. The path of the village was soaked with red blood.

But there was great joy when we found the Isarnos women, all tied up together in the bottom of one of the curraghs, ready to be taken across the sea into slavery. They were all uninjured, except for the old Granny who had a broken leg.

We began to make a tally. All the older men were dead. They appeared to have made a brave stand near the beached boats. The lower houses too were all burned and the women and children had gone to the Otherworld. There had been no time for them to make a getaway to the Forest.

We carried our dead reverently to our burying place, and laid them carefully until we could begin the digging and burying.

Gradually the woman began to come back from the Perilous Forest. They had been alerted by the noise of the battle at the landing stage, which had delayed the raiders for the vital few minutes, allowing them to run for the Forest, dragging their little ones behind them, or snatched up to safety.

We looked to the burned houses. Some might be repaired with a new thatch. But Julius and Titus, thatchers and carpenters, were lying dead in our burying place. What would we do without a carpenter and thatcher? The round houses, the ones Aella had protected with her spells were intact, except for the cleansing needed to clear the blood and send the ghosts of their owners on their road to Annwn. and we wondered how the other small villages along our river had fared.

I thought suddenly of the Weaving Hall and tore down to see, my heart in my mouth. From the front it looked as though it had escaped but at the back, shards of flaming wood had embedded themselves in the new stored fleeces, rolled ready to spin, which were still burning. Our whole year's wool gone in a few minutes! And the looms, even Ailidh's, the largest in the village, which had made so much wonderful, magical cloth, were burned. The tears poured down my cheeks. I could not stop sobbing. What would I do without Ailidh? How could I learn without her genius?

When I got back, the others were discussing what had happened to the people in the other parts of the village. Merewin whose mother lived in one of them was like a taut wire, unable to settle, and volunteered to go see, and Seirial went with her. The rest of us turned to clearing up and making a great feast.

Merewin and Seirial came back before sunset, shaking their heads and looking sick. With them came a dazed small boy and his dog, and two chickens in a basket.

'Surely that's not all,' said Aella, and I could hear her voice shaking. We had healed people from all three villages and had made friends among them.

'Your mother?'

Merewin wiped away tears. 'Dead. Houses burned to the ground. Nothing left, not even the bodies. The cattle butchered. The sheep driven off. The goods taken. Maybe among the stuff in the boats.'

'Surely some must have escaped?'

'I think the raiders came upon them very quickly, while they slept. Only here, later, was there resistance.'

When the sun went down, we feasted on the meat of some of the animals the raiders had slaughtered. We built a huge fire of all the broken and blood-sullied things to drive away the ghosts, and we got drunk on the skins of honey-mead that we found in one of the raider's boats. Riotously drunk now, we cleared the curraghs of their stolen plunder and together, we all began to drag the bodies of the raiders to their boats, cleansing the village of their hated presence, not satisfied until they were all gone. We flung the bodies in without care or pity, like offal for pigs, shouting with hatred and pleasure, set the curragh's alight, and cast them off down the river to the sea, with howls and shrieks, worthy of a Wild Hunt, that loosened a little of our pain of loss.

The next morning was a gloomy heavy time. Ashamed, we went about our necessary business with heavy hearts and heavy heads.

'We behaved like animals,' I said to Aella, crying. 'And I killed in hate, using my magic for a dark thing. A destroying thing. It is very bad.'

Aella sighed. 'There are forty-five men dead from my healing herbs. Forty-five mothers birthed them, and I destroyed them. How do you think I feel? I settled old scores. I have waited for my revenge for many years. I thought I would enjoy it after this long time. We put them down like the mad dogs they were, but it is in my mind that we must make some sacrifice to the Goddess.'

'I will never do that again,' I said. 'I vow that I will never again use my magic to destroy, whatever the reason.'

Aella looked at me doubtfully. 'Perhaps you should, after all, keep that option open, Rhianna.'

Liath we kept under close care. She slept the snoring sleep, until early evening and then passed into normal sleep and we began to hope that she might get better. We bathed her hurts and dribbled spring water and herbs into her mouth and spelled her into forgetfulness and good health and hoped.

The little boy, Edryd, he said his name was, not yet eight years old, we fed and cuddled and spelled him into a deep sleep. He had been burned on his arm, and we bound it up and settled him with his dog. And the chickens escaped their basket and went to join our chickens that were still roosting in the trees at the edge of our garden.

Brigitta, our neighbour, returned, gleeful at the way she and Aella had spiked the kegs of ale with the poisons. She came in and threw her arms around Aella crying and laughing at the same time. 'It worked! I never thought it would. We were so clever! I've just burned the kegs in the yard. No chance of mixing them up with my next brewing!'

Aella smiled weakly. 'Death came close, but the village has survived. We will have a council to decide what must be done before the winter comes and our men return.'

'I came to ask if I could have the boy,' said Brigitta. 'Twenty years I was married, and twenty years I longed for a child and now I am too old, but I would love him dearly.'

Aella nodded. The Alewife was a cheerful, happy woman and she thought the boy would do well with her. She smiled. 'The boy and his dog. They won't be parted.'

The Alewife grinned. 'I wouldn't turn him away. I like dogs.'

* * *

The council convened under the oak in the centre of the upper village, a pitifully few people and fewer children, sombre in the sun. Rhoswen was another great loss for the community. The raiders had taken her for slavery but when she'd cursed them in the name of the Goddess Sabrina, they had simply thrown her in the water and the cruel currents had borne her away immediately.

Aella seemed to have been automatically chosen as the new Head woman, but she quickly set that right, insisting that they must choose someone born in the village.

'I might not always be here,' she said. 'You will need a sensible good-hearted person, who you all trust. I would nominate Lania. She would have the help of her girls, and her sons when they come home.'

Lania was trusted and much liked. She had been organising parties for the clearing of the blood and offal of the slaughter, so that the wolves would not be attracted by the smell, and cleansing the village well, so that disease would not follow the violence as it did so often.

The women decided on the allocation of the houses, and went to inspect and divide up the stolen goods left by the raiders, and to store the food in a spare hut. A party set to, salting the butchered meat to preserve it for the coming winter. And Brigitta, with helpers, began to brew again. Her barley sacks and grains had been blessedly preserved in the underground cellar she used for the purpose.

The raiders had taken woven hangings and clothes, and the women sorted and gave them out according to need, for the most part without serious disagreement as far as I could see. I suppose escape from death had made us all see that petty quarrels were nothing worth.

For all that, it would be a hard winter, lacking the grains and vegetables that had been burned, and other supplies like leather and cloth. We would have to weave in the old way of our people with the warp threads tied to stones, until a carpenter could be found to make new looms. Julius wife said that she had watched her husband all their married life and would try to do some of the repairs needed, until Tegus came home.

And so, gradually the village returned to life. No one suggested that we should go to the other villages and clear away what remained. My ravens had been noticeably absent for a few days and I shuddered to think what they were about.

It was a while before we thought of Master Merlin. I was ashamed that his welfare had gone out of my head, and I had failed to go to my usual lesson, or take his bannocks. But next day, he came limping into the village, grave and anxious, asking if we needed help.

I ran to him, hugging him with delight that he had escaped the attention of the raiders. He sat with us at our evening meal, listening to our stories tumbling out and grunting with distress at the atrocities.

Later I spoke to him, telling him how I had killed the big man and he said that my punishment would be in the shame lodged always in my memory, and I should do as the Christ had said, 'Repent and go and sin no more'.

'Master,' I said, 'Although we have worked hard and cleansed the village, the violence is still here. The ghosts are still here, moaning in the night wind. The hate is still here. How can we drive these things away?'

He said he would see to it, and he walked through the village, scattering sweet smelling, seeds, chanting, and then, suddenly, screaming and howling terrifying spells in a language I did not know. Everyone quickly dispersed, very frightened, and as the moon rose, Master Merlin left, without a word to any of us.

In the morning we set about the worst job of all, the mourning and burying of our dead according to their several beliefs. Those of the old religion went back to the Mother lying on their sides their legs bent, ready for their rebirth, those of the new religion were buried lying straight, wrapped in their cloaks with the white Christ's prayers to send them to Paradise, and some went to the Feasting Hall on a pyre as high as we could make it.

Liath woke fully, asking for water, and lay quietly, dozing. But she took broth and willow bark tea, and slept again. The lance injury was healing well, with no sign of the heat or fever, we had feared; she had good healing skin.

'Will she stay with us?' I asked. 'Her foster parents are dead. The father didn't come back from the spring campaign last year. She has no family.'

Aella looked at her. 'It must be as she wishes. But who is she? Where are her birth parents? Perhaps they will come.'

'How will they know?' I was surprised.

'Oh, this news will fly beyond the Forest, never fear. Or rather, perhaps we should fear it. We must be prepared, my love. There will be changes.'

And I remembered that the Lady had said 'Danger and changes.' So it was not over yet.

Rhianna 19

On the third day after the raid, when we were still clearing up and trying to repair the broken houses, Bethan's older boy came pelting along the path. He was shouting as he came, half hysterical, 'They're coming. They're coming.'

The women's council had posted watchers around the paths to the village, and on the landing stage, fearful that more raiders might be about. They had chosen the fleetest runners, and the boy was sobbing for breath.

'They're coming. Half a mile.'

The women poured into the pathway, their worst fears realised

'How many?'

'Scotti? Irish?' asked Lania,

The boy gulped and tried to catch his breath. 'On horses.'

'Horses?!' Aella stopped and pushed her way back through the crowd. The boy gulped again, and scrubbed his tears away with his fists. 'With swords and lances.'

'You saw them? Where are they?'

'In the burned villages. They came along the road through

the Forest to West Stillwell. One said, 'No bodies. Nothing left here. We're too late.' And their leader, he said, 'There were three villages, I think.' And then I slipped away and came straight here. I expect they will be here soon.'

'Bad news?' said Bethan.

'Better not take chances,' said Aella, 'They may be a patrol, but into the Forest, everyone, until we get a look at them. Keep well hidden. I'll stay, and signal when it is safe to come out.'

'But Aella,' I said, as they melted away into the green depths.

'You too,' she said.

'No. I'll not leave you. I won't.'

She didn't argue. 'Up in the thatch then, let me know what you can see.'

I scrambled up the ladder and kicked it away, and lay snug in the little space. The hole in the outer thatch gave a clear view down the street. I could see already mounted men moving in single file along the track.

'They're here,' I said to Aella, who had settled herself next to the hearth, and had begun to stoke the fire under the cauldron. Oh Goddess, was she getting ready to poison this lot too? 'About twenty horsemen. Not raiders, I think.'

The first horseman turned to shout over his shoulder 'More round houses here, sir. This must be the main village. No bodies.' The others came trotting up, about thirty in all, and clustered under the oak, looking about them, the horses restless and fidgeting.

They were all dressed in serviceable leather body armour, breeches, boots and helmets. On their bare arms were wonderfully wrought gold armbands, long swords glittering by their sides, and lances couched against their horses. Thick scarlet woollen cloaks held large gold brooches. 'There's a boy carrying a pennant with a red dragon prancing on gold.'

'Arthur's men,' groaned Aella, under her breath.

'Arthur's horses!' I whispered, entranced by the horses, bigger than I had ever seen, shining and dancing with impatience.

The younger officer said, 'Deserted. Where is everyone?'

'It's been cleared up. Someone is still living. Look for them, Gawain.'

Then I saw Lania emerge from her house very bravely, walking stiff and dignified, her face rigid, followed by her daughter Ardra. 'Sirs?'

At once the leader dismounted, holding his horse, lightly. 'Madam, we come too late, I think. I'm sorry.'

Lania did not relax. 'Who are you? Where do you come from?'

'King Arthur's men. The High King has sent us to help. I am Bedwyr. You have had trouble.'

'Raiders came from the sea. Here, eight men dead, seventeen women, four bairns. We have buried them. In the other villages, all the houses burned, all dead.'

I glanced down at Aella, expecting her to go out to support Lania, but she did not. Instead, she glanced up at me and went and stood by the door to hear better, signalling to me to keep quiet.

'We had reports that raiders had been seen in the Sabrina Estuary, heading up the river. They have burned other villages. Scotti from Ieune.'

'Three keels here,' affirmed Lania

'We came as quickly as we could. We are too late. I'm sorry, very sorry indeed.' Bedwyr looked upset and at a loss.

'Homes burned, loved one's dead, women raped,' Lania's voice broke and she turned away to hide her tears.

'What happened to the raiders?' said Gawain, clearly Bedwyr's second in command. 'We would dearly like to catch up with them. Where did they go?'

Lania took a deep breath. 'They are dead.'

'What, all of them?' he was astonished, dismounting and calling an order to the other riders. 'Where are their bodies and their boats?'

'Dead, and sent to the wrath of the Goddess.'

'But, forgive me,' said Bedwyr. 'I believe that your menfolk are away with the King's army?'

'Six of our menfolk, elderly and lame, fought bravely at the landing to give some of us time to get away to the Forest, and they killed eight of the raiders...' she faltered to a stop. 'We killed another five or six on the path...'

'And the rest?' he said, gently.

'The Alewife and the Wise Woman poisoned them.'

There was a subdued intake of breath from the listening troop.

'After the raping they would eat and drink and the kegs were poisoned and the cauldron of broth was poisoned. They saved us all.'

The soldiers looked at each other. 'We could bury the bodies for you,' said the younger man, helpfully. 'A difficult job.'

'We have buried our dead already. The raiders we burned,' Lania said, with grim satisfaction. 'We burned them in their boats and sent them to Annwn, down to the Western sea, so Arawn could set the Wild Hunt upon them.' No mention, I thought, of the drunken witches' night!

'Where are the survivors?' Bedwyr asked, looking around.

'In the Forest, well hidden. We did not know if you were friend or foe. Look, they are coming back.'

And, indeed, I could see that the women had seen the red dragon standard and had begun to crowd down around the patrol, relieved and joyful that the danger was past and help had come. The children were whooping among the horses

The soldiers had all dismounted now and were accepting the proffered mead and honey cakes.

But Aella was still not moving, watching, to my astonishment, through the door leather.

'I'll come down,' I said, 'Put up the ladder.'

'Stay where you are,' she said sharply.

'But...'

'Do as I tell you!'

She was pale and more frightened, I think, than I had ever seen her, yet these were warriors from Camelot, King Arthur's men, and we all knew that he was our friend.

I looked out of my roof hole again to see what was happening.

Bedwyr was still looking around, carefully scrutinizing every woman, and seemed increasingly worried. He said, at last to Lania, 'Madam, I have been asked to find someone – a woman. The King asks for her specially. He is very worried. She is a woman with a child. I cannot see her here.'

'Too many have died. What is her name?' Lania said.

'Gwenaella.'

She shook her head. 'No one of that name here.'

'In the other villages?'

Lania shook her head. 'I have never heard it.'

'She would be an older woman. Came here perhaps ten or eleven years ago, with a young child.'

Lania hesitated, and looked around, realising suddenly that Aella was not there.

'The King is most anxious.'

'Aella? Aella!'

Aella cursed under her breath, and impatiently pushed aside the leather door and walked out into the path.

'You are looking for me, Sir Bedwyr?'

'Madam!' he said, joyfully, and fell on his knees, seizing her hand and pressing delighted kisses upon it. to my great astonishment. 'You survived after all, I was beginning to think we had lost you.'

'Still alive, Sir.'

'The King has been enquiring.'

'That is very kind of him. You may tell him that we are safe, and send him my dutiful greetings. The Goddess go with you on your return journey.' She turned, clearly intending to go back into the house, but his voice, soft and gentle, stopped her.

'And the child, Gwenaella? What has happened to the child?'

She hesitated, clearly trying to think up a plausible lie.

'I have to report to the Bear, Gwenaella. I have orders from him, and from Morgan le Fay too.'

She breathed deeply and turning, called 'Rhianna, show yourself.'

I had already dropped down from my nest and was straightening my skirts and running my fingers through my disordered hair, wondering why Aella had been living here under a false name. Now I walked outside, like Lania – tall, my shoulders stiff, with as much dignity as I could muster. I had no idea what was going on, why Aella was so fearful and trying to hide me, but I would not creep and crawl like some timorous creature, whatever the great Arthur wanted with me.

It was strange. As I emerged into the brilliant sun of midday, I had a clear sense that I was stepping, willy-nilly, from my child life into another.

'Sir?' I said, coldly and curtsied, standing impassively, staring at him, and absorbing all of him as he stared back at me surprised. I thought he had a strange face for a soldier, narrow and gentle, like a bard, with brilliant blue diamond like eyes. Arthur's great friend, they said, the Leader of his army.

Why was he staring? What had he expected? What did I care? But all the other men had turned round and were staring too. I had a feeling that he did not quite know what to say.

'You are much taller than I expected. There is a great likeness.' He bowed and kissed my hand too. 'Lady Rhiannon.' My secret name. And Lady? Was he mad?

'Rhianna.' I said, firmly.

'Rhianna, we have come to take you home to the King.'

'I am home. I live here with my grandmother,' I said proudly. 'This is my home.'

Bedwyr looked at Aella, and she looked away, tears in her eyes.

'She will come too,' he said, although there was a question in his voice.

Aella said, expressionless, 'Of course.'

'But...why? Where are we going?'

Aella said 'The King has sent for us, Rhianna. We have to

go to Camelot.'

My first thought was that at last I would see my mother, but this was all too strange. Questions tumbled through my mind, and why was Aella looking so white and strained and tearful. If there was danger I would just as soon stay here with my work and studies.

I said, 'I don't know the King. Why would he send for me? I would rather stay here, thank you. The danger has passed.'

Before Aella could say anything, Bedwyr said sternly and finally.

'The raiders may come back. The King would have you safe at Court. The High King has sent for you. You have no choice. I have orders to bring you to Camelot.' He stared at me. 'He has long desired to meet you.'

And there was something in his eyes that made me believe he was speaking the truth. I sighed. Another mystery.

He turned to Aella to ask how quickly it would take to pack our things. He wanted to be way be away quickly to get a good few miles in before the sun went down. 'The King is anxious. Meanwhile, my men will make themselves useful about the village and help restore the houses.'

I was very annoyed. So, the King was anxious, so why should we be inconvenienced? We had been here ten years; the King could have sent for us at any time. I said firmly. 'Tomorrow morning. We will be ready to travel tomorrow morning, Sir Bedwyr. Your men can bed down in the round houses that are empty now.'

'But...'

'It is not just a question of packing a few clothes. We have much to do. Closing down our house and making arrangements for our garden to be looked after. Animals. Wonderful friends to say good bye to. People who have loved us and looked after us. And many patients, of course. We must make arrangements for their treatment and medicines. There are no other doctors in the area. We will try to be ready tomorrow morning.'

I did not wait for a reply, but followed Aella. She trudged away, her shoulders drooping, and I do not think I had ever seen her look so old.

'Aella,' I said, when we were inside the house, 'Look at me. I must know. Why have we been hiding all these years with false names? Why must we go with Sir Bedwyr? Is there danger?'

She would not meet my eyes. 'I think so.'

'From King Arthur himself?'

'No. I think not.'

'Who then?'

'Others. The Court will not be easy'

'Why has he sent for us? What does he want? Why did they keep looking at me so strangely?'

'You will have to ask him.' Then she broke out desperately, 'Rhianna, I can't tell you what you want to know. It is not in my remit. All will be made clear to you when we get to Camelot.'

I watched her for a few seconds, and she looked at me, apologetic, upset, her eyes filled with tears but determined. And I knew that it would be useless to go on. She really wasn't able or willing, perhaps, to talk, and I would have to wait and find out later.

'I will see my mother?'

'I expect so.'

There was a moment of silence between us. 'Aella... Gwenaella, Goddess! I don't even know what to call you now.'

'Call me Aella, it was ever my pet name. Nothing has changed.'

But everything had changed it seemed to me. Our life here had been a lie. We were not who we had pretended to be, simple village people. Sir Bedwyr had knelt to Aella and kissed her hand. Who was she? And who was I?

'Aella, we won't be coming back here ever again will we? This life where we have been in hiding is over.'

'It is over,' she said, finally. 'I am sorry. It was for the best. It has been a good life and safe.'

'I'm sorry too,' I said, surprising myself. 'It has been a good life. I would like it to go on.'

'The High King decides, Rhianna. We must do as he says. We have no other option.'

After that there was nothing to say, and we packed our things speedily. I had only three gowns, and tunics, Aella even less. She said, 'Put on the best of your gowns tomorrow. We shall look like beggars.'

I said, 'You must wear your new cloak,' and Aella brightened. 'Indeed, no one will have one like it.'

'If we are not coming back I will take the rarest of my herbs wrapped in damp cloths. I will not go without. And I must take the book Master Merlin gave me – O Goddess! what am I to do about Master Merlin, He will be so angry when I don't go for my Greek lesson, and I haven't thanked him properly for teaching me... '

Aella said, 'You must write a note, telling him that Bedwyr has come. He will understand. You can give it to Lania to give to him.'

'And there are all my friends in the Forest, and the Lady of of the Pool – it's no good, Aella I really can't go. Not without saying 'goodbye' They will think I have forgotten them.'

'Tonight,' said Aella, 'Late, when the men sleep. You must slip away quietly. There is a full moon.'

I was so relieved, that I was able to concentrate and make up the medicines and salves for all our patients. It was fortunate that the dried herbs in the forest were already packed. I told my bees in the garden that I was going to Camelot, and that Brigitta would look after them and they settled down again quietly and seemed happy. Other small creatures who had come to live with us, gradually disappeared back into the Forest.

Aella had been to see all our friends, and asked them to look after the garden and the chickens. And gave away all our household goods including the wall hangings I had made, which gave me a pang, as I wondered if I would ever make another weaving.

In the morning we assembled all we wanted to take, and it turned out that there was much more than they had room for. But Gawain helped to stow it all in the saddle bags shared among his troop. I wanted so much to take the remains of Ailidh's half-burned loom, but Gawain said desperately that was too heavy and bulky, 'We cannot carry it on these horses. We will have to send for it later. There will be as many looms as you want where you are going!' But I did not believe him and felt bereft.

Aella had insisted that little Liath should come with us, and Sir Bedwyr agreed, assuming that she was our maid servant and we did not enlighten him. She had stood mute and frightened while the village activity swirled about her.

But when he heard he was losing Liath, little Edryd, burst

into tears and was irreconcilable, so Brigitta said she would take Liath too. It would be better perhaps if she stayed in familiar surroundings until she recovered fully from her injuries.

And so, it was with a heavy heart that we left the village, the women hugging us, all in tears and calling down the Goddess's blessing on our journey. I did not know what they would do for a healer in the time to come. I felt that my own life was destroyed utterly, friends dead, dear friends, animal and human, left behind, my loom lost forever, and my studies abandoned. The wild Forest was lost to me. It was a nightmare.

Then, without ceremony, we were mounting up, Aella and I riding pillion, and I could see nothing, blinded by tears.

Sir Bedwyr, rode ahead, annoyed at our late departure, taking the shadowy path through the Perilous Forest. The troop rode swiftly, alert, looking over their shoulders uneasily, and after a while I began to recognise the faces of my friends, human and animal, peering through the leaves, smiling and waving, whistling and roaring, which made me smile and then the big black cat lying above us on a branch let his tail dangle down to frighten the horses, and I had to laugh.

All was not lost. I was still a healer, still a mage, still able to talk with the animals even if I did not know what the future held for me. I would find another loom, and another garden, whatever happened. I would look for another teacher for my studies.

And then, glancing up, I found that my Ravens, flying high overhead, were coming with me.

Ingram Content Group UK Ltd.
Milton Keynes UK
UKHW021905200623
423768UK00011B/592